fat
hoochie
prom
queen

Also by
Nico Medina

••

The Straight Road to Kylie

fat
hoochie
prom
queen

Nico Medina

Simon Pulse
New York London Toronto Sydney

This book is a work of fiction. Any references to historical
events, real people, or real locales are used fictitiously. Other
names, characters, places, and incidents are the product of the
author's imagination, and any resemblance to actual events
or locales or persons, living or dead, is entirely coincidental.

SIMON PULSE
An imprint of Simon & Schuster Children's Publishing Division
1230 Avenue of the Americas, New York, NY 10020
Copyright © 2008 by Nicolas Medina
All rights reserved, including the right of reproduction
in whole or in part in any form.
SIMON PULSE and colophon are registered trademarks
of Simon & Schuster, Inc.
Designed by Mike Rosamilia
The text of this book was set in Adobe Garamond.
Manufactured in the United States of America
First Simon Pulse edition May 2008
2 4 6 8 10 9 7 5 3 1
Library of Congress Control Number 2007938111
ISBN-13: 978-1-4169-3603-9
ISBN-10: 1-4169-3603-3

*For everyone who put up with me
while I wrote this book. Especially Aaron,
who* still *wanted to visit me every month,
despite my insanity. I love you, buddy!*
—*Nicopottamus Crabbypants*

Contents

1

The Pink
Bermuda Triangle

••

I hate Bridget Benson. I know "hate" is a strong word to use, but she leaves me no choice. It's gone too far. Some other strong words I'd use to describe her would be: conniving bitch, evil manipulator, non-benevolent dictator, shallow label whore, hateful Wasp, horrible actress on-screen (but amazing *off*-screen, ironically), and . . . and . . . two-faced bastard child of a Tijuana *whore*!

Hey, I usually don't hate people. I *love* people! And I love myself. I love my big ol' body and I love who I am—and people respond to that accordingly, which has given me a life full of amazing, astounding, and all-around awesome friends. I might have even been *friends* with Bridget Benson—if I didn't want to expose her bullshit in all its stinky awfulness to the misinformed student body.

Okay, truth be told, I *used* to be friends with Bridget. Back when we were six years old, we were child actors in a couple of kids' shows that filmed here in Orlando. I don't know how it happened, since we were on *different* shows, but I guess our parents must've met at some event or something, because all of a sudden, *boom!* we're play-mates. At that point, I had a tutor, so no school for me—so Bridget was pretty much my best and only friend. At six, I guess it's hard to be a raving, uppity biotch, because we got along pretty well for a couple years . . . till Bridget all of a sudden stopped calling me.

Ugh. Bridget Benson.

She plays the angel on TV and at school, but people should know about the *real* Bridget Benson. The Bridget Benson who embarrassed me on national television when we were sixteen. Who had the nerve to call me a "fat piece of Puerto Rican trash." Who acts all friend-of-the-environment but drives a gas-guzzling SUV and litters like it's going out of style faster than trucker hats did *oh*-so-long ago. Who violates the dignity of heart attack victims! Who thinks that everyone we know can be bought off—because she has the money to do it. . . . Really, the only thing she *hasn't* done is kill puppies and kittens and sell the skins to Chinese black-market fur traders!

It wasn't always like this. There was a time, just a few weeks ago, when hearing Bridget's name did hardly anything to me. But that was before my life was turned into this huge, messy *tele-novela* (minus all the slapping) with unpleasant surprises lurking around every corner.

So! Welcome to the fucked-up, crazy story of how Bridget

Benson turned mild-mannered me into a hateful rage-o-maniac hell-bent on changing the face of "prom queen" forever!! (Yes, that was a DOUBLE exclamation point!!)

A few weeks before I left my sanity at coat check, I was driving in my car and *basking* in the luxurious love I was experiencing for the brand-new blouse my sister had just made for me, when my best friend and right-hand homo, Lucas Ellison, had called me on my cell and frantically told me through choked sobs and violent sniffles that he and Zach, his boyfriend of a year—more than 365 consecutive days, babes—had just broken up, and that I needed to get to his penthouse condo, "like, stat."

Twenty minutes and a few run-through red lights later, I was in his bedroom, doing my best to comfort him. I could not *stand* to see my poor dear Lucas crying his little blue eyes out. In fact, seeing my friend's adorable baby face streaked with tears and smeared with hysteri-snot made *me* want to cry.

"What happened?" I asked.

"He's just—I mean, he—Oh, goddammit!" He broke down again and put his face in his hands and continued to cry.

"Lucas, sweetie," I cooed, handing him a paper bag, "just breathe into this and tell Mama what's wrong."

Without even looking up, he took the bag from me and breathed in deeply . . . then started coughing. "Did I just breathe in eau de Burger King?" he asked, then looked at the bag I'd handed him, answering his own question.

"I was finishing my fries on the elevator ride up. Sorry—I wanted to get here as soon as I could."

"You mean after you docked at The Mothership." (This is what he's taken to calling The King.)

"Bitch, I was boxed in at the drive-through line when you called—gimme *some* credit."

"Zach and I fought about prom again." From the way Lucas blurted it out, then immediately welled up, I could tell this wasn't about his desire to wear a wrist corsage. This was not a Crying During *Grey's Anatomy*–type thing—Lucas had truly blown a gasket.

I pointed to the Burger King bag, and Lucas nodded and resumed his breathing.

"This is kinda yummy, actually," he added meekly. "Guess you got onion rings, too?"

Zach is (or *was*, I guess) Lucas's boyfriend. They'd stayed together this whole school year, even though they were no longer at the same school. See, Lucas had transferred to Winter Park just this—our *senior*!—year, during which we'd become superfast, supertight friends.

"Madge, *why* did I have to date a closet case for this long?" Lucas wailed. "I *knew* it would get old!"

Madge is me. Well, actually Margarita Antonia Diaz is me. "Madge" was born in Spanish class with Lucas. (Yes, I'm Puerto Rican and I take Spanish, and *besa mi culo*, baby, because it's an easy A.) So one day we did this exercise to learn about the different forms of traditional Spanish names. I'm Margarita Antonia Diaz normally, but if you added my mom's maiden name, I'd be Margarita Antonia Diaz-Gallegos. Then Lucas and I figured out that if we got married, I'd be Margarita Antonia Diaz-Gallegos de Ellison—and thus, "M.A.D.G.E." was born. Lucas, Madonna-crazed homosexual that he is, immediately started calling me "Madge" exclusively (except for when he called me "Your Madgesty"), which I wasn't all that crazy about at first, but when that little blond angel had said all melancholically, "But, Margarita, you might be the only Madge I'll ever get," I couldn't help but grin and bear it.

"Why don't you tell me what the fight was about?" I said now, as soothingly as I could.

"Well, you know, prom's coming up," he said, calming down a bit.

Prom *was* coming up. My health-nut freak show of a mother—in the grand old PR tradition—was insisting on making my dress for me, and since she paid the bills (actually, she just signed the checks; my often-absent workaholic father made the money), I'd pretty much resigned myself to it. So long as there weren't bows or sashes or ruffles on the thing . . . unless, of course, they were made out of vinyl or faux fur.

"And remember how you told me I shouldn't be afraid to ask Zach to prom and that we should totally go together?" Lucas asked. "Well, I *agreed* with you. And Zach's my fucking *boyfriend*! My boyfriend of *forever*. So I asked him. And you know what happened?"

"He didn't wanna go."

5

"Give the lady a prize! You guessed it—he *still* hasn't come out to his parents, and he's 'not comfortable being gay in public'! What the hell?! I couldn't *take* it anymore!"

"Gay in public" was sort of Lucas's specialty. He'd been out since ninth grade, and frankly I'm surprised he and Zach lasted so long. Not that I didn't like Zach. I actually *really* liked Zach—he was the sweet, chill ying to Lucas's flamboyant and manic *yang!yang!yang!* Which I thought would ultimately be enough to win Lucas over and make him be more patient with Zach—because everyone deserves to come out on their own terms. But I guess Lucas's impatience had won out. Sucks for Zach.

"So then," he went on, "it escalated into this big fight, and he was saying that prom isn't such a big deal—which I said of *course* it is and that *you* and *everyone else in the world* agreed with me—and before I knew it, Zach is *screaming* at me, telling me he could take the pressure from me *no longer*, and that it'd just be better if we weren't *together* anymore." Now the tears started back up again, and back to the BK bag Lucas went.

Shit. I guess Lucas had been the dump*ee*, not the dump*er*. No *wonder* he was freaking out so much. I guess I should've guessed it from his hysterical condition, but this whole time I figured he'd been the one to get fed up with Zach. Though not to sound mean, but it seemed like Lucas might've instigated the breakup, even if he didn't perform the follow-through. I'd only meant Lucas should *ask* Zach to prom—not freak out and get into a huge blowout over it. It wasn't worth that.

But I kept doing my best to ease Lucas's pain—back-rubbing, hand-holding, shoulder-to-cry-on . . . the whole bit. When Lucas wanted to trash-talk his "venomous" and "straitlaced" ex, I would nod and agree (though it was hard for me). When he wanted to reminisce, I would happily join in. I heard the story of their first date, when Lucas was made to pretend that he and Zach were going on a double date with two girls from their chemistry class, and how mad it'd made him—but how once they were out of sight of Zach's house, Zach reached over and took Lucas's hand oh-so-sweetly. I told him I liked how Zach had an insane capacity for geography trivia, and that I'd found it way interesting that South Africa had three capital cities: one for judiciary, one for legislative, and one for administrative.

It was almost like having a eulogy for their relationship (except for the trash-talking part, of course). This seemed to help Lucas a little bit.

Eventually, we ended up leaning our faces against Lucas's floor-to-ceiling windows, gazing onto downtown Orlando. We wound up here often . . . people-watching at Lake Eola from four hundred feet in the air. Everything just seemed so tranquil from up here—and it was our favorite activity to do together at his house. (Well, other than making chocolate-covered, frozen-whipped-cream-and-graham-cracker sandwiches, and watching *Arrested Development* DVDs . . .)

"You know what?" Lucas said, staring down onto the city. "I've spent the last year of my life dealing with someone else's gay hang-ups. Maybe I should look at this as an opportunity."

"An opportunity for what?"

"Well, first of all, you and I should *totally* go to prom together now. Wait." He smiled and backed away from the window, then knelt down on one knee. "No-Salt-on-My-Margarita Diaz, will you go to the prom with me?"

I smiled big and said, "Of course." I hadn't had a boyfriend since the fall—long-distance shit with college guys just isn't my thing, I guess—and the only real crush I'd had as of late was on the scrumptious BK drive-through guy (Thursdays, Fridays, and Saturdays), so I'd been planning on going stag. But having a cute little blond boy on my arm—even though I'd probably tower a few inches over him in my heels—wouldn't be *such* a bad thing.

"Good!" Lucas beamed, standing back up to give me a big hug. Then he continued, "Anyway . . . *other* good things about this breakup. Now that I'm a free man, I get to play the field again!"

"Lucas, I don't think you've *ever* really played the field . . . even metaphorically."

"Exactly! Now's my chance to slut it up!"

"Oh." *This* caught me off guard. "Seriously?"

"Yeah!" He looked off into the distance, as if staring into a future of sexual encounters with every available eighteen-year-old gay boy in metro Orlando. He had quite the cat-grin going on. (Though I didn't completely buy it. Lucas really seemed like the nesty-boyfriend type, despite all his talk.) "Oh, Madge . . . let's celebrate! Let's go to Parliament House!"

"No! We've got Madison Whiteman's party tonight." (Plus, I wasn't in the mood for the trashy sights that the Parliament House Motor Inn club-slash-motel had to offer, as hilariously divine as they could be at times.) "Don't you wanna see Bridget Benson treat Madison all shitty like she always does?" I asked.

Poor Madison. She used to be the school's Top Dog, till Top Bitch (f'*sho*!) Bridget Benson came onto the scene in the fall of sophomore year, the year we turned sixteen. Bridget had been homeschooled and tutored through most of elementary and middle school, but once she hit high school, her "momager" and publicist thought it'd be a good idea for her to film only during summers and holidays, so she could slum it in the public school system for brownie points with Middle America. Winter Park High, the area's highest-rated institution (and the overall poshest school district), was the natural choice.

Miss Madison Whiteman's fall from the top of the cheerleading pyramid came rapidly, and can be explained only by a minor drug scandal that I'm pretty sure Bridget (or the previously mentioned momager or publicist) coordinated single-handedly. Why Bridge and Mad were such good "friends" now, I didn't really know, but maybe there's some truth in the adage "keep your friends close and your enemies closer."

As for me, Bridget was hardly an *enemy* at this point. Besides the fact that years ago, she had dropped me as hard as a coke-hungry starlet drops rehab—and besides, of course, the *Super Sweet 16* incident—I was pretty much neutral on her. Since she came back into my school and my life two years ago, we'd hardly spoken outside of the few cold and uncomfortable social exchanges in the classes we shared—and that was just fine by me. Hey, at this point, I didn't *need* any more friends—pretty much everyone at school loved me, so what difference would it make to have one more? Especially one who I was pretty sure harbored some mysterious resentment toward me. I mean, why *else* would someone stop talking to me? I was like *Super* Friend!

But a lot of people loved Bridget. And—I *guess*—what's not to love? Money and fame; impossibly bright and shiny smile; blonde-highlighted-to-perfection shimmery hair; a rock-star body that would get her hired for a WB show (I'm sure she was holding out for a guest appearance at some point); "friend of the people" as student-body president; hot item, everyone-wants-him boyfriend . . . the works.

(Okay, let's go ahead and add a side of "mild distaste" to my previous order of "neutral." I ain't gonna lie. She did sometimes get to me.)

Lucas laughed. "Benson and Whiteman, together forever . . . Okay, okay, we'll go to the party. I'm sure I can find guys there. . . ."

I gave a little half nod/half smile. I gotta say, I wasn't too sure about this new Lucas. I'd only known him one way—attached and in love—and I wondered if things were gonna drastically change now. . . .

"Wanna have a drink, hoochie?!" Lucas asked suddenly, his smile widening mischievously.

Okay, I guess things were pretty much the same so far.

"It's kinda early, isn't it?" I asked.

"You were gonna come over and pre-party tonight anyway," he said. "So why *not* start early? It's a special occasion! I'll make mango margarit—"

"Sold!" I yelled, smiling.

Maybe it was because it was my namesake drink, or maybe it was just because Lucas's are always so fruity and delicious ("Just like me," he always says), but I can never say no to a mango margarita.

"Comin' up!" he said giddily, and skipped down the stairs and to the foyer.

Lucas's mom, who insists on being called "Mitsy" (and I love it–love it–love it), keeps a supply of mini liquor bottles in a pink magazine basket by the front door. She used to keep a closer eye on her liquor supply, but since Lucas and I only had a few weeks left of high school and had already each gotten full rides to University of Florida (Go, Gators!), she'd put out the basket as a sort of reward.

Her one rule was that we—really, *truly*—had to keep an eye on each other.

Oh, and that we take her car service, which always makes for a pretty fabulous entrance . . .

. . . and that if there was only one bottle of Grey Goose left, we were to leave it precisely where it was.

(I *heart* hanging out with Lucas Ellison!)

Lucas found two itsy-bitsy Jose Cuervos and ran to the

kitchen, sliding in his socks on the swank cherry-wood floors.

As cool as I usually played it, it was hard not to be humbled by Mitsy and Lucas's *schweet* pad, which apparently was Mitsy's idea of "downsizing" after divorcing her big-shot TV-producer husband. Thank the real-estate gods for no prenup on *that* one! Thirty-five floors up, 2,800 square feet? Yeah, I'd like to downsize to that.

It was the kind of place I'd always dreamed about owning one day—big, not too showy. Simple and elegant. It was basically one gigantic room that included an expertly decorated living room—with the cushiest white leather couch I've *ever* had the pleasure of meeting—a chef's kitchen *swaddled* in stainless steel and marble, and a clear glass staircase that led up to the two bedrooms and TV den.

"So, Margarita-*sita*," Lucas said as he broke up an ice tray, "who do you think I should make out with tonight?"

"Um . . . I dunno, sweetie. It's kinda slim pickins, no?"

"Yeah, I guess . . . But there's always Kenny Daniels."

"If he's not too cracked out of his mind," I warned.

We'd actually had a Kenny Daniels discussion already, back when Lucas told me on the first day of school he thought he was cute. Kenny *was* cute. But it pretty much stopped there. Unless you counted constantly moving your head like you're dancing to a never-ending trance song in your brain as evidence of a personality, Kenny simply didn't have one. Not to mention being a nineteen-year-old second-year senior. *Hells* no!

There was also this weird mystique surrounding Kenny. Last year, he mysteriously didn't show up to prom. Apparently, he'd had a little run-in with the cops and spent the night in jail. Next thing we know, Kenny's expelled from school for the rest of the year, and now he's back, doing Senior Year the Sequel. Since no one knows for sure what Kenny got arrested for, there are naturally a lot of rumors floating around as to what it could've been. My favorite one—right now, at least—is that he was busted for underage drinking at a strip bar. Thing is, it wasn't the *drinking* that caught the bouncer's attention. It was a ridiculously drunk and giggly Kenny pouring ice water on a dancer's boobs that got the bouncer's attention.

Honestly. No class.

(I'm fairly convinced he would've been doing the same at a full-frontal *male* strip club, but there weren't any of those in O'Town—or *I'd've* been there with him!)

"So *what* if he's cracked out?" Lucas asked me now, dropping a couple globs of mango sorbet into the blender. "He'll still be able to *kiss*, right?"

Oh, Jesus. I was already concerned that Lucas was entering the ever-dangerous rebound-boy territory. It was like a Pink Bermuda Triangle—once you got sucked in, you never got out . . . unless you treated yourself by therapy-splurging on Prada shoes.

"What?!" Lucas asked, in response to my nonresponse.

"Nothing!" I yelled. "Finish up those margaritas!"

High-Stakes Drama, for the Bargain Price of Fifty Dollars

· ·

The party at Madison Whiteman's sprawling lakeside house on Lake Sue was *sick*. Madison was sort of top-tier popular, in that so-called "popular" crowd that everyone kind of dislikes. You know who I'm talking about.

Since Madison's a bit of a MySpaceSlut (and not the brightest bulb in the hardware store), when she posted a bulletin with an announcement of her party, a couple hundred of her closest "Friends" showed up. But the beer would never run out—when one keg emptied, money got passed around, jobs were delegated, older friends or siblings were summoned, and another would show up.

After I'd seen the announcement for the party, I'd checked out the comments on her page, just for shits and giggles. It was so discouraging. Reading all the horrendously misspelled "words" and nonexistent punctuation was like witnessing the slow and painful death of the English language. Some choice gems were:

omfg Mad you look sooooooo prettiiii in thos pixxx. im so therr on fri.
sorri I 4got2callu yesterdayyy but ill c u at the partyyyyy!!!!!!!
omg saturday! idk if I work or not but ill call u lol hehehehe. hope we
can hangout work is so gayyyyy! NE1 fill u in on my latest DRAma yet?

Ugh. You know, I usually don't have a problem with most people, but sometimes people can be so gayyyy. Know what I mean?

As our driver pulled up to the house, I noticed the whole street was lined with cars: shit-ass Camrys from the nineties, shining new Beemers, Mercedes SUVs, Volvo station wagons—a pretty mixed Winter Park crowd. Cars were covering Madison's sprawling front yard, too, and as we got out of the Town Car, Lucas was downing his second bottle of Sprite and Grey Goose (luckily Mitsy had recently restocked). He'd made the switch from tequila to vodka after the first batch of margs. Not really the *smartest* idea—especially since we'd started so early—but he wasn't gonna listen to reason tonight.

"Easy there, killer," I told him as we got out of the car.

"Pish-posh, Madgie," he responded, arching an eyebrow in a dead-on impersonation of his über-proper Waspy mother. "It's a fucking *party*!"

Lucas had definitely pulled out all the stops for tonight, his

I'm-a-Slut-Now Debutante Ball of sorts. He was compulsively squeezable in his skinny-leg Levi's, and his skintight faux-vintage David Bowie shirt definitely showed off the little guns he'd been working on lately. (He was also sporting his favorite pair of pink Hello Kitty socks I'd given him as a joke for his eighteenth birthday, but inside his favorite pair of Marc Jacobs sneakers.)

I wasn't looking so bad myself. I was in my worship-my-booty Seven jeans, silver pumps that were surprisingly (and blessedly) easy to squeeze into and walk in, and my amazing new blouse— my sister Vanessa's latest creation. It was a three-quarter-length-sleeved black silk blouse with the ends of the sleeves slit in two places to make them burst open. The slits were studded with tiny silver ball bearings, and the rest of the blouse had all these random, swirling lines made of metallic silver thread. The deep neckline, which pretty much exploded open at the chest (always gotta show off the breasteses, baby), was lined with these amazing silver-and-lime-green paisley embellishments. I know it all sounds kind of showy, but . . . well, fuck yeah, of *course* it is! I wanted to *marry* this blouse.

Vanessa works at a bank in the big shopping center next to her apartment. She never went to college—never really wanted to— but she does pretty well . . . even if she regrets her decision sometimes (especially when our mom rubs her face in it on a weekly basis). Her big dream is to maybe go to fashion school, and eventually have a clothing boutique somewhere, where she can sell the *delicious* clothes she makes—for people of *all* sizes. She totally deserves it, too—I only wish she could get out of that awful dead-end job to make it all work.

Vanessa's sort of my hero, because:

a) If she didn't make these plus-size masterpieces of silk, satin, faux fur, feathers, and elastic for me, I'd be doomed to an eternity of shopping at Gap and Old Navy and the Dress Barn,

b) Um . . . well . . . she does it for *free* (for me, at least!), and

c) Even if she's a little behind, she's still trying to follow her dream, despite the soul-sucking lectures from our mother.

Lucas tripped over himself as soon as we stepped onto Madison's grassy front lawn.

"Shit!" I laughed as I took him by the arm. "Hey, let's have *water* be our first drink."

"Fuck water. Moderation is best *in moderation!*" Lucas cried semi-maniacally, and took off running for the front door.

I'm a big girl, and Lucas is way faster than me—and I wasn't in the mood to run an obstacle course, like Lucas obviously was—so I just weaved my way slowly through the mess of cars covering the yard to the front porch . . . or *portico*, rather. (Gotta love gaudy Greek columns in suburban Orlando.) When I finally opened the door and headed into the party, I heard someone call, "What's good, Rita, you lookin' *fine* tonight!" from the side of the house.

"Hey, Alejandro, *gracias*, baby," I purred, heading into the house. *God*, that boy was hot. This blouse was already paying off.

The party was like a cross section of our school. There were my Gs (as in *Wuddup, G?*) and my Gs (as in the Lucas variety);

my Puerto Rican countrymen drooling over my *fine* be*hind*; all the bored-looking, skinny, pseudo-intellectual hipster kids (why even *go* to a keg party?); overenthusiastic athletes; stoner-chill skater/surfer/beach-bum kids; the way-diverse group of computer geeks; even some kids from the drama department. Pretty much everyone was in their own individual cliques, but I went around and said hi to everyone. I sorta had friends all over the place. Everyone *loooved* the new blouse, of course. And it was so nice to see everyone in one place outside of school.

Then I saw Bridget Benson chatting it up with Lindsay Taylor, who was voted Most Likely to Marry a Colombian Drug Lord . . . by me and Lucas. Lindsay had been in a show with Bridget waaaay back when—and hadn't worked since, except maybe a Dr. Scholl's commercial or two. She'd kind of gone the Britney route, only ten years sooner. She was all messy, curly, red-streaked amber hair and skank-ass makeup, and was wearing a way-too-short white skirt (which served up that flat white ass of hers like an order of mashed potatoes), with a baby-doll tee that read HEARTBREAKER. Right. More like I'M COKED UP AND EASY SO COME AND GET IT. Totally hotttt. JK!

Bridget, of course—*May she one day get uncontrollable acne!*—looked predictably perfect.

And while all the lowly plebeians in the house were drinking the same Bud Light keg beer out of red Solo cups, Bridget and Lindsay were taking delicate little sips on red cosmos . . . in martini glasses with sugar-dusted rims, no less!

Bridget's latest TV role—on a super-successful Saturday morning tween show produced by a certain Orlando-based mega-company whose name I don't think I need to spell out for you—has set her up to be the next big breakout actress . . . and probably musician, too, eventually, since that's how it goes nowadays. Some really wholesome blah-blah-blah. And up until recently, I'd noticed that she'd been very careful not to drink at parties, probably for fear of being photographed and having her perfect image called into question by the execs at her family-friendly production company. But I guess she was throwing caution to the wind tonight. Go, Bridget! You *drink* that badass cosmo! Next thing we know, she'll be riding her hog topless at Bike Week!

And here came poor doormat—and our hostess for the evening—Madison Whiteman, with a shiny cocktail shaker full of refills for the exclusive duo.

If *this* wasn't proof to people that Bridget Benson sucked, I don't know what is. Just drink the beer like everyone else, ho!

Whatever. That Bud Light was calling my name now, as was Lucas.

"Beer, Madge!" he called from the keg, which was in the screened-in back pool deck. I headed over to him, squeezing my way through the crowd. When I got up to Bridget and Lindsay, they hardly budged to let me by, so I had to just keep moving.

"Ugh!" Bridget huffed at me. "Watch the cosmo! This blouse is *silk*."

"So's mine—'scuse me," I replied.

This was the most Bridget had said to me in a long time. Most of the time, she couldn't even look me in the eye. Maybe that had something to do with the fact that right around the time she'd friendship-dumped me, she'd pulled the perfect part in a new TV series *right* out from under my feet.

And then went on to become a superstar.

Well, as much a superstar as an eight-year-old can be.

And please: don't think she got the part because I'm fat and she's not and I'm an idiot for thinking I'd have a *chance* at a part that beyond-compare Bridget Benson got. Because for the record, I didn't start getting chubs till *after* the disastrous audition, when I quit acting and went to normal-kids' school. And before you go on making *more* assumptions, I didn't pork up because I was depressed or anything. Acting was hard. I wanted to have *friends* and a more normal existence. And the only reason I got fat is because, well . . . *everyone* on my dad's side started gaining weight when they were around my age.

Now, as I passed Bridget, I heard her mumble something about sweatshop silkworms working overtime on my garbage bag of a blouse. "Lucasito!" I called now, deciding to ignore the super-witty anti-fat comment. "How's that delectable brew?"

"I'm gonna *funnel* it!" he said excitedly as I walked out onto the porch. He pointed to the beer funnel this basketball-player guy Jon was holding.

"All right, Ellison," Jon said. "Stick your thumb at the end of

the tube and get ready. I'll pour the beer into the funnel and tell
you when the foam's gone."

Funneling, while having the potential to be gross and messy, is a
fine method for binge-drinking piss-water beer. It's also a bit of an art
form, and it takes some practice. So as I caught Lucas's nearly imper-
ceptible, momentary look of confusion in regard to Jon's directions, I
realized that *I* had funneled before, but Lucas hadn't. Before I could
interrupt the process to give my friend a few pointers, it was too late.
The beer had been poured, the thumb removed, and Bud Light was
splattering all over Lucas's face and the back porch.

As Lucas belched and blew foam out his nose, Jon was laughing, saying, "Nice job, Ellison—what the fuck was that, dude?"

"Never send a woman to do a man's job!" another b'ball boy
named Tristan said, laughing.

"Maybe you could give him a few *pointers* on suppressing the
gag reflex, Tris," I said, burping Lucas like a baby. "Here," I said
to my buddy, "watch how it's done. It's actually really simple. You
just relax your throat and let the whole beer sort of . . . *fall* into
your stomach." I took the tube from him, placed my thumb over
the end, and sat in the chair next to the keg. "*Cerveza*, baby!" I
yelled at Jon. "*Dame!*"

Jon obeyed, pouring a cupful of beer into the funnel. Once he
said the foam was gone, I gave myself a three-second countdown
and let the beer rush into my stomach in two seconds *flat*! (New
record for me.) I let out a bellowing and very satisfying belch as
a finale.

I smiled graciously, bowing to accept the cheers and applause of everyone on the porch.

I summoned Lucas to the funnel. "You ready, *amor?*" I asked him.

"Sure."

I noticed we had a few more people around us now, notably Bridget and Lindsay.

"Okay," I said to Lucas. I took the funnel from Jon and gave the end of the tube to Lucas. I slowly poured in a cup of beer, and waited for the foam to work its way out. For some reason, I was feeling very protective of Lucas right then. Maybe because of his recent heartache, or maybe because I just didn't like Bridget being so close by—but I *really* didn't want him to embarrass himself. He was all fun and games now, but I had a feeling he could crack at any moment.

"All right," I said. "On the count of three. One . . . two . . . *three!*"

Lucas removed his thumb, and at first, I could tell he was a little surprised at what gravity will do to a funnel full of beer, but he recovered quickly, and seriously just in*haled* that beer. Down the tube it drained, and within five seconds—he'd get better with practice (though Mitsy would probably frown on such a vulgar habit) the beer was all gone and Lucas had his pride back.

"Yes!" he cried, throwing his hands in the air and belching. "I'm a *maaaaan!*"

I saw Bridget roll her eyes. Grr.

"Hey, Bridget," I called to her. "You wanna do a funnel?" I all of a sudden needed to embarrass her. Nobody rolls their eyes at my boy Lucas. "Deeeee-*licious* Bud Liiiight . . . !" I coaxed, my voice singsong-y.

"I don't drink Butt Wipe," she said, shrugging. "Sorry."

"Ah, c'mon . . . Whaddya think, people?" I called to everyone around me. "Who thinks our little student-body president should kick off the prom season with a nice funnel of beer?!"

Everyone laughed and cheered in agreement, seemingly eager to see their leader debase herself to domestic keg beer. By now, some more people were hovering on the other side of the sliding-glass door. She'd have to do it.

"You gotta listen to the fans, Bridge," I goaded.

"Fine," Bridget said quickly, placing her empty martini glass delicately on the patio table. "If anyone takes pictures of this, you're *banned* from prom. Seriously." She turned to Jon and ordered, "*Pour*, please!" and he respectfully poured half a cup of beer into the funnel.

There are really only two words to sum up what happened next: Beer everywhere!

Okay, maybe two more:

Everyone laughing.

Bridget, looking uncharacteristically mortified, stormed back into the house, nearly running right over a *very* characteristically spaced-out Lindsay.

"That was fun." Lucas smiled. "Let's do another!"

By the time I'd had a couple more beers, the party had really picked up. Props to Madison for getting someone cool to deejay, because the music was great, and it just didn't *stop*. And unlike most gigantic house parties, this one had a pretty decent dance floor going, which I took *full* advantage of. I shook and grinded my way around the room, my hair flying in all directions, my boobs bouncing in my hot new shirt, my booty shaking furiously, sweat forming in all *sorts* of places.

When I got the hankering for a little Lucas–Madge grind time, I noticed my friend was nowhere in sight. He'd funneled his fair share of beer, too, so it would probably be smart if I made good on my long-standing promise to Mitsy and checked up on him. So I headed upstairs to look around. The only interesting things I saw were some half-naked people making out in a bedroom, a couple of freshman girls puking in a bathroom (one in the toilet, the other in the tub), and my friends Steve and Lance taking hits from their big glass bong they'd lovingly dubbed Walter Cronkite (they were big TV-production geeks at school and had their own Wednesday morning show).

I decided to kick the party up a notch, so I joined them for a few minutes. Steve and Lance were my boys. Totally cool. We'd known each other since freshman year—I really couldn't believe how grown-up we all looked now. They'd turned into little men. It was so cute.

Little men with strong weed, though. *¡Coño!*

"So, Madge . . ." I heard Steve say.

All of a sudden, I was craving chips something fierce.

"*Madge*," he said again.

"What?" I asked, reluctantly snapping out of my food fantasy, which now involved green onion dip.

"You hear the latest scoop on our school's little starlet harlot?"

"No!" I said excitedly. Too excitedly. Why the hell should *I* care? (But I guess I did.) "What is it?"

Lance took over for Steve (who was in mid-hit), saying, "We heard she's, like, *running* for prom queen."

"*Really?*" I asked shrilly. Too shrilly? I felt as if I sounded like a chipmunk or something. "Can you even do that? I mean, who *runs* for prom queen?"

"I guess you can do it," Steve said, exhaling a monstrous cloud of smoke. "Man, I thought everyone knew about that. It's been news for a couple weeks. But isn't that lame?"

"Totally lame," I agreed, though part of me was wondering why she'd do it in the first place. Bridget being Top Bitch at our school—not to mention a major TV star—she was sort of a shoo-in for the position. I wonder why she'd make such a big deal out of it.

"You gonna vote for her?" Lance asked Steve.

"I dunno . . . I don't really think about it. But if she wants it that bad, I don't see why not."

"See, I'd rather vote for someone who *wasn't* running," Lance said. "Margarita, *you* should run. You'd have *my* vote."

"Aha," I said, wagging my finger, "but if you wouldn't vote for someone 'cause they were running, then why would you vote for *me* if I were running?"

Lance just stared blankly at me for a few seconds, then burst out laughing. "That's some deep shit, Diaz!" he giggled. "I dunno how to answer that, but I *like* you!"

"I like you, too, Lance." I smiled and patted him on the back. By now, the laugh bomb had gone off, and Steve was rolling around on the floor, giggling with his buddy. They were so adorable. Like Bert and Ernie—only not gay.

"All right, boys," I said, standing up a little shakily. "I gotta skedaddle and procure myself some snacky-snacks. Thanks for the hit."

I made my way back downstairs, itching to gab with Lucas about this latest prom-queen development. I mean, come on! What freak runs for prom queen? Is it not enough that she's got everyone in the palm of her hand—she's gotta go ahead and be *crowned* for that shit? I guess it's just her constant need to be number 1. That particular need bit me in the ass one time, hard, so I knew all about it.

Where *was* Lucas anyway?

Crap! The whole reason I'd gone upstairs in the first place was to look for Lucas.

I hoped he was okay, and had the good sense to switch to water soon after the funneling.

Madison's place was even more packed than it was before. I'm talking, like, can't-make-it-to-the-back-door crowded. But it was fun, because I was running into practically everyone I knew. I loved being in school and seeing all these people in classes and at lunch and in the hallways and everything, but it's so much more fun to see them all in one place together, however hazy and muted the random conversations I was having with them were seeming.

(Eek. Those boys smoked some strong shit.)

Crap *again*! Now I'd forgotten why I'd gone *down*stairs: food!

I pushed my way hungrily into the kitchen and found an unguarded bag of Lay's. Taking it, I headed through the throng out the door to the pool deck. Finally, after making my way to the front of the keg line and getting another beer, I went outside to the gigantic back lawn to look for Lucas.

Now, yes, I'd gotten sidetracked a couple times while looking for my best friend, but before you think I'm a *completely* horrible faghag, allow me to inform you that I know Lucas's alco-limit better than he does. I doubted that in this amount of time, he could have gotten drunk enough for me to worry. I mean, that boy was the blue-blooded Wasp Son of Mitsy, and he could hold his liquor pretty well. He was probably just outside for some air.

I headed down the grassy slope toward the lake, figuring he might be on the bench I saw near the shore. And, as it turned out, he was . . . but he was kind of horizontal, and making out with that cold-sore queen Kenny.

"Ew—I mean, um . . . *sorry*!" I yelled, which made Kenny jump about three feet in the air, right up from on top of Lucas.

"Heeeey, Madge . . ." Lucas slurred at me. "Don't worry about it . . . Kenny was just leaving, anyway."

"Yeah, *toooh*-tally," Kenny said. "Hey, Margarita. Fab shirt."

"Thanks."

"Okay, see ya." And off he went. Quite the conversationalist.

"So, Kissy McKisserton . . ." I teased Lucas when Kenny was out of earshot. "What was *that* all about?"

"Nothing." Lucas sat up slowly and shrugged. "Just Kenny looked cute, and I wanted to kiss somebody."

"Cute? Lucas, he had on a shirt that said TIGHT END. That's not only stupid, it's passé."

"Look, *don't* tell me who I can and can't kiss!" Lucas blurted out suddenly. It was literally the closest thing we'd ever had to a fight. That little outburst. Craziness—Lucas had never talked to me like that. But as quickly as it came, it was gone. "I'm sorry, Madge," he said. "I'm just still broken up about Zach."

"Um . . . *hello*, Lucas?! You guys just broke up *today*. Take your time, sweetie—it's *okay* to be sad."

"I know, I know . . . It's just . . . I feel guilty, because I already *like* being single again."

"Really?" I asked, surprised by this. I thought I had my Lucas pegged as a one-man guy. But then again, I'd never seen the boy as angry as I'd seen him a few seconds ago. So who knew?!

"Yeah," he said. "It's like . . . now that I can be with people who are *okay* with being gay and out . . . I'm kind of all about it." His shoulders slumped now, then he leaned forward, elbows on his knees, head in his hands. "But that makes me feel *guilty*! I was *devastated* this afternoon when Zach dumped me. And now I'm making out with someone else not twelve hours later, and I don't care! Does that mean I *wanted* us to break up all along?!"

Wow, talk about conflicting emotions! Pink Bermuda Triangle, indeed. See? I know my shit.

"I don't know, Lucas," was all I could say, because it was true. I had no idea. All I knew was that I had to support my friend, right then and there. Never mind how much I liked Zach, how *little* I liked Kenny, and how thrown off I was by Lucas's new go-with-the-flow-and-be-a-slut attitude—I had to be there for my best friend. For now, at least.

But just as I was about to continue with earning my gold medal in the Comfort Olympics, we heard a piercing cry of "*Ew*, I don't want this shit beer!" in that signature *eh-mi-gawd!* voice of Bridget's. Lucas and I looked down the lakeshore, and saw Bridget throw a cupful of Bud Light into the water. The poor sophomore guy who'd obviously tried to impress Bridget with a nice cup of beer practically *ran* back up the hill to the house. Bridget, all alone, crossed her arms and stared angrily across the lake.

"Hey, Lucas," I said. "Know what might cheer you up?"

"What?"

"Bridget gossip," I whispered conspiratorially.

So I told him all about what Steve and Lance had told me,

about how dumb the whole thing seemed. And it did sort of perk him up a bit. But not all the way.

"C'mawwwn, baby," I urged. "This sort of shit always makes you happy!"

"I know, I'm sorry . . . I'm just tired of talking shit about that girl. It's not even worth our time."

"Oh, *please*! Don't 'act all above gossip—you read *Us Weekly* cover to cover every Saturday!"

"True, true . . ." He sniffed and put his face in his hands.

"Hey, Lucas," I said again. "Know what might *really* cheer you up?"

"What?"

"You pay me twenty bucks, and I'll go over there to Bridget, and I'll ask her why she's running for prom queen."

He lifted his head, his face lit up. "Twenty bucks?!" he said. "Hey. Offer to be her campaign manager, and I'll give you *fifty*!"

I was up and on my way before he even finished the sentence. I heard Lucas's laughing fade away as I approached Bridget. This was the first time I'd *really* talked to her since I don't know when, so it was a little surreal. Luckily, the weed and alcohol had emboldened me.

"'Sup, Bridget," I said as I approached.

"Yeah?" she asked, eyeing me suspiciously. "What do you want?"

"Why the attitude?" I asked.

"Um . . . how 'bout, I can't get the taste of that cow-piss domestic *beer* out of my nose, thanks to you?"

"Sorry!" I said, holding my hands up. "Didn't know you couldn't handle half a cup of beer," I teased.

She just glared at me.

"Look, the reason I came over here," I said as matter-of-factly as possible, "is to ask if there was any truth to what I heard. . . ."

"You'll have to be a *little* more specific than that, Margarita," she said, seeming annoyed. "There're a *lot* of rumors about me."

"Right, right—the whole big-important-star thing," I said under my breath. "No, I was just seeing if it's true that you're running for prom queen."

She rolled her eyes and sighed. "Yes. That one's true."

"Um . . . mind if I ask *why*?" I said. "I mean, it's . . . kinda . . . lame."

"Right, okay. Well, I don't think I need *you* to tell me what's lame and what's not," she said, all nasal and obnoxious. "But I'm running because if I *don't* get prom queen, what's that gonna *say* about me? I can't get into the good sororities if I got beat out for prom queen at some ghetto public school."

"You sure you wanna be the typical shallow starlet who has to be the best at everything she does?" I blurted out, surprising myself with how much emotion was evident in my voice. "I mean, *I* wouldn't want to be that. . . ."

"Yeah, well, *first* of all, there's a difference between not wanting and not being able to get there in the *first* place."

I tried to remain calm, but it was hard. This whole experience was somehow striking a nerve with me. "Oh . . . I get it," I replied slowly, "I was probably *never* prom-queen material. *That's* why I never made it as an actress—and why we're not friends anymore."

"Listen," she said sternly, "this is *business*, okay? Not something you'd really understand."

"Okay, what's *that* supposed to mean?" Now I was just pissed. She was taking it there, and I had not been expecting it.

"I can't believe you're still not *over* all that, Margarita," she said, tilting her head in what I could only assume was supposed to be an empathetic gesture. "It's just unhealthy. Look, it was *one* part, *one* audition. I got it and you didn't. It was no reason for you to drop your career and *gain* eight hundred pounds—"

"Why do you *hate* me so much, huh?" I yelled all of a sudden. I'd called her for *months* after that audition, and I got nothing back! "What *is* it about me? We used to be cool with each other!"

"Why do *you* hate *me?*" she fired back. "And what on *earth* makes you think I have the time or the *energy* to hate you?"

"Um . . . I dunno . . . the *Sweet 16* show? The silkworm remark earlier? How about when you asked Mrs. Grant if obesity was contagious when we were lab partners that one day in bio, before you transferred out of the class? Stop me whenever you want. . . ."

"Okay, what do you want, Margarita—an apology? Fine. I'm *sorry*. I'm *sorry* you didn't get that part, and I'm *sorry* you showed up uninvited to my *Super Sweet 16* party, and I'm *sorry* about what I said inside, and I'm *sorry* that you have issues with your grossness. Anything else?"

"I didn't ask for an apology," I said. "Just an explanation."

"Oh, *GOD*, I *HATE you!*" Now *she* was hissy-fitting. "You wanna know what it is? Well, here ya go . . . I just don't get why you think you're so *fucking* fabulous. I mean, come on! That shirt? It's like a flea market, with sleeves! And *why* you think people like you so much, I just don't understand. It's really kind of *sad*! You're sweaty, you're loud, and you dress *hideously*! I mean, can't you see how *disgusting* you are? You think those people really like you as more than just an overweight novelty item?! Don't you see? You're nothing but a fat piece of Puerto Rican trash!"

My vision went momentarily white with rage, and my anger exploded like Mount Saint Madge, my voice booming out, full force. "*¡Puta!* How can *you* think you're so incredible?! You think everyone truly *likes* you? You're just a cookie-cutter student-body president that everyone voted for because no one else bothered to run against you—'cause no one would have even *dreamed* of running against the fucking TV star *Bridget Benson*! But you're nothing but *default* popular, Bridget. Those people in there care about *me*, not you. *¿Me entiendes?* You get it? You're a soulless, *hateful* person, and you know it, and I cannot *wait* till you're pregnant with some no-namer-wannabe-punk-rocker's baby and in rehab at twenty-one with your career down the toilet—"

"Yeah, wouldn't *that* make you happy? But you know what they say: eating—I mean, *living* well is the best revenge."

"Look, Bridget," I said, breathing deep and ignoring her last comment, "the fact remains: I might be fat, and I might have to have my clothes specially made for me, and I might sweat a little bit more than a hundred-and-two-pound sunken-in waif like you. But I have friends. *Real* friends. People who actually *give* a shit about me, which is more than I can say for you."

"Wow." She paused—for dramatic effect, I'm sure. "How long've you been waiting to say *that*?"

"Say what?"

"That you have friends, and I don't."

"You know the real reason I came over here?" I asked her, ignoring her question (and picturing the fifty dollars from Lucas in my head). "Because I was gonna offer to be your campaign manager for the race."

"Right. You really think I *need* that, Diaz?" She cocked her head again, and gave me a pitying look.

"Well, no, but I'm gonna enjoy the fifty dollars I just earned."

"What?"

"Nothing," I said, trying hard not to smile. I decided to savor this a little, so I egged her on. "Hey, all I know is that you've supposedly been running for weeks, but not everyone knows about it. That's kinda pathetic."

"*This*," she said, gesturing around my general vicinity, "is pathetic. Just get out of my face, all right? There's no way you'd know what you were doing anyway."

"Oh, yeah? *I* could probably get prom queen easier than you could."

Bridget cackled evilly (you never see her do *that* on the D

34

Channel!) and said, "I'm so certain I'd win, that if you beat me out, I'll let you *personally* dress me in your freak-chic garb at my *OK* shoot this summer."

Whoa, put on the brakes!

Did Bridget just challenge me to run against her for prom queen? And let me dress her for a major photo shoot if I won? This could be just the jump start my sister's fashion career needed! (And it might be fun to watch this girl cry after all the horrible things she just said to me.)

"Are you for real?" I asked her, disbelieving.

"Sure, why not?" she said, shrugging her narrow shoulders. "Seeing you lose out to me *again* is gonna be a sad thing to witness, but it'll be cute watching you try to impress me for the next few weeks."

So then I had to ask, "Well, what do you get if *you* win?"

"Please. Watching you grovel is gonna be reward enough. But if you throw in never *talking* to me all randomly like this again, I'll be plenty happy."

"Works for me," I said quickly. "Just get ready to lose by a landslide."

She let out one of those fake "Huh-*ha*!" laughs. "Honey," she said condescendingly, "the season premiere of my show fucking broke Nielsen *records*, okay? So we'll just see about your little theory." She turned around and strutted back to the party. "This is gonna be *so* fun, Diaz," she called over her shoulder.

A minute later, she was back in the house, and it was just me and Lucas out on the lawn. I headed back to my friend, who—good man that he is—was holding out a crisp fifty-dollar bill.

"Did you do it?" he asked, still holding on to the bill.

"I did indeed."

"You should get an extra ten for the fireworks display!" he said, handing it over to me. "What the hell happened?"

I told him everything—well, almost everything. I didn't wanna mention how much she'd gotten my goat by bringing up that whole audition thing, and the unspoken implications about what all happened *after* it. It'd just make Lucas feel sorry for me, and that's the last thing I needed right now.

What I needed right now was . . . to *celebrate*! Bridget was gonna *finally* be humbled like the subpar TV actress that she was, my sister's fabulous clothes were gonna take the world by storm, and *I* was gonna be the first 200-plus-pound prom queen Winter Park High had ever seen. . . .

And I think that called for at *least* a celebratory round of shots!

3

The Jungles
of Central Florida

· ·

I woke to the sound of swirling ice, and could feel my aching head practically splitting in two. My eyes struggled to open against the bright light and caked-up mascara, and I was momentarily disoriented until I took in the view of office buildings backed by endless expanses of flat suburban sprawl, with Mitsy stirring up a Bloody Mary in the foreground.

I groaned, and sat up in the white couch I'd passed out on the night before, after taking the car service back to Lucas's condo from the party. I noticed a (thankfully empty) wastebasket on the ground next to me.

"I know that sound," Mitsy said sagely, taking a bite out of her celery-stalk garnish. "That's the sound of . . . *regret*."

"What the hell happened last night?" I said. "The last thing I remembered was doing that Jäger Bomb. . . ."

"You're asking the wrong person, dear." Mitsy pointed to two white pills and a glass of something icy on the coffee table next to me. "Take those. You'll feel better."

"What is it?"

"Vodka and ecstasy."

I gagged and almost upchucked all of my fun from last night.

Mitsy cackled, way too loudly for eleven in the morning after a night of heavy libations. "It's just water and Tylenol, Madgie. Take the pills—Oh, *shit*! Hangover's hard *enough* on your liver, no need throwing Tylenol into the mix. Let me get you an Advil. We need to get you and your luscious caboose back in working order."

"Make it two Advil." I smiled.

Mitsy smiled sweetly back, and hustled to the bathroom as I took a sip of water from my glass.

I love Lucas's mom almost as much as I love Lucas. First off, and this sounds pretty superficial and all, but she's just so damn *hot*! And hot middle-aged ladies are pretty much automatically a-okay in my book. Mitsy's body is rockin', and her chin-length bouncy-bob-blonde hair totally just . . . *shimmahs*. She's, like, *Madonna*-hot—their one fundamental difference being that Madonna keeps in shape with all the power yoga and personal trainers, and Mitsy pretty much sticks to her three Ls: liquor, laxatives, and Lean Cuisine. But aside from her amazing looks and impeccable taste in clothing (the kind of taste that only *mucho dinero* can support), she is really easy and fun to talk to. Half the time I hang out at Lucas's, she's right there hanging out with us—which drives Lucas crazy sometimes, but I don't think he knows how good he has it.

But I'm in no mood to discuss *my* mother right now.

"So, should we try and piece together your evening?" There was a note of giddiness in Mitsy's voice—she loved hearing all about our parties. I would say that she missed the good ol' days, but it's not like she's hurtin' for things to put on her social calendar or anything. Lady seems to have plenty of fun as it is. "It's best to start from the beginning," she advised.

"Um . . . okay . . ." I gulped the last of my water and recounted the story of the party, from the car service on. I told her about the breakup—"I heard, I heard, I liked that Zach"—about the funneling—"Oh, how *barbaric*!"—about the dancing—"Did they play that 'Humps' song I like so much?"—the bong hit— "Oh, Madgie, you're just too much!"—and finally made it up to the conversation by the lake—

"Oh my God!" I cried, when it all came flooding back to me. I started laughing hysterically, despite my intense brain-pain.

"What?" Mitsy asked. "What happened next?"

"Madge decided to run for prom queen against everyone's favorite TV star," Lucas said, coming down the stairs into the living room.

"Lucas, darling!" Mitsy said, hopping up from her seat and running to greet her son at the foot of the stairs. "I'm so sorry about you and Zach. Is there *anything* I can do?"

"Um . . . yeah. Don't *ever* say his name again—I just can't take it." Lucas groaned tiredly and collapsed onto the couch, right on top of me.

"You couldn't wait for me to move my legs?" I asked him.

"Have a heart. I'm *dying*!"

"Wait," Mitsy interjected. "What was that about prom queen a minute ago?"

I jerked my legs out from under Lucas and kicked him lightly on the shoulder. "I just remembered what I *did* last night!" I said to him.

"How could you *forget* it?! It was brilliant!" Lucas turned to his mother and quickly recounted the story of my confrontation with Bridget, and Mitsy was lovin' it. (Lucas left out a few Kenny details, but whatever—I wouldn't wanna tell my mom that shamefulness, either.)

"So what happened after that?" Mitsy asked.

"Nothing much," Lucas said. "I just told her it was a great idea, but all Madge wanted to do was party more."

"Guess I just wanted to celebrate. I think I drunk-dialed my sister, too, to tell her the news." I grinned. "Hey, Lucas, when did *you* sober up?"

"I'd pretty much sobered up right when I started crying about Zach," he said pointedly.

"Oh," I said. "I'm sorry—was I not much of a comfort toward the end of the party?"

"Let's just say you gave me something *else* to worry about, Miss Jäger Bomb. . . ." he said.

"Sorry," I said sheepishly. "So I guess I overdid it last night." My stomach gurgled now at the thought of all that alcohol.

As if reading my mind, Mitsy asked quickly, "How 'bout some grilled cheese sandwiches, kittens?"

"*Yes!*" we both cried. Mitsy shuffled off happily to the kitchen, and Lucas reached for the remote.

"Wait," I said, grabbing the clicker from his hand. "So you *do* think this prom-queen thing is a good idea?"

"Why wouldn't it be?" he asked. "You said she, like, *majorly* insulted you, and you have a chance to get your sister's designs into a national magazine. What more could there be?"

"No . . . no, nothing. It's just, I wonder if I was too messed up when I said I'd do it. I was kinda out of it, Lucas, and she really got me angry. Like, maybe so angry I wasn't thinking straight . . ."

"Hey, all I know is what you told me, and from what you *told* me, I think it's definitely a great idea." A big grin spread across his face. "Plus, imagine the *drama* that's gonna unfold. It's gonna be *huge!*"

"I dunno . . . I'm all about helping my sister out and every-thing, but . . . *prom queen?* It just seems so stupid."

Lucas laughed. "I'm hearing about *stupid* from the girl who jumped into a lake last night?"

I looked down at myself. Somehow my latest Vanessa blouse was gone, and I was wearing a men's T-shirt that said, in big bold text, THAT'S JUST HOW I ROLL.

"Don't worry," Lucas said. "I was the one who made you change out of the blouse."

"When did I get this?"

"When you led the conga line downstairs and through the laundry room."

"Shit."

"Yeah, and I thought *I* was having an interesting night. . . ." He looked at me slyly and raised one eyebrow.

"Boy stuff?" I asked quietly.

"We'll talk later." He grinned. I almost lost the contents of my stomach again.

"I can hear you!" Mitsy yelled as she fired up the stove.

"*Anywaaay,*" Lucas said, ignoring his mother, "you *have* to do it. When you told me about your conversation with her, I was totally with you on every word of it. I don't think *anyone* really cares about that girl. She's just wedged her way into this weird sort of figurehead position, and everyone likes her 'cause they feel like they're *supposed* to. I mean, of *course* people are gonna like her. The girl is famous and has money. But everyone *already* and *truly* loves you, Madge—and I'm sure they'd love to see you become their prom queen."

"Yeah?"

"Would I lie?"

"No. But you'd exaggerate, Miz Drama Queen."

"Me? Exaggerate? Please."

"Didn't you tell me not five minutes ago that you were dying?"

He thought this over for a second, and said, "Point taken. But I'm serious."

"Huh." I hadn't really thought it out, I guess. Well, I hadn't really had much *time* to think it over, since I'd only just now remembered it all. But I recalled my conversation with Bridget in detail now, and I completely agreed with what I'd said to her. Wow, agreeing with myself . . . imagine that! Bridget was a mean-spirited, hurtful bitch, and the sooner people realized that, the better everyone would be for it.

And all of a sudden, a minor pang of hurt resurfaced from my storage-tank memory. Just a little pang. I suppressed it quickly, because it really wasn't that big a deal.

But maybe it's time for me to talk about the *Super Sweet 16* incident.

Bridget was on that god-awful MTV show that follows around vapid, spoiled *putas* that get their mommies and daddies to rent out clubs and hire pop stars to perform at their extravagant and "exclusive" Sweet 16 parties. Her episode—a Special Celebrity Edition, of course—was actually kind of awesome, in that pathetic sorta way. For some inexplicable reason, she'd themed it "Jungle Boogie," and had hired a bunch of "actors" to get into grass loincloths, put big fake tusk piercings all over their faces, and introduce her to the crowd of partygoers as she emerged from a cloud of rain-forest mist (dry ice from Party City, no doubt). Whether it was the fact that hired white-boy actors from Orlando don't exactly look Amazonian or the fact that no amount of rented foliage can transform the Winter Park

Farmer's Market into a lush, tropical forest, I don't know. But it just didn't work.

I think the only one who fully embraced the South American theme was good ol' Lindsay Taylor, Cokehead Extraordinaire. Actually, the producers had frozen a frame of Lindsay dancing like a spazzed-out maniac, and put it up next to a screen shot of her in her adorable ten-year-old-lil'-actress days. Kind of a before-and-after-skanking-out situation. Hilarious.

Later on during the show (though it was actually earlier in the evening, thanks to crafty MTV splicing and editing), I showed up at the door to get in with my glittery green invite. I *had* to take advantage of the opportunity to show my fabulous ass on television (it *had* been years, after all) . . . and to see what lame-ass has-been rapper the Bensons had gotten for the performance section of the evening. But when I got to the bouncer (who wasn't that big—I probably could've taken him), I was told quite rudely, "Yo, you ain't on the list."

"Oh, okay," I'd said, "but I should be—I got this invite."

"Sorry, I don't see no Diaz on here."

"Listen, handsome," I'd said nicely, "could you please just call Bridget over here? She knows me. We were friends when we were little."

(*That* made me look supercool on TV, for sure. . . .)

It was when the bouncer started talking into his headset, asking for someone to bring Bridget to the door, that I'd started to get an idea of how this was all gonna turn out. This was TV star

Bridget Benson's Special Starlet Edition *Sweet 16* show, and lord *knows* it needed drama!

Then Lindsay Taylor stumbled next to the bouncer, sniffing furiously and screaming all dramatically, "Wh-*at* the <bleep> is *she* doing here?"

Fantastic.

Even after she yelled into the club, "*Bridgeeeeet*, unless you ordered a fat Mexican *bitch*, I think we have a party crasher on our hands," Bridget never showed. I guess she was too image-conscious to be a complete and blatant bitch on TV. I just couldn't believe she'd set me up, and was petty enough to not let me in in the first place!

It was ten years ago, all over again—but meaner.

I didn't even bother pointing out to Lindsay, Professor Geographica, that I was Puerto Rican, which is a good 1,500 miles from Mexican. Or that this entire thing had clearly been staged. It was all too stupid for words. But still . . . national TV. It *was* embarrassing. But I think I did an okay job of not showing it. At least, I *hope* I did.

I turned around and walked back to my car. I felt a little crappy, but it's not like that was the first time I'd been made fun of for being fat, or even been dissed by Bridget Benson. But I'd gotten over that kind of shit a long while ago. . . .

Back at the penthouse, upon reflecting on this little gem of a memory, I decided officially: "Yeah, I'm gonna do it."

"Yay!" Lucas cheered. A genuine smile played across his cutesy little face, and I knew I had at least *one* true fan. And that was enough to start with. "Now, can I have the remote back?" he asked.

"No!" I told him. "We don't even know how someone *runs* for prom queen. It's not exactly like there's some sort of campaign for it. We have to brainstorm!"

"Oh, we have to do all that *now*? What happened to your hangover?"

"I dunno—maybe the grilled cheese will help . . . ?"

"*Madge*. A second ago you didn't even *know* you were running. Are you telling me you're gonna turn down a *Project Runway* marathon in favor of racking your over-boozed brain for ways to run for prom queen without looking like a tool? *Come on!*"

"God, you're dramatic."

"And you're repetitive." He snatched back the remote and smiled. "We'll deal with this on Monday. You should take today to relax. 'Cause tomorrow, we've gotta figure out how you're gonna blaze down the campaign trail."

Streaking
for the Cause

"... and today's lunch is crispy, *delicious* chicken tenders, fresh out of the freezer-oven, with a side of corn niblets in lukewarm water, iceberg-lettuce salad-equivalent with your choice of seven delectable dressings, and a square of the finest brownie-brick this school district could offer," I said into the loudspeaker. "And those are your mouthwatering morning announcements. Have a crap-tastic Monday!"

I spend first period in the front office. Not for money or anything, but for the volunteer hours. Eventually, all the office people ended up loving me so much that they let me do the morning announcements, any way I wanted to, as long as it didn't get too nasty. They figured it didn't do much harm, and it made the students actually *listen* to the announcements.

"Nicely done, Miss Diaz," Mrs. Kellerman, the old secretary, said. "Though I *like* those chicken tenders."

"Who doesn't?!" I said excitedly. "Who cares how they're prepared as long as they taste good?!"

"'Scuse me," I heard suddenly. I looked up and there was Bridget, waving a piece of paper in my face. "I have to make an announcement. Student-government thing." She looked me in the eye, a very slight grin tugging at the corners of her thin-lipped mouth.

"Can I see the announcement?" I asked her suspiciously.

"Of *course!*" she answered, all helpful. She handed me the piece of paper (which was typed up all kiss-assy and memo-style), smiling sweetly at Mrs. Kellerman the whole time. "How are *you* today, ma'am?" she asked her.

"Fine, dear, fine," Mrs. Kellerman said. "Keeping the students happy, Madam President?"

"Most definitely."

I tried not to puke as I listened to the ensuing exchange about how much Mrs. Kellerman's grandkids just *loved* Bridget's show, and read over the announcement.

Damn. From the looks of the "memo," it seemed that Bridget was actually stepping it up in the race for prom queen. First stop, the Environmental Club. I couldn't believe she'd—

"You know what, Margarita?" Bridget said, interrupting my reading. "Why don't *you* announce it? I *love* it when you do the announcements; it'd be a total honor."

Who knew that Evil Personified could be so chipper?! I tried to keep my eyes from bugging out as I took in the sight of her, all perky and brown-nosey, her little lips shiny with gloss. I felt a poke at my shoulder.

"Go ahead, dear," urged Mrs. Kellerman. "Read it for her. You *do* do such a nice job. . . ."

Well, I *could've* tried to say no to Bridget, Whore of Satan, but I couldn't turn down a sweet old lady . . . who was sort of like my boss, too.

"Okay . . ." I grabbed the mike again, and pressed down on BROADCAST. "Attention, students." I lifted my finger for a moment and took a deep breath. Cartoonish homicidal flashes played across my mind's eye: flattening Miss Flat Ass with an ACME safe, feeding her to a tank full of sharks with a hankering for skank, stringing some dynamite to her—

I exhaled.

"This announcement is to inform you that student government, headed, of course, by your student-body president, Bridget Benson, has joined the Environmental Club in the effort to make our community a better, cleaner place to live."

Gag me!

"Please find a student-government officer during your lunch period to sign up for Lake Cleanup Day, to be held this Saturday. Bridget will be at all lunches today, to kick the week off right." I sighed slightly. "Thanks again, and sorry for the interruption."

"You do have a lovely voice, Margarita," Bridget said to me

after I'd put away the mike again. And with another award-winning smile and a movie-star swish of her hair, she was gone.

Bridget was definitely working the crowd at lunch, hopping from one group of students to another, laughing and chatting it up with everyone from the IB kids to the water-polo boys and the over-it indie-rock crowd. And, much to my chagrin, no one seemed to mind. Guess she was pretty good.

"I can't stand what I'm seeing," Lucas said, munching on his tuna-and-celery sandwich. "Madge, if we don't think of something soon, she'll have schmoozed her way into prom-queendom."

"There's nothing *to* think about," I replied. "Gimme that sandwich."

"Come on, Madge!" Lucas cried, trying to snatch back his food.

"Oh, you gotta keep your slim little figure somehow," I told him, taking a big, delicious bite of the sandwich. I loved that Mitsy still made Lucas his lunch a couple of times a week. Tuna sandwiches, along with grilled cheese, is one of the things she can make *so* well.

Lucas twitched suddenly and reached into his pocket. "My vibrator," he said, grinning, as he took his phone out of his pocket. He looked at the display screen and frowned. "It's Zach."

"No way."

"Yes way." He paused. "Do I answer it?"

"Yes!" I cried, and he hopped up immediately and answered

it. I motioned for him to walk off and get some privacy, and he motioned for me to finish his sandwich. I was really excited about Lucas talking to Zach, not just because I liked the guy but because the Lucas and Kenny situation was a little more icky that I'd thought.

Once Lucas and I had gotten some alone-time the day before, he'd told me all about Kenny. Apparently, the little make-out session I'd stumbled on at the lakeside bench was only the first of many that night. (Guess Lucas had abandoned his look-after-Madge duties a couple times.) And like what sometimes happens with gay boys in semi-drunken lust, their relationship quickly pro-gressed to third date–type activities by the end of the evening.

Though the hooking-up stuff *had* surprised me a little bit, it hadn't thrown me as much as the fact that Lucas seemed like he might actually become *friends* with this Kenny character. I mean, it's all well and good to have a little rebound fun, but when it's with someone as blah as Kenny, it oughta stop there. (I mean, c'mon! On any day ending in *y*, you could see the outline of nipple piercings bumping out from under his skintight Abercrombie graphic tees. Not sexy.) But after I'd left the penthouse the day after the party, the two of them had met up for a magical day of bonding at—where else, for two gay boys in Orlando?—the Millenia Mall.

Whatevs.

The guy had *ulterior motives* (among other things) written all over him. But as long as he didn't sit with us at lunch, I guess a little shopping wasn't such a big deal. Though I'd have to keep an eye on things.

I just hoped Kenny wasn't the one to drive them that day . . . 'cause another prom-night rumor about dear Kenny was that he was either so slap-you-in-the-face high or don't-even-know-your-own-name drunk that he got pulled over by the cops for driving *under* the speed limit on I-4.

Fifteen miles per hour, I'd heard.

In the grassy median.

I mean, come on, dude. Call a cab. Or a friend. Moron.

And in stark contrast to Kenny, there was Zach.

I was *such* a Zach fan. He was the nicest, funniest, most endearingly geeky guy—and he so adored Lucas, even if he couldn't show it in public yet. I could totally see Lucas's frustration with all that—and there's no question as to where my loyalty is—but I couldn't help but feel that Zach couldn't really help his situation yet.

Poor Zach had some pretty awful parents. I'd never met them, but I'd certainly heard about them. I mean, we're talking, like, "God created AIDS to kill off gay people—Homosexuality is an abomination—Birth control is evil"–type of parents. I always figured he'd come out when he decided he could—like when he was out of the house, more financially independent, and more in the mood to get . . . I dunno, *disowned*—and that Lucas was gonna stick around for it. But I guess I'd been wrong.

I'd call Lucas a jerk, except that it couldn't have been easy for him to bear Zach's burden with him. . . .

Thinking about this whole thing had kinda sapped my appetite, and by the time Lucas returned—looking at the ground, bewildered—I'd barely touched his scrumptious Mitsy-made sandwich.

"What?" I asked him after he'd been sitting a full forty-five seconds in silence. "Say something!" I tried my hardest not to cross my fingers—and my legs and my feet and my arms and my eyes—for a Lucas–Zach reunion.

"Sorry," he said suddenly, finally looking up at me. "That was just weird."

"What was weird? How he was begging for forgiveness so hard-core that you could almost *picture* him down on his knees with his hands folded, screaming, *'Forgive me! I love you! I want to be your gay prom date!'"*

Lucas laughed a little, taking his sandwich back from me. "Not exactly. He pretty much called me up to see how I was doing. There was, like, *no* hint of wanting to make up in his voice." He shook his head. "And he actually *said*, 'So you're okay with the fact that we're broken up for good?'"

"He did?"

"He did." Lucas was talking faster now. "And he even got a little mean about it—he was like, 'Because I know how you get and how you always think that you're right, and I'm through with that,' which *really* pissed me off."

"That doesn't sound like him," I said softly. "I'm sorry." Maybe I'd given Zach too much credit. Was it possible for the sweetest gay boyfriend of *my* sweetest gay boyfriend to go from zero to bitchy in one breakup? Did I know *either* of these boys at all?!

"Yeah," Lucas said, "it really *isn't* like him—you're right."

(Okay, well, that made me feel a little more sane.)

Lucas shrugged his shoulders and stood back up, looking out toward the main courtyard, where Bridget was probably still schmoozing like crazy. Lucas snorted. "Ugh. She's putting up another one of those goddamn posters. Tackiness! Enough is enough!"

"You sure you're done talking about Za—?"

"I'm done talking about Zach for a good long time, Madge," he interrupted pointedly, looking down at me. "My mourning period is officially *over* as of right now. So, *please*."

"Okay," I told him. Wow, another dose of Testy Lucas. I decided to back off, and got up and joined him, checking out Bridget. "I just can't believe that the irony's not lost on anyone," I said as Bridget finished putting up her poster. "I mean, Lake *Cleanup* Day? We saw her throw litter *into* a lake at Madison's party! *So* ridiculous . . ."

"Oh. My. God," Lucas mumbled all of a sudden, and pointed. "Naked boys!"

I heard it before I saw it: the screams and hollers of five naked guys, streaking through the outdoor lunch area, yelling, *"Wooooh! Lake Cleanup Day! We love you, Bridget! Wooooh!"* I turned my head and saw them: five of the school's fittest, hottest, A-list-iest guys, streaking for the cause, with nothing but a huge, long banner running across their midsections. The banner was circular, so if the boys held both sides of the paper on either side of them, they were covered up. Pretty much. I still saw some junk flying around, and every one of their asses.

Not that I was complaining, but this was definitely one way to get everyone's attention. And I was a little mad that I hadn't thought of it myself.

Everyone at lunch started laughing and cheering, and even a few people from the cafeteria came outside to see what was going on. Luckily for the boys (but not Lucas, who was busy trying to mop up his drool), no administrators came outside in time to stop them, and within a minute, they were through a half-open fence and safely off school grounds.

"I love my life," Lucas said simply. "At this moment, everything is right with me. . . ."

Before I could say anything, Bridget Benson's voice crackled loudly through a megaphone. "Hi, everyone. And, um . . . thanks, boys . . ." She giggled. "See what lengths some of us will go to for the environment?" she said to the crowd that had gathered. "Well, while I do *not* condone breaking school rules—and I'm sure there *must* be one about running around campus naked—I *am* happy that some people are serious about Lake Cleanup Day. And I want to get all your help, because I love this school and this community *so much*, and I'm super-proud to have become part of this really worthwhile event. Anyway, please—"

"*Bridget for prom queen!*" the streakers called, now all piled into a car and driving past. The crowd erupted into laughter and cheers again.

That conniving, evil . . . brilliant woman. I wonder how she convinced them to do all this. Tawdry sexual favors was my best guess. Or maybe she just whored out Lindsay. That's what washed-up Dr. Scholl's commercial actresses were for, after all.

"Ha-ha," Bridget laughed all fake-embarrassedly. "Well, sure, I'll take *that* endorsement." She ran her fingers through her gorgeous head of hair and did a little pose that Tyra *and* Janice Dickinson would've been proud of. "As I was saying, please do consider signing up for Lake Cleanup Day. We need all the help we can get. Oh! And I have a bunch of cookies"—she motioned to Lindsay, who was holding a big tray of chocolate-chip cookies— "so whoever signs up can get one. While supplies last! Thanks!"

"Lindsay probably laced them," Lucas said.

I just smiled and shook my head.

"So, what now?" Lucas asked me, biting into a carrot stick.

I thought about it a second. "I guess the only thing to do is become just as visible as Bridget. Go where she goes, that sort of thing. Starting with . . ."

". . . wiiith . . . what?" Lucas raised an eyebrow questioningly.

"How do you feel about manual labor on Saturday mornings?"

Lucas collapsed in a dramatic full-body sigh, his bones apparently having turned to Jell-O. "Why do you have to drag *me* into this?" he asked, lying on his back and whining.

"Because it was you who helped convince me to do this in the *first* place, buddy." I smirked. "And your new man Kenny might be there. . . ." I ventured, hating myself a little bit.

"Yeah, hoping for more nakedness, probably," Lucas scoffed.

"And aren't *you?*"

Lucas raised an eyebrow. "Fine. But you have to go sign me up yourself. And grab me a cookie. I can only hope it *is* laced with something. . . ."

I snatched the rest of his sandwich back from him before he could protest and nibbled it happily on my way up to the signup table. When Bridget saw me approaching, she rose gracefully, handed the signup sheet to Lindsay, and walked over to greet me.

"Hey, Margarita," she called from afar, loud enough for everyone to hear. "*Great* job on the announcement today!"

"Thanks!" I said, all chipper. When we were finally face-to-face and only a few feet apart, I said quietly, "You seriously think you should be so confident just 'cause you paid a few hot boys to streak for you?"

"Um . . . *yeah*, I think I should be. 'Cause what've *you* got?"

"I don't need to rely on such crass and blatant advertising," I told her. "My ass is its *own* advertisement."

"I'll say. Too bad we don't have an elephant to parade around campus in a little white dress for you—*that* might get your message across."

"Bridget, come on. Elephant jokes?" I snorted. "You can do better than that."

"Well, *you* can't do better than this." She gestured to the long line of people waiting to register for the cleanup. "So it looks like you've got your work cut out for you."

"It suuure does," I said, nodding dumbly with widened eyes. "Starting with Saturday morning."

Bridget cocked her head. "What do you mean?" she asked, a little confused.

"I'm here to sign up for the cleanup. I *love* the environment. Almost as much as your gas-guzzling SUV loves to destroy it!" I punched her shoulder lightly. "So sign me up. I don't wanna wait in the line. Oh—and Lucas Ellison, too. He's coming."

"You're *sure* you can handle a day outside in the heat?" she asked, a note of nervous expectation in her voice. "You're not gonna, like, *faint* or anything, are you? I'm not gonna have to hose you down or make sure you get a mud bath to keep the mosquitoes away?"

"Cute, but no. Just let me grab some cookies, and I'll be on my way." I surprised her by leaning forward to give her a little hug and kiss-kiss on the cheek, and I whispered in her ear, "It can't be *your* show the whole time. You don't know what you've got yourself into."

And before she could give me what I'm sure would've been a bitingly witty retort, I skipped over to the table, picked up some cookies, and sashayed back to Lucas, feeling tons better already.

I was *not*, however, feeling all that great on Friday night, the night before Lake Cleanup Day. Don't worry! The cookies weren't laced, and I wasn't feverish or puking or stationed at the toilet for any sort of long period of time. It was just another Friday night dinner with my mother that was getting me down.

The rest of the week at school had been great, though! Word had started getting around that I wanted to run for prom queen, and I was getting almost nothing but good reactions. When people asked me why I was doing it, I would pretty much say, "Um . . . why *not*?!" People seemed very much into it, and I couldn't help but feel that I almost had it in the bag. I figured all I had to do for the next couple of weeks was get people talking around school, try not to spaz out too much, and show up to as many parties and events as I could, just to stay on people's minds. And with the last days of high school rapidly approaching, I was in quite the party mode anyway. . . .

Unfortunately, this Friday, there were no big parties to speak of. Vanessa was out on a date, and Lucas was having dinner with his aunt and Mitsy (though I made him *swear* to call and rescue me as soon as he could!), so I was left to dine at home with *Madre* Dearest.

Well, *home* is a term I use loosely. I kinda have three "homes," and, in order of how much I like each one of them, they are as follows: 1) Lucas and Mitsy's penthouse, 2) my sister's apartment, and 3) my parents' house.

It's not like I hate my parents, really. I'm sort of indifferent about my dad since he's a total workaholic-lawyer guy who's hardly home to begin with. But I'll give him credit for wanting to pull me out of acting after the whole audition thing.

My mom, on the other hand, on a daily basis makes me crazy

enough to eat rice cakes. Actually, correction: *no one* could make me *that* crazy. But she's a gorgeous, health-nut *psychopath* of a woman who was put through too many mind-warping beauty pageants as a little girl and seems to hate the fact that I inherited my most apparent traits from my dad's side of the family—those traits being mainly my husky five-foot-ten frame. I won't say how much I weigh—because *no* lady does that!—but let's just say it's at least a deuce . . . plus the weight of a beagle, *mas o menos*. But I inherited my *telenovela*-star good looks from my mom, so she seems to think it's possible to reverse half of my genetics and make me into the daughter she always wanted.

Basically, I think she wants me cut in half, but since that's not really an option, diet and exercise (or at least a constant sound-track of *nagging* me) are her weapons of choice. Meals with my mom generally included a very bland piece of meat (grilled, dry, unmarinated chicken breast is her specialty), a pile of steamed veggies (what *is* kale, anyway?!), and brown rice (since bad carbs are outlawed in this household). And you can forget eating any snacks in peace—I can hardly pop open a cookie package and party with the Keebler Elves without hearing the goddamn *tsk, tsk* sound my mom is so famous for. And the biggest kicker is that when my dad can actually be bothered to join us for dinner, my mom manages to make him something fried or fatty or flavorful, and I'm stuck with the same brown-rice-and-vegetables BS.

Maybe she thinks that a life of overexercise, denying yourself happiness and decent sustenance, and tracking the development of wrinkle lines more than, say, the state of current affairs is what I want for myself.

But it's not what I want.

On this particular Friday night, I was practically *finished* with my whitefish and steamed spinach before my mom had even taken her second bite. When she's not having one of her trademark screaming-in-Spanish hissy-fits, she's so damned slow and deliberate about everything. Makes me *loca*.

"So, *amor*, how was school today?" she asked me, delicately preparing herself a bite of the wilted dark-green spinach. The sick amount of gold she was wearing around her wrists jangled as she worked her eating utensils.

"Not nearly as fun as this lightly salted catch-of-the-day," I answered sarcastically. "*Really*, Mom, I don't know what I do to deserve this."

"I don't understand why we have to have this conversation again and again, Margarita," she said tiredly. "I'm only trying to get you into some healthy eating habits so that when you go away to Gainesville next year, you'll know how to cook for yourself."

"You realize the only habits you're teaching me are to sneak food from Dad's dinners and to hightail it to the closest drive-through the second I leave this house, don't you?"

Mom sighed. "I wish you wouldn't."

"And you did the same thing to Vanessa, and it's not like it taught *her* anything."

"*Hija*, I only try my best," she said. "You know it's because I care about you. And you *know* I wish Vanessa would make better choices . . . starting maybe with some actual *college*."

"*Mami!* You *know* she wanted to go to fashion school instead!"

"And we weren't paying for that! Why would we? So she could waste our money and fall flat on her face?" she asked, dropping her fork and looking me in the eye. "*No*, Margarita—we didn't want to take that chance. College degree *first*. If she wants to go to fashion school, she can do it on her own time. She should've gone to a university when she had the chance."

"It's not like college has an expiration date," I informed her quietly. "And I like this whole use of *we*. Is that the royal *we*, since Papa's never here?"

"*Coño-carajo*, Margarita, enough!" She looked back down at her plate, and cut herself a minuscule piece of fish. Maybe she figured that if she took smaller bites, it'd feel like a real meal. I'm surprised she wasn't eating with teeny-tiny silverware.

The thing that bugged me about my mom and Vanessa was that it seemed like I was the favorite daughter. Which really isn't saying much, believe me. But I'm the one with the leftover acting money, and then the scholarship. And I *know* my mom would've helped me out with school, even if I didn't have all that. So why wouldn't she help Vanessa, when fashion design is, like, the *one* thing she's ever wanted? I got to act when I was little—why couldn't Vanessa pursue her own dreams? It was so aggravating, and it made me want to win prom queen all the more, for her sake.

"So. Let's talk about something else," Mom said quietly. "You have any plans for the weekend?"

"Well, I'm probably sleeping over at Lucas's tonight—"

"*Oye*, this is the first *I've* heard of this," she interrupted me. "I wanted to take some more measurements for your dress!"

"*More* measurements?" I let out a little chuckle. "Mom, I'm still as big as I was last weekend—just use those measurements."

My mother rolled her eyes.

"Anyway, I'm going over to Lucas's, because in the morning we're going to this Lake Cleanup Day thing."

"Why don't you have him over here?"

Because all you'll do is criticize me in front of him in the hopes that pure, torturous embarrassment will miraculously cure my love for the magic of fast food.

"Because my room's a huge mess."

"So what is this . . . Lake Cleanup Day?"

"Just something that student government thought up—get everyone involved in cleaning up this nasty lake near school. No big deal."

"Well, I think it sounds *fantástico*, Margarita." She leaned back a bit and smiled. "It's nice to see you get involved."

"Mm-hmm," I said. I didn't want to let her know about the prom-queen thing. She'd probably flip out and yell and scream in that crazy way I was talking about earlier and say that I was just gonna get my fat feelings hurt. And I didn't need to deal with that. "And it'll be some good exercise," I said to appease her. Plus, it'd make her less mad that I was going to sleep at Lucas's for, like, the third time this week.

"That's true," she said, nodding and wiping her mouth with her cloth napkin. "Okay, *bueno*. When are you going to Lucas's house?"

"As soon as he's done with dinner with his aunt, he's gonna call me," I said.

"You know, if it's exercise you're looking for, you can join my spinning class!" she said, getting a little too excited. "We could go at six, right before school—"

"Oh, wait!" I interrupted, touching my pocket. "I think my phone's vibrating." Sometimes lying just came too easily. I took the phone out of my pocket and ran to my room, pretending to have a conversation with Lucas. "Sure!" I said deliberately, good and loud. "I'll be over soon. Bye-bye!"

"Gotta go, Mami," I said, walking back to the table. "I'll call you tomorrow after the lake."

"Oh. Okay," she said, sighing a little sadly. "Your papa should be home in a couple hours, though."

"Well, tell him I said hi, and to stop working so damn much," I said, taking my plate to the kitchen.

"*Callate su boca, hija.* He does what he can to provide for us."

"Okay," I said, running back to the table to give her a kiss on the cheek. "Bye." I think I heard her start to say something in the way of a lame apology, but I was out of the room too quickly. I just couldn't deal with it right now.

Within ten minutes, I was free—out of the house and on the road. I know it might be a tad on the bitchy side to ditch my mother, but she could really stress me out. Maybe if she wanted me to stick around more, she'd just chill out about everything.

My mom wasn't *always* like this. For one thing, the separate-dinners thing only started a few years ago, I guess when she realized that Vanessa hadn't been a fat-fluke, and that I wasn't gonna growth-spurt out of *my* chubby body. And she used to be a lot more fun to hang out with . . . like back when I thought *Bridget* was fun company. One of my clearest Mami-memories, actually, was when she helped me sew an octopus pillow for Bridget's seventh birthday. It took *forever*—and she probably did most of it, since she's a whiz at everything crafty—but it's one of those burned-in-my-brain-cells happy memories that I relive a little anytime I see sea creatures with tentacles.

I'll bet Octavian the Octopus went right in the Dumpster after Bridget dumped me. Whatever. Why the funk did *I* care?

I figured I could cool my jets by going to Sonic and having some tater tots and a burger brought to me while I waited for Lucas's call. Nothing better to do for the next couple of hours, especially at my house.

Almost like clockwork, as I finished off my strawberry shake and collected up my wrappers to throw in the trash, Lucas called me and said he was ready to hang out.

Saved!

I reached out my car window and threw my trash away in the

nearby trash bin. I love Sonic—you don't even have to get out of your car!

I reversed, pulled out onto the road, and headed downtown.

I found rock-star parking on the street right outside Lucas's building and made my way into the lobby.

"Hello again, Miss Diaz," Carl, my favorite doorman, greeted me as I walked toward the elevator bank. "What's shakin'?"

"Hey, Carl, just the usual," I answered, doing a playful shake of the hips.

He chuckled embarrassedly (even though this was our usual greeting) and told me to go on up, the Ellisons were expecting me.

"Thanks, toots," I said, punching him on the shoulder as I walked past.

After the thirty-five-floor ride, I was greeted at the door not by Lucas or Mitsy . . . but Kenny Daniels.

"Hey," he said, flatly and nasally. "Lucas is in the shower. I was just leaving." That was the extent of the greeting. A far cry from Mitsy's usual "Madgie! Madgie!" chorus, which was generally followed with a bear hug. Kenny spun on his heel and returned to the penthouse, grabbing a shopping bag from the kitchen counter and getting ready to leave.

"So . . . what are you doing here, Kenny?" I asked, trying to sound nonchalant. "Did you guys go shopping or something?" I felt a little stupid asking this, since it was late, and Lucas had just finished eating with his mom and aunt. Of *course* they hadn't been shopping.

"Yeah, well, we went last weekend. I just forgot this bag, so . . ."

"Oh. Okay."

I wondered if Kenny had bought whatever was in that bag *himself*, since I'd noticed during his five-minute guest appearances at our lunch area that aside from a total lack of *personality*, Kenny also seemed to have a blatant lack of *money*. Lucas was always giving him handfuls of change or dollar bills so he could eat his skinny-club-kid-figure-keeping lunches of Coke Zero and animal crackers. And since it was common knowledge that Lucas was pretty loaded, I hoped Kenny wasn't taking advantage.

Kenny was making so little effort to be friendly or sociable as he tied his shoes and danced to that beat in his head that I considered ripping off my clothes and screaming at the top of my lungs, *"IS IT TRUE THAT YOU DIDN'T MAKE IT TO PROM LAST YEAR BECAUSE YOU ATTACKED A FRYCOOK AT DENNY'S?!"* just to get a rise out of him.

Thankfully, Lucas came down the stairs at that point, all fresh and clean and polished looking, already in his pj's.

"Hey, honey," he called as he approached us in the living room.

"Hey," both me and Kenny replied.

Ick. Now *I* needed a shower.

"Bye again," Kenny called up to Lucas, and with that, he was gone. Thank God. I didn't need any added stress to my evening right now. I just wanted to curl up on that cushy white couch, watch some DVDs with my best friend, and forget about the fact that I had to wake up at the ungodly-for-Saturday hour of eight A.M. to go clean a mucked-up lake.

"What was that all about?" I asked, masking my concern with a playful smirk and wink.

"Oh, nothing—I just had that bag of his," Lucas said, all nonchalant.

I raised an eyebrow.

And Lucas moaned, exasperated, "I'm being serious!"

How *Does* One Recover
from a Wooden Animal Party?

After everyone's words of prom-queen encouragement through-
out the last week, I was feeling pretty confident Saturday morning,
as Lucas and I ate our delicious McDonald's breakfasts on the way
to the lake. Pretty confident, that is, until I fully took in the
scene at the lake.

Bridget had outdone herself. And me, clearly.

A big Home Depot truck was pulled up to the park, and
people were unloading dozens of small trees, bushes, and flowers
from it. Bags of mulch, potting soil, and fertilizer were already
out and stacked on the ground. Lindsay handed out gift bags—
filled with Luna bars, bananas, granola from Whole Foods, jars
of natural preserves from the farmers' market, and a reusable

water bottle with LAKE CLEANUP DAY and the date printed across its middle—to everyone as they signed in. A gigantic tub filled with ice sat next to the signup/gift-bag table, bottles of Vitamin Water, Gatorade, Fiji, and Evian sitting inside. And amidst it all stood Bridget, clipboard in hand, moving cheerfully from person to person, doling out their duties for the day.

To make matters worse, it was one of those awful Central Florida mornings where—despite it being early March and not even close to "summer"—it was already in the mid-eighties, with air so humid it's like a brick wall of mugginess.

I was so not in the mood for this anymore.

But I grabbed a Focus-flavor Vitamin Water anyway—hopefully it'd do its job.

"Wow," Lucas said. "This is kinda nuts."

"Yeah," I agreed. "I was not expecting this."

The turnout was impressive. Bridget had done a bang-up job on collecting those signatures. At least a hundred people were there already, with more showing up by the carload. Kids were already swarming all over the area surrounding the lake, picking up trash, digging holes for the new plants, and getting orders from Bridget.

"Oh, God," I moaned, "it's too early in the morning for any of this. Look at me! I'm already *sweating*. And I just got a mosquito bite! Fuck! *This* is why I don't ever do shit outdoors."

"I can't believe you roped me into this," Lucas said. "I *knew* it'd be awful. Let's just go home."

"Wait, hey . . . maybe it won't be so bad," I said. "I mean, we're near a lake. . . ."

"A lake that's a virtual nursery for bloodthirsty insects!" Lucas complained.

"C'mon, let's just do this thing. You know I have to."

Lucas groaned, and we made our way into the crowd to do a little prework mingling—since that was sort of the whole point of it all—but were quickly intercepted by Bridget.

"*Hi*, Margarita," she said enthusiastically. "Thanks for coming out and lending a hand. I think I'll put you two on"—she looked deliberately, importantly at her little clipboard—"shore duty."

"Okay . . . ?" I said unsurely.

"Just grab some trash bags and pick up all the garbage you see along the shore of the lake."

Fantastic, I thought. *We're trolling through mud for trash.* But what else was I expecting? And I couldn't help but notice that no one else seemed to be on shore duty. But I couldn't say anything in front of all the other students without seeming like a petty bitch, so I just said, "Cool," and got a trash bag and went to work. "Let's go, Lucas!" I said with as much gusto as I could muster.

"This is some awful, torturous *bullshit*," I wailed at around noon, after way too many hours of trudging through slippery, slimy, skuzzy mud. I had completely soaked my T-shirt in sweat, my face was probably beet-red from all the exertion and sun, and my shoes and jeans were caked in mud up to my knees. Not to mention the virtual all-you-can-eat buffet my body had become for the local mosquito population.

And Bridget was trying her best to keep us isolated from the rest of the volunteers. Every time I took a break to walk up to the water tub, Bridget was already there, intercepting me with a bottle of Fiji water: "One step ahead of you—now, could you please go and do" blah, blah, blah. Each time I strayed too far from my post, she'd be right there in my face. "Looking for more garbage bags? Here's some." "Here, I brought you another banana—you looked hungry."

I really don't know why I was obeying her blindly and just doing whatever she told me to do. Well, it *could've* been because my general apathy about the whole thing was rising in direct correlation with the increasing heat and humidity. I just couldn't care less now.

"It's not *that* bad, Madge," Lucas told me.

"Easy for *you* to say, Mr. Popular. I wish *I'd* gotten four 'urgent' phone calls in the last two hours." I eyed him suspiciously. "Just how urgent *were* those calls?"

"Very," he said, smiling. "And I can't control who calls me when. I'm in demand, baby."

I ignored him and set my garbage bag down. "I'm about ready to strip naked and jump in this lake." But instead I just collapsed onto the ground, exhausted.

"Skinny-dipping is always superhot," he replied, coming to

join me on my patch of dry grass. He opened my new bottle of Fiji and poured it over our faces.

I squealed as a few drops of the hoity-toity water got sucked up my nose.

"Ohhh, you look *super*sexy now!" Lucas joked.

"Stop it!" I screeched.

"Awww, c'mon, *Maaar*-garita," I heard a deep voice say from behind me. "You know you look *damn* sexy all the time."

That deep, drawly Southern twang—and the sudden warmth in my cheeks—could only mean one thing: Randy Larson was nearby.

I sat up quickly, trying feverishly to wipe the water from my face, which was probably only making matters worse with my appearance, and turned around to face Randy.

Okay.

Remember my crush on BK Drive-Through Guy? Maybe I forgot to mention my little crush on Redneck Randy (which is what he lets me call him). I can't believe it took all these years of knowing him to notice it, but he was *so* damn cute. In that not-trying-hard kind of way, because really, he didn't have to. He was a little bit pudgy, but he still had some *niiice* muscles; you could tell from how his clothes hugged certain parts of his body, even though he always wore large T-shirts and baggy Levi's jeans—and not that waifish-hipster-kid skinny-jeans nonsense. No frills. I liked that about Randy. And those baby blues set deep in his tanned, well-proportioned face didn't hurt much, either. Nor did the thick, curly sandy-blond hair held down by his Bass Pro Shop hat.

What? You expect me to occupy all my time with gay-boy drama?

"So'm I gonna have to rough up this guy pourin' water all over you?" he said good-naturedly.

"No!" I exclaimed, getting to my feet and laughing hard. Probably *too* hard. I hated turning into a giddy schoolgirl around guys. "Randy, this is my friend Lucas. Lucas, this is Randy—he's having that party tonight."

"Indeed I am," Randy said as he shook Lucas's hand. He totally wasn't Lucas's type, but I could tell by the slight blush in Lucas's cheeks that he was appreciating the understated *hotness* that was Randy Larson. "So, you guys comin'?"

"Yeah," I said, answering for the both of us. I'd told Lucas about the party on the way to the lake that morning. He'd seemed a *little* wary, but I'd made him promise.

Randy has this blowout at his grandparents' house every year around this time. His grandparents have this annual trip to Vegas for some good old-fashioned gambling and NASCAR-ing, and that leaves the house—and the acre of backwoods land it sits on—empty, just *begging* to have a party thrown at it. The place is out in Chuluota, a little hickish town about a half hour outside Orlando.

Every year, Randy and his fucking crazy friends try to top themselves from the year before. Sophomore year was pretty nutty in itself, what with the keg-stand tournament and the mud wrestling, and last year they added in a diving competition—but using an enormous trampoline and an aboveground pool. I wondered what was gonna happen this time.

I felt a little privileged to have been to the inaugural Randy bash. And if anyone had been able to lift me, I would've *so* kicked ass in the keg-stand competition.

"Cool," Randy said. "Well, I better get back to plantin' trees before Bridget comes over and yells at me. Just wanted to make sure you'd be there, Margarita."

That made me smile.

"And you, too, Lucas," he said. "Nice meetin' you."

"You, too!" Lucas called as Randy headed off. Once he was gone, Lucas slapped me playfully and teased, "Looks like the Fiji isn't the only thing gettin' you wet!"

"Naughty!" I yelled, hitting him back.

"I can't *believe* you haven't introduced us yet, Madge," Lucas said, putting his arm around me. "You clearly wanna keep him for yourself."

"Get away from me," I said, laughing. "I just don't hang out with him that much. . . . But, yeah—he *is* yummy, no? Lucas, you *have* to come tonight, okay? 'Cause—"

"Hey, Rita!" I was cut off by Annabelle Turner, the Environmental Club president, as she came up and joined us. "I'm glad you came out to help," she said, plopping down on the ground next to us. "Did you get a Luna bar?"

"I did," I told her. "I even grabbed some extras—this is hard work."

"I know, isn't this all . . . great . . . ?" She looked at me and sighed heavily.

"What?" I asked her, intrigued.

"Can you keep a secret?" she asked me.

"Please. You know me." And she *did* know me. Annabelle and I had been friends since ninth grade—she was a cool girl. Really passionate about the environment—we're talking no paper plates, recycles her class notes at the end of each year, takes the bus to school even though she has her own car. . . .

"Okay," Annabelle said now. "I mean, it's *really great* that Bridget decided she wanted this thing to be student government's latest pet project. If she hadn't, we wouldn't have, like, a *third* of the people we have here today."

"Right . . ."

"It's just . . . gift bags—which are completely nonrecyclable in the first place—and all this other elaborate stuff . . . I just can't help but feel like it's detracting from the whole *point* of it all."

"Are you thinking of the twenty-odd SUVs in the parking area?" I asked her.

"Yes!" she cried. "I mean, who here really gives a hoot about the planet?"

"Well, all the Environmental Club kids, for sure," I said. "Other than that, though . . ."

"And you, too," Annabelle said quickly.

I laughed a little. "Annabelle, baby, I *do* care about the environment. But I'd sooner replace all the lightbulbs in my house with those special fluorescent ones than do this again. I'm sorry, but I'm seriously about to *die!*"

"Hey, at least you're honest," she told me, "and that's more than I can say for most people here. . . . But whatever. Today's a big success, so I should just shut up and go with the flow." She pushed herself up off the ground and we said our good-byes.

I slapped another mosquito that'd landed on my arm. I knew I was delicious and all, but this was just ridiculous. I stood up and turned to face Lucas, stomping my foot against the ground, since it had fallen asleep.

"All right, Lucasito," I said, still working out the pins and needles. "I think we've done our part, don't you?"

"*God* yes!" Lucas cried.

"You guys aren't leaving so soon, are you?" I heard Bridget ask, having appeared out of nowhere.

"*Soon?*" I said. "We've been her for, like, three hours. That's plenty. And the lakeshore has *never* looked better. We're outtie."

"Ohhh . . . m-kay . . ." She feigned sadness. "But you're gonna miss the big finale."

"*Please* tell me it's a pool party."

"Funny. No, just stick around—I want you to see this."

"As long as it's happening in the next five minutes," I told her, smacking myself in the neck as I felt another mosquito burrowing into my flesh.

"You want some repellent?" Bridget asked.

"Um . . . no. No, thanks," I replied, a little thrown off by the random kindness. "We're leaving soon anyway, so . . ."

"Okay, okay, just . . . head over to the coolers," she said. "I have to get something out of my car."

So Lucas and I—curious as could be—left the shoreline and headed up to where all the coolers were. I grabbed myself a bottle of Gatorade, and followed Bridget with my eyes, watching as she opened the back door of her shiny champagne-colored Escalade ('cause she was so ghetto-fabulous). She pulled something out. Something big, and covered with a sheet.

"Is that a machine gun?" Lucas asked me. "You think she's gonna end the prom-queen race now, once and for all?"

I laughed, putting my sweaty arm around my friend. "At least we'd be in *Us Weekly*, right?"

"A dream come true," he said, putting on a big fake smile, then relaxing into a real one.

Bridget made her way down the hill from the parking area, calling out to all the volunteers. "People! People! I have a little announcement to make."

Within a couple minutes, everyone had left their posts to gather around Bridget, no doubt wondering what the four-foot sheet-covered shape was all about. Once she had everyone's attention, she got into her whole student-body-president groove and spouted off the same BS that she did when she'd plugged Lake Cleanup Day at lunch on Monday—helping hands, pitching in, bettering the community, all that shiz.

I caught Lucas's eye, and he looked truly baffled at what was going on. His eyes were wide as he mouthed, *What the fuck?*

All I could do was shrug.

Then I noticed Annabelle, who looked a mixture of curious, perturbed, and exhausted. Poor girl. Bridget was totally stealing the Environmental Club's thunder to make herself look good.

"And so," Bridget concluded, "to commemorate this day, and all our hard work, I give you the Lake Cleanup Day memorial—"

"Wait!" I yelled.

I think that if Bridget *had* been holding a machine gun at that moment, I would've been dead.

She sighed and asked, "What?" as calmly as she could.

"Don't you think we should hear from Annabelle, President of the Environmental Club?"

Without missing a beat, Bridget just said, "Of course!"

"Annabelle," I said, catching her eye, "go on up there and say a few words."

The crowd of people sort of broke apart a little for her, and Annabelle emerged, looking a little embarrassed. I ran up to her quickly and whispered in her ear, "Just do your thing—let's get some of these kids into hybrids next year."

She smiled, quietly thanked me, and went up to stand next to Bridget.

"Well, first of all," she said, "I wanna thank Bridget and all of student government for making today so special—we wouldn't have had such a successful day if it hadn't been for them, so let's give 'em a round of applause." Annabelle started the applause, and Bridget did a gracious little curtsy. "But I was hoping you all would take something else away from this experience. This is just one tiny lake in one tiny city in the world. But it *will* make a difference. Each tree you planted will absorb up to *one ton* of carbon dioxide in its lifetime. And it's little things like that—if we do them every day—that can help save our planet. Seriously—it doesn't take much. A different kind of lightbulb. A more fuel-efficient car. Carpooling when you can. Come and see me if you want more specifics, but I wanted to let you all know that, if you truly care about your planet, Lake Cleanup Day isn't where your involvement should stop. So, again—thanks to everyone!"

I felt like a proud parent when the crowd erupted into real, sincere applause. I mean, I guess it didn't surprise me—Annabelle is sort of an adorable and inspiring figure, and is really the sweetest, most genuine girl around. But still. I was glad it'd gone over well.

"So, back to you, I guess," Annabelle said to Bridget. "Show us what you got us!"

"Thanks, Annabelle," Bridget said. "So, again—I give you the . . . Lake Cleanup Day memorial plaque!"

And with that, she grabbed the sheet and pulled it off with a dramatic flourish, clearly expecting everyone to be impressed beyond belief. Instead, what I saw at that moment made me want to laugh hard enough to pee my mud-caked pants.

I don't know what had possessed Bridget to do what she'd done. Yeah, the girl dressed like a high-priced hooker every now and then, but she usually had *some* taste, which was why I was a bit surprised by this . . . *Thing*. Let's just say it was pretty freakin' *feo*. Super-ugly and tasteless. It was some sort of upright trophy-plaque Thing, about three feet tall, the base of it carved out of wood, with hand-carved fish, birds, and an alligator all sort of twisted into and around each other as they climbed up the length of the . . . Thing. The wooden animal party—which kind of looked like a scene ripped from *Snow White* and whittled on the spot—finally ended in a flat piece of wood at the top of the stand that held the bright gold plaque, which I'm sure had all sorts of inspirational jibber-jabber engraved on it.

Um, *baarrrrrf!!!*

Did poor Bridget really think this was gonna impress people? This wasn't a family-friendly TV show where togetherness saves the day and we can all go out for ice cream afterward. Kids here are *mean*!

Dead silence all around.

Okay, better than jeers and catcalls and torches and pitchforks.

Then there were a couple of claps . . .

. . . and a few more pity-claps.

Bzzzzzz . . .

I slapped a mosquito that had landed on my forehead, and a

few people laughed—probably because it looked pretty funny—and before I knew it, it had spread and almost everyone was laughing.

Although this was almost too good for words, I felt a *wee bit* bad as I watched Bridget squirm. Her eyes had grown large, and I could see her power-hungry mind working feverishly on a solution behind their iciness. And then . . .

"Pool party!" she screamed suddenly. "At my house! Right after we're done here! Bring whoever!"

Fuck! Come on! Bitch stole my idea!

The laughs turned quickly to cheers (oh, the fickleness!), and Bridget's expression returned to its usual smug, self-assured look. She did, after all, have one of those sprawling, immense behemoth castles that looked like it was three or four real-people houses stacked on top of and alongside each other—and allegedly threw the most legendary parties, though I'd never been invited.

I walked up to Bridget and said quietly to her, "Can't believe you stole my pool-party idea."

"Too shy to squeeze into a bathing suit?" she asked, feigning concern.

"So what the hell is this plaque?" I asked, reading over the inscription. "Some bullshit you spent a bunch of money on that you think is gonna make you look good?"

"It's just good politics, Diaz—you'd better get used to it. If you can't, you don't have a chance against me."

"I think good politics would've been to put the Environmental

Club before your own name. Or leave your name off it altogether."

"Please. I did *way* too much work on this to not be on that plaque, and people understand that," she shot back. "If it weren't for me, it'd just be ten Environmental Club kids out here with trash bags and Dixie cups of watered-down Gatorade."

"Yet you still have to rely on throwing an impromptu pool party at your McMansion to win everybody over." I cocked my head, in a very Bridget-like manner. "I'm noticing a pattern here."

"Make it past upper-middle class, Diaz," she whispered into my ear, "and maybe this'll work for *you* one day." And with that, she said, "And weren't you just leaving, anyway?"

As I looked around me at everyone finishing up their work at super-speed, chatting excitedly, I realized something scary:

Maybe this wasn't gonna be the cakewalk I'd pictured.

Sit Back, Breathe, BeDazzle

. . . .

I know I've been talking all about showing my face more in public, keeping myself on everyone's minds, yada, yada, yada. . . .

But after Bridget's small victory at Lake Cleanup Day, I was just *so* not in the mood to attend her little fiesta. I further justified not going to the pool party because the blazing sun and *stank* humidity had really drained me—not to *mention* all the bending and lifting and cleaning and mud and muck—and I needed to recharge.

Because I had to look *way* more fresh-faced when I saw Randy at his party tonight than when he'd seen me covered in sweat, mud, and bottled water.

Lucas, though, *did* want to go to Bridget's pool party—hey, I won't hold it against him, 'cause there were a lot of cool people going—so I headed home to put in some face time with the folks. My dad was absorbed in some crappy Western on cable—"Nice to see you, *too*, Papa . . ."—and my mom was puttering around in the yard—"I think I've done enough outdoor work today, Mami . . ."—so that face time quickly dissolved into a long-ass shower, guzzling around a gallon of Gatorade, and collapsing onto my bed for about three hours.

I wasn't complaining.

After waking up from my nap *super*-refreshed, I took care of all my homework (which, thankfully, wasn't too much—I could tell our teachers were going a little easier on us) and told my parents I was going to sleep at Vanessa's apartment—"*Hija*, I feel like I never see you . . ." "Um . . . *ditto*, Dad"—and headed out to the east end of town. Since my sister had dicked me over for her date last night (thus forcing me to eat unbuttered fish and steamed spinach!), she'd promised me we'd have dinner tonight. So after about thirty minutes in the stop-and-go traffic, toward one of those coal-black scary-ass-looking Central Florida storm clouds, and past the endless strip malls, supercenters, and fast-food restaurants of East Colonial Drive (I really should've sprung the $1.25 for the expressway), I finally made it to the Waterford Lakes Town Center—a *ginormous* shopping center that had not only a Petco but a Pet*land* and, of course, multiple Starbucks (including one in the SuperTarget), and just about everything else.

The most ironic thing about this place is that they called it a "Town Center," and expected people to actually, like, *walk* around the place. I'm sorry, but with the Florida heat and the general spread-out-ness of this place, I don't care how many shaded breezeways you build—people are just gonna *drive* from store to store.

And that's what I did. From SuperTarget to Jo-Ann Fabrics, and finally to Qdoba, to pick up some Mexican to go. After pulling out of the "Town Center," I was at Vanessa's apartment complex within minutes. I punched in the security code, drove through the slowly opening gates, and found a spot right in front of her building. I'd just started on my way up the covered staircase when the sky opened and started dumping buckets—yeah, I'm not exaggerating—of rain.

Maybe Randy would bring back mud wrestling this year. And *this* year I won't drink so much beforehand. (Yeah, it had been an ugly situation.)

I shuffled up to the second floor and knocked on my sister's door.

"Hey, *mami*!" Vanessa cried excitedly as she opened the door and leaned forward to give me a kiss on the cheek. "I just finished your newest."

"Lemme see!" I said, barreling into her foyer. The AC in her place blasted me with its cold, sweet relief. I wish they could just put a bio-dome over us and air-condition the whole state. Vanessa's crazy pug, Olive, bark-snorted her greetings, running around me in circles and trying to bite her curled-up tail. "Where is it?" I asked my sister, walking into the living room–slash–kitchen.

"Well, where's my money, bitch?" she asked teasingly.

"My money's no good here, you know that." I smiled. "And I brought you food. Seriously, though—lemme see!"

"Thanks for the food. But at least say hi to Olive first."

"Hi, Olive."

Olive looked at me with that silly openmouthed pug grin, her buggy eyes open wide. Then she barked for some love, and I reached down to give her some.

"Good enough?" I said, after Olive had sneezed and licked on me enough.

"All right, all right, it's in my bedroom."

I squealed and bolted for the room, Olive snorting right at my heels. I *always* got this excited when I got a new article of clothing from Vanessa. Not only did it make me proud, it also made me positively *gleeful* that I'd get to add another super-choice garment to my wardrobe . . . since there isn't ever much selection at the cute stores for girls like me.

This year for Redneck Randy's, I wanted to go all out. So a couple of weeks ago—right after Vanessa had started working on that *hot* blouse I wore to Madison's party—I asked her to concoct something white-trash chic. Nothing too tasteless, nothing that would hurt anyone's feelings, but something with a certain *yo-no-sé quois* . . . I put it totally in her hands. And it was worth it.

"Oh, V, you've outdone yourself," I said when I walked into the room.

"You really like it?" my sister asked hopefully.

"Are you *kidding* me?"

I was looking at a hoodie vest made entirely of camouflage hunting material, under which sat a simple black T-shirt that read, in sparkly green rhinestones (Be*Dazzle* that shit!): YOU TOTALLY CAN'T SEE ME.

Of course I stinking liked it! I *adored* it as if it were my own child!

"I'd cover up a *murder* for this outfit," I told Vanessa. "I'd *commit* murder for it!"

"Really? Maybe you should kill my boss, then."

"I said I'd kill for the *outfit*, not for you," I said, acting all serious. "Why? Is he on your case again?"

"*Carajo*, when is he *not* on my fuckin' case?! It's all just micromanagement *mierta*. . . ."

"Explain?"

She sighed. "Too boring and stupid to explain."

I hated seeing Vanessa sad. The thought of anyone giving her a hard time made me scream inside—I just wish I could go into Vanessa's bank and set her little pencil-pusher/taskmaster of a boss straight.

But I couldn't.

'Cause she wouldn't tell me his name or what he looked like. I was lucky I knew the sex.

"So, how's things?" Vanessa asked me. "Mom still on *your* case?"

"Micromanagement *mierta*," I quoted back to her. "Too boring to go further." Vanessa, as I've explained, knew just as well as I did how Mom was, since she'd also inherited our dad's build.

"Don't worry," Vanessa said, leading us back into the living room and emptying out the Qdoba bag. "You're almost outta there, anyway. Your grades are gonna end up okay, right?"

"Now *you're* micromanaging," I said defensively. I plopped down on the sofa and leaned forward to the coffee table, opening up my salad. (Yes, I picked salad over a scrumptious Qdoba burrito. I liked to starve myself *just a little* before Randy's big food parties.)

"Rita." I could feel my sister glaring at me. "You know if you screw up your final-semester grades, you might get that scholarship taken away, and Mom will have a shit-fit. She's dealt with enough crap with me."

"Oh, *please*, sis—don't be so hard on yourself. You know Mom's the biggest *puta* to you."

"You're a little hard on her sometimes, too, you know," she told me. "She's not as bad as you think."

"Oh, *right*! I just love that if she doesn't approve of your life goals, she completely refuses to help you out."

"Well . . ." Vanessa smiled at me. "She called today and told me she wanted to give me money for fabric shopping. . . . So, go easy on her."

"She did?" I asked, surprised.

"Yeah!" Vanessa said, still smiling. "Kind of outta *nowhere*, but still . . . better late than never!"

"*Claro.*" Huh. I wondered if my latest spat with Mom had had some effect on her.

"Anyway," Vanessa said, "back to you and your grades. This *is* your second party in two weeks, you know. I was just checking up on you."

"It's under control," I assured her. "You think I'm gonna mess up my ticket out of the house? Please."

By some miracle involving lots of studying, some friendly pressure from my sister, and a couple of very helpful scholarships, I got into the University of Florida up in Gainesville with Lucas. It's not like I *needed* the scholarships—since turning eighteen, I'd had full access to all my child-acting-days money—but I still wanted to get them, to sort of prove my worth. (Also, it wouldn't hurt to have a bunch of money in college, just to make the experience easier and more fun!) Lucas and I were gonna live together and start classes in August. It took a fair amount of convincing—my parents did *not* want me rooming with a guy, gay or not gay—but eventually I got what I wanted.

Lucas and I hadn't found ourselves a fabulous apartment yet, but we were getting to that pretty soon. Maybe even next weekend. I was totally gonna miss my sister and everything, but I was way too happy to have a free ride away from my mom to give it a moment's hesitation.

Plus, Gainesville's only two hours away.

"So! What's goin' on with this whole prom-queen thing?" Vanessa asked me, all giddy. "You still gonna make me famous?"

"I think so," I said. "I'm not as sure as I was earlier, 'cause this girl's got some major skills. But I'm still workin' it."

"I'm gonna have to adjust my designs for her skinny little body," Vanessa said, taking a bite out of her burrito. "That might be hard—and it kinda goes against my whole philosophy."

"V, exposure is *exposure*—and you'll do fine. You're brazilliant!"

"Thanks, babe." She put her arm around me and pulled me in for a little hug. "But I'm mostly concerned about you. How're you doing with this whole thing?"

"Fine. Why wouldn't I be?"

"I dunno . . . maybe 'cause you haven't talked about your old friend Bridget Benson since she dropped you all those years ago?"

"Thanks," I said, working my way out of her hug. "But I'm fine."

"Rita, come on!" my sister said, flicking my shoulder. "You were a *wreck* when she got that part."

"*Look*, it's *fine!*" I said, getting louder. "I only rehearsed and *rehearsed* until I was living and *breathing* those lines, and then my perfect little 'best friend' swoops in, with her big-shot dad and his fat-ass checkbook, and takes the part right out from under me. I was *made* for that part, Vanessa. And she took it from me. Because she *always* gets what she wants. *Siempre.*"

Olive snorted in agreement.

Vanessa just looked at me. "So you're fine, huh?" she asked. "Somehow I don't believe that."

"I don't wanna talk about it."

"Fine . . . So's she gonna be there tonight?"

"Ha!" I screamed, startling a panting Olive. "I don't think

she'd slum it *that* hard-core. . . . She wouldn't grace the place with her presence."

Vanessa looked at me all concerned again.

"What?" I asked.

"I just wanna make sure you're doing this for the right reasons. You're sure you're not all weird about Bridget and your whole history?"

"Look, the bitch stopped wanting to be my friend forever and a day ago, okay? I'm over it. I'm doing this for you."

"Okay," she said, eyeing me as she finished off her meal. "What about Lucas? Is he going tonight?"

"He's supposed to call me." I looked at the time. "*Shit*. He was supposed to call, like, an hour ago. Lemme go see. I'm sorry." I got up from the couch, went into my sister's room, and shut the door. I wondered what the holdup was. Lucas was a lot of things, but flaky wasn't usually one of them. The boy was *always* on time.

The call went straight to voice mail.

Shoot. I hope he wasn't having another Zach-related break-down or something. I mean, Lucas *seemed* okay most of the time, but he *had* been rather snippy and weird about the whole thing. Maybe the sheer gravity of losing such a great guy was finally dawning on him.

"Hey, Lucasito, it's Madge. Look, I thought you were supposed to call me about Redneck Randy's. It's freakin' *epic*, Lucas, you don't wanna miss it. Call me. I'm at my sister's, but call my cell."

I flipped my phone shut and returned to the living room, where Olive was staring expectantly at my salad from my old seat on the couch.

"Move, pugalicious," I said, pushing her off and sitting back down. "That was strange," I said to my sister.

"What was?" she asked.

"His phone was off."

"Maybe it's out of batteries, and that's why he didn't call you."

"Really?" I hadn't really thought of *that*.

"Well, I've used that lie before, so I'm sure he could, too." She smiled and laughed in my face teasingly. "I'm only kidding. How is that sweet boy? And *his* sweet boy?"

"Oh! I can't believe I left that part out! Those two are no more. That's why he was depressed at Madison's that night, why I cheered him up by messing with Bridget."

"Oh, no."

"Yeah, tell me about it," I said, rolling my eyes. I brought Vanessa up to speed about the Lucas/Zach/Kenny stuff (Oh, off with you, Pink Bermuda Triangle!), including the fact that I was Lucas's new prom date.

"Wait, what about this Kenny kid?" my sister asked.

"What do you mean 'what about him'?"

"Just . . ." she spoke slowly. "I hate to break it to you, sis, but . . . don't you think Lucas will want to take his new boyfriend?"

"What?" I asked, then quickly added, "They're not boyfriends."

"They're not?" she asked, looking at me funny.

"Well," I said, "he's saying he and Kenny only hooked up, and that they're only hanging out. . . ."

Vanessa shrugged. "Just be prepared, that's all I'm sayin'."

"Whatever," I said, mimicking Vanessa's shrug, not wanting to entertain the idea. *But thanks for the seed of doubt, sis*, because now I saw that she might've had a point. Crap, I hadn't even *thought* about prom.

I rose to take our trash to the kitchen, then checked my outgoing calls. I'd called Lucas more than thirty minutes ago, and still no reply. The guy has a charger in his car at all times, *and* he and Mitsy have one permanently plugged in right next to the liquor basket. So he'd be able to charge his phone if he needed to.

Argh.

Fantastic, I was already worried about Lucas hanging out with that sketch-ass, potential gold-digger Kenny, but now I had to worry about losing my prom date, too?

Plus, of course, Lucas was majorly missing out if he didn't call me back tonight.

But then I looked in the Jo-Ann bag at the packet of little plastic googly-eyes I'd bought and the bandanna I'd gotten at Target and smiled. A little fun with my sister and her glue gun was due to be had, and after that, if Lucas hadn't called back, *then* I'd be worried. And by then, it'd be time to go to Randy's to drink some Coors Light and eat some barbecue and play in mud, and everything would be perfection!

Bridget Benson Caters
to Your Every Need!

....

"Perfection is overrated," I told myself as I drove out of my sister's apartment complex, alone.

Okay, Problem #1 was that I was talking to myself.

And Problem #2 was that Lucas *still* hadn't called by the time I'd finished gluing an entire bag of googly-eyes onto my red bandanna, the resulting product of which gave the illusion that my skull was doing something between swirling and exploding. So now, of course, I was worried as I drove back onto East Colonial, heading farther east and out of town.

What if I *was* dateless for the prom again?

Not that I completely minded. I mean, I hadn't had a boyfriend since that long-distance debacle, so it wasn't like I'd been planning on having a date. But when Lucas offered last weekend,

I was pretty psyched about it all of a sudden. *Please* don't get the idea that I have a crush on my gay best friend—that would be so typical and dumb, since I've known from Day One that Lucas wasn't a fan of the ladies in any more than a platonic way. (And he wasn't my type anyway—too delicate. Boy couldn't handle all the love I've got to give!) I was just happy to have a date—like it made the prom more . . . more promlike or something. Corsages, boutonnieres, pictures—that whole thing.

Also, the thought of Lucas and Kenny going together was very "eh," but I refused to entertain the idea further. I needed to clear my head if I was gonna have *any* fun at Randy's tonight.

Listening to a little vintage Missy Elliot, circa her Fat-and-Hot-Miss-E Days, made me feel a little better. I missed those Missy Days. "Get Ur Freak On" lives on as a timeless classic, in my mind.

So I danced around in my car while my *So Addictive* album played on and the scenery changed from suburban strip mall to tacky subdivision to sparse, rural scrub forest. I hung a left on Chuluota Road, just before Bithlo—because once you've hit Bithlo, you've gone too far in *so* many ways—and within ten minutes, I was there.

Randy's grandparents' house was down a small dirt street just off the main road. Actually, this little street doubled as a sort of *gigantic* private driveway, since there were no other houses off it. A few tall pine trees sprang up here and there in clumps along the street, and I'd never seen so many stars at one time. Had there not been so many cars parked in the vast front yard, I might've been a little scared-shitless at how isolated this place was. I couldn't believe places like this *existed* forty-five minutes from my house—and *twenty* from my sister's!

Damn, there *were* a lot of cars here. This party not only gets crazier each year, it also seems to get *bigger*. More and more of the *actual* cool and savvy kids—pretty much anyone who wasn't a tool or in Bridget's inner social sanctum—were finding out about it and showing up, and it was never a problem. Randy and his crew are always super-welcoming, and all that clique shit doesn't seem to matter to them. I think they figure as long as you're out to have a good time and not start up a bunch of bullshit, who the hell cares? In that respect, Randy seemed almost like my male counterpart—big, friendly, and sexy as hell.

I took my car off the street and to a spot on the lawn far separated from the other cars. I didn't wanna get boxed in before I left in the morning. (Yeah—no Lucas, no car service.) Thank goodness Vanessa had told me the colors of my surprise outfit earlier today, because I had the perfect dark-green liquid eyeliner to go with my camo hoodie. So I did a little touching up, made sure my bandanna was securely holding down my slicked-back-and-ponytailed hair, kissed myself in the rearview, and got out of the car.

I walked through the muddy maze of cars and pickups and jeeps (glad I wore my black All Stars!) and went around the side of the house to the open backyard—this wasn't really a knock-on-the-front-door kind of party. And from the sounds of it, the backyard—or back-*acre-of-land*, rather—was already filled with a lot of activity. The first thing I heard was some drunk girl yelling, "Bob, if you keep distractin' this dog with all that food, we're never gonna get him to drink this *beer!*"

I laughed as I got to the back-acre, where there were about fifteen lawn chairs—all filled with people—spread around the large concrete back porch. Two kegs—one labeled BUD, the other labeled IMPORTED SHIT—floated in icy plastic tubs while two joints weaved their way among the crowd. I thanked my lucky stars and was about to make my way to the imported shit just as I heard the familiar howl:

"*Maaaaar*-garita!" Redneck Randy called to me from the set of sliding-glass doors that opened the overflowing-with-food kitchen onto the back porch. "Todd, pump that keg for my prom queen—*where're* your damn manners?!"

He smiled at me, and I smiled back. A minute later, I had a cupful of Heineken, and all was right with my world. Gotta love that Southern-boy hospitality.

"Randy, you've classed this shit up *just* enough," I said, air-toasting him. "Thanks for the Heinie."

"For *your* heinie, anything." Randy smiled again and motioned me to join him in the kitchen. He was looking so cleaned up and cute in his big white polo shirt, I was getting butterflies. Mmm!

"Hi, Randy," I said, and gave him a little hug. *"Feed me!"*

He laughed hard at that. His eyes were a wee bit on the glazed-over side of things, and his cup of beer—probably not his first of the day—was almost empty. "I like how you're not one of those girls who won't eat in front of a guy," he said, his voice deep and booming and a little scratchy.

"I like it, too," I said. "Otherwise I'd be a little bit thinner but a *lot* more cranky." Yeah. When I'm hungry, watch out. Lucas calls me "Miss Crabbypants" when I've gone too long without food. I loaded up my plate with some wings and blue-cheese dressing—and a little celery, too, why not?—and then some coleslaw and potato salad.

"You have fun planting trees today?" I asked him, dipping a celery stick in the dressing.

"It was all right. I mostly went to make sure y—to make sure everyone was comin' tonight," he said, looking almost bashful.

"You go to Bridget's pool party after?" I asked.

"Naw. Had to get back here and set up."

"Right."

"So how's all that prom-queen stuff goin'?" he asked.

"Fine, I guess." I sucked the meat off a buffalo wing and chewed for a minute. "I don't really wanna talk about it now," I decided.

"Hey, no problem, baby—you know you've got *my* vote."

"Excellent," I said, nodding. After a couple semi-awkward seconds, I gestured to all the food in the kitchen and asked, "So you didn't, like, make all this shit, did you? I never pictured you as being all that homey."

"*Hell* naw," he laughed. "Got it all at Publix." He cocked his head and smirked. "Know what else we got?" he said devilishly. "Deep-fried turkey."

I nearly wet myself and screamed with glee.

You simply haven't *lived* until you've eaten deep-fried turkey. If my family and I still lived in Puerto Rico, and if Puerto Rico wasn't already a part of the U.S., I think I'd have to immigrate to Florida simply for its deeply rooted deep-frying culture.

I was not a fucking idiot—I knew this stuff is bad for me. But blame it on my mother (for practically starving me) for my love of bad-for-me food. I'd straighten up one day and eat what a human being was built to eat . . . but not *now*, when I'm going to be tipsy and *hungry* in T-minus sixty minutes.

Lucas who?

Like I cared!

What the hell did it matter to *me* if Lucas never got to experience Randy's brand of legendary party—forget the damn pool party at the grotesquely oversize and probably unimaginatively decorated mansion, where people could sip delicately from martini glasses and feign their overall importance. This was the real deal—a party full of good kids who just wanted to have a drama-free, all-out good time, away from all the bullshit of everyday life. So what if he didn't get to experience that? Because *I* was going to. And the only thing that could derail me now was . . .

Oh, c'mon . . . you *knew* it was bound to happen.

"I come bearing gifts!" I heard someone trill shrilly.
Bridget "The Buzzkill" Benson.
Weighing in at 105 pounds.

Plus the weight of some big trays of barbecue.

"I got Sonny's catering," she said. "I called when I heard about this party last week and just ordered a bunch. Could someone grab the other trays out of my car?"

Then there was that awkward moment in a get-together, when one of those cluelessly annoying people that has no idea that they're not really welcome shows up at a party. Everyone has that split second of *"whuh?"* as they turn and see the person . . . and then just as quickly as it comes, it goes away, as people discreetly—if they haven't been spotted gaping—resume their previous activities, pretending not to have noticed anything out of the ordinary as they get back to their Wii-ing or drinking or just-passing-through.

But you know what?

The clueless person remains clueless and lives to attend another party.

I just couldn't have even *imagined* Bridget was this clueless.

But Randy, always the welcoming gentleman that he was, immediately greeted Bridget with a hearty, "Why, hey there, Madam President!" and led her into the kitchen to drop off her gifts of catered food. "Thanks for the grub! Uh . . . the more the merrier."

"Thanks. Sorry I just barged right in," Bridget said softly. "It's just . . . I was knocking at the front door for, like, five minutes, and eventually I just tried and it was unlocked."

"Uh, yeah . . . it was open," Randy said, scratching his head and suppressing a cute and tiny grin. "You coulda just gone around . . . Or you shoulda come right in . . . Aw, whatever—you're here now! Nice to see you, Bridget."

"Thanks," she said bouncily.

"Now, I'll just, uh . . . go out to your car and get the rest of this stuff."

"Thanks," she said again.

"Thank *you*!" Randy said, heading out of the kitchen. "I love Sonny's."

Once Randy had left the room, Bridget said quietly to me, "Cute boys always do what I say."

Bitch.

Bridget didn't deserve to have someone like Redneck Randy doing her heavy lifting.

"Anyway, hi, Diaz," she said, leaning forward to give me a little hug and kiss-kiss on the cheek, same as I'd done to her after signing up for the cleanup day. I flinched and stepped back.

"What the fuck?" I asked her.

"Just doing a little friendly campaigning," she answered quietly. "You wanna eat some of this, don't you?"

"Well . . ." I thought about it a minute. As little as I liked her here, she *did* come bearing Sonny's. And it's not like I had to worry about her winning over this crowd. And maybe, just maybe . . . "Did you get corn nuggets?" I finally asked. (Battered and deep-fried globs of creamed corn, with a ranch dipping sauce. Appetizer of the *gods*!)

"Corn nuggets?" Bridget's left nostril flared a bit, giving the impression that her little button nose was sneering at me. "No. I don't even know what they are."

Okay, this was officially not worth it anymore.

"See ya," I said, turning to head back outside.

I felt Bridget's hand grab my shoulder, squeezing it slightly.

I turned around. "What?" I asked. "I'm not hungry."

"Right," she said.

"Good-*bye*!"

"No, no, no, wait!" she pleaded softly, pulling me back. "I'm sorry. Just . . . you're the only person I really know at this party."

"So the hell what? Why'd you come, then?"

"You *know* why I came." Bridget paused, sighing. "I thought I could—Look, I'm ex*hausted*. I thought I could breeze through this, but all of a sudden, I don't have the energy. So . . . will you just hang out with me a minute? Please?"

"Bridget, this is a low-pressure crowd," I told her. "Have some beers, eat some food, and try not to look like an uppity, cosmo-drinking stick insect!"

"Please?"

I looked at Bridget for a moment, regarding her deer-in-the-headlights expression, the circles under her eyes, the haphazard makeup job she'd obviously done in the car on the way here. I flashed back to us on her seventh birthday, after her mom had given her her first makeup kit. I remembered laughing so hard as I'd smeared lipstick on her face, the end result looking something like a freakish circus clown. She'd been laughing along with me till she'd caught a glimpse of herself in the mirror, at which point she ran to have her mom fix it up.

A prissy little perfectionist, even way back then.

I almost felt bad for her, so I said, "Sure. We can hang. Could we just . . . ix-nay on the om-queen-pray? I'm too tired."

"Ditto," she agreed.

And so we did. We loaded up our plates (well, Bridget pretty much had a dollop of potato salad and a few spears of celery), found a couple empty lawn chairs, and just chilled out. We made small talk about nothing in particular—school, teachers, summer plans—until she made the mistake of bringing up our past.

"So . . . what the hell happened back then?" she asked me.

"What do you mean?" I asked warily.

"Y'know . . . when you went all psycho on me forever ago. What did I do wrong?"

What did she do *wrong*?

Was she *kidding* me with this?

How about the fact that the casting directors had said I had that part in the *bag*, and then who do I see coming into the office next but my "best friend" Bridget Benson, swooping in for a last-minute audition—without even *telling* me she was gonna audition in the first place—with her mom and dad and their bags and bags of money, to steal a part from me that was a better fit than half of Vanessa's custom-made outfits?

How about how when I called her and called her after that, trying to make sense of it—or at the *very* least, trying to live vicariously through her and her newfound success that should've been *mine*—and she didn't once call me back?

And what about the second, third, eight *millionth* chance she had to make it up to me when she started going to my school again, but never bothered to even *glance* at me, except in disgust?

"So . . . fun pool party?" I asked, changing the subject. I could *not* make a scene here—not in this, my Happy Deep-Fried Turkey Place. And I didn't wanna give her the satisfaction.

"It was fun. . . ." Bridget said, though I didn't quite believe her. Girl looked freaking tore *up*—I guess when you insist on organizing a major environmental cleanup and then an impromptu pool party at your house, you pay the price.

"I went home," I bragged. "I took a shower. *And* a bath—a really long bath, with candles and body salts. We're talking, like, total Zen. I even had one of those rain-forest CDs playing in the background. Then I slept for, like, three hours, and—"

"The party *was* a blast," Bridget interrupted, the edge back in her voice. "I got the house staff to run out and get a bunch of tequila and mixers and . . . *cervejas*—"

"It's *cervezas*."

"—and we had a margarita party. In honor of your absence! Too bad you had to go home and pass out like a loser."

"Sounds like my *name*, at least, was on everyone's mind," I said sharply. "Thanks for the free advertising."

"It could only *help* me, Margarita, to have people think of you and me at the same time. . . . I'm always gonna win out."

All of a sudden, I felt like Bridget and I were Alexis and Krystle from *Dynasty* (Lucas and I liked to watch them on YouTube), and that we were gonna get into a daytime soap–style catfight involving glitter, mud, feather boas, and lots of hair-pulling, looking like a couple of idiots. . . . It just felt ridiculous, and I realized I had better things to do, like enjoy the party that I had driven all these miles to attend.

"Have fun, Bridget," I said, getting up from my chair and heading to the keg for a refill. "I'm *so* glad you made it out tonight."

We studiously avoided each other for the next hour or so. Despite feeling like I'd taken the high road by walking away from our latest little spat, I was weirdly paranoid that Bridget was gonna randomly show me up again, like she kinda-sorta did at Lake Cleanup Day. I wasn't really digging the suspense. And I wasn't digging the fact that I *wasn't* digging it. I didn't like being put on edge—I liked to think of myself as pretty unshakable.

Lucas finally called, though.

"I'm so sorry, Madge, but I had a few too many margaritas and *totally* forgot to call you."

"What the fuck, Lucas, my *name* is Margarita, what kind of excuse is that?"

"Um, no. Your name is *Madge* to me, and I really did only forget. Kenny was at the party, so he drove us back to my place and we went shopping together. *Stop rolling your eyes!*"

I stopped, even though Lucas was forty-five minutes away

and I had every right to be rolling my eyes. (We had plans!)

"Anyway, I'm really tired and my mom's at my aunt's for the night, so I think we're just gonna hang out here in the condo."

"You have no *idea* what you're missing, though," I said, a little too pleadingly. "There's deep-fried turkey and all sorts of food, there's Heineken, I can teach you how to play Beer Pong . . . and you can watch me shamelessly flirt with Redneck Randy. . . ."

"Oh, *Maaaadge*," he whined. "Why do you have to tempt me? I *can't*. I'm *tiiiired*."

"You just wanna get laid."

"I *doooo*." He laughed. "Come on, Madge. It's like gay-guy code. If I can get some tonight, then it's cool if I . . . pursue that. You gotta get used to Single Lucas. . . ."

"That's not *our* code, though," I said. "At least it *wasn't*, up till last weekend."

"Please don't bring up Zach right now—"

"*Coño*, Lucas, Bridget is here and I feel like having you here and I—"

"Bridget's there?!" he squealed. "At *Randy's*?! Oh, this is *too good*, I'm getting the car service."

"Will you drive me back here tomorrow so I can pick up my car?"

"Roger. I'm cute-ing up, and'll be there in an hour."

And with a click, he was gone.

I just hoped the "and'll" was short for "and I'll" and not for "and we'll." I couldn't take another unexpected visitor tonight.

Showdown at
Redneck Randy's

An hour later, around eleven—right on time, like Lucas *usually* was—Lucas got to the party. I was helping set up Beer Pong under a tent in the muddy backyard, when I heard a "Hey, hoochie" come from behind me. I turned around and there he was, looking all cute and conservative in a salmon polo and light (and tight) blue jeans.

I was happy to see he was alone.

"Well, *you* cleaned up good," I said, glancing at my watch. "And quickly." I gave him a little peck on the cheek and went back to pouring beer in Solo cups.

"Sooo . . . ?" Lucas looked at me expectantly. He leaned forward and whispered into my ear, "Is there any dirt?"

I shook my head. "Not really." I finished pouring out the

beers, and people started putting the cups into position, on the two opposing sides of the Beer Pong table. I told everyone I'd be back in a second, and went out into the yard with Lucas.

"So nothing?" he said desperately. "Where's the drama, Mama? I didn't come out here for nothin'." He smiled and put his arm around me.

What the hell was this about? Don't get me wrong, I was happy to have my best friend at my side now, but I wasn't too keen on the fact that the first thing he asks me is where the dirt and drama are. Aren't I *enough* to justify the forty-five-minute drive? (Okay, don't answer that, but c'mon! Forty-five minutes is nothing! It's the length of an album, or a *Veronica Mars* episode.)

"I thought you were comin' out here with me tonight *anyway*," I said, shrugging him off. "Thanks for forgetting, by the way."

"I'm *sorry*, okay? It won't happen again. It's just . . . me and Kenny had a really fun day together. And I got all distracted."

"Spare me the details, lady."

"No, nothing like *that*—we just went to Millenia again and did some shopping. Just *wait* till you see the pair of jeans I got at Neiman Marcus. I actually have an *ass* in them! It's, like, a miracle!"

Wow—two trips to the mall in as many weeks. Why was this raising some red flags in my mind? "Did Kenny get anything?" I asked, leaving out the *Maybe some T-shirts with sophomorically homoerotic slogans? Ass-less underwear? VD?*

"Yeah, he um . . . well, *I* got him something from Zara—"

"Interesting," I said, cutting him off, not wanting to hear any more.

Lucas paused, furrowing his brow. "Wait, *why* is that interesting?" he asked. "I had my card, so why wouldn't I—?"

"Nothing!"

Lucas stopped justifying himself for a moment, looking a little hurt. Finally, he said, "What is it, Madge?"

"Look, I'm sorry," I said, shifting uncomfortably. I really didn't wanna get into this right now, but I guess I had no choice. "But don't you think that maybe Kenny's using you? The guy's got no money, and he's always driving you guys to the mall. And don't you think this might be happening too close to you and Zach breaking up—and Zach being an ass to you—that maybe you're not seeing things as clearly as I am?"

"This coming from the girl who's drunk as a skunk right now?" he said, smirking.

"No, I— Well, yeah, I am, but you're not listening to me—"

"I am, Madge," he said soothingly. "And I appreciate it. I think I can take care of myself, though. Kenny's just a friend, okay? And I'm *fine* with the Zach stuff—I just need some gay-man fun now, and if Kenny's anything, it's a gay man."

"You're sure?" I asked warily.

"Yes," he answered quickly. "*Please* don't worry about me so much."

I tried my best to smile, realizing I'd said enough, and if I said more, Lucas would just freak on me. "I promise I won't," I said to him slowly, "if you'll go get us some beer."

"Done." He smiled back, and hopped off toward the keg.

I probably didn't need the beer right before the game of Beer Pong, but one of the advantages to being a big girl is having all that extra body mass to soak up alcohol. Actually, I wasn't sure if that was scientifically true or not—it might have been that my and Lucas's recent end-of-senior-year party habits had built up my tolerance—but, point is: I knew my limit. I was nowhere *near* pukey-sick yet, and since it was Saturday night and I didn't have any plans in the morning and I had done all my studying and homework and I was at this crazy party all night, I was gonna take it as close to the brink as I could. God bless the car service. If only Paris Hilton and Lindsay Lohan had been this smart.

I smiled as Lucas returned with our beers. "Thanks, *chico*," I said, taking a sip.

"So you're now officially cool with my friendship with Kenny, right?"

"Sure," I managed. Try as I might to be nicer, it was gonna take more for me to see Kenny as anything other than a gold-digging meth-head. But like I said, if I pushed it any further, I risked pushing *Lucas* away.

But, hey—at least he wasn't *dating* the guy!

"Good," Lucas said, "'cause when we were at the mall, we sorta rented tuxes . . ."

"What?"

"Madge, Kenny and I think we should go to prom together."

Shit-cakes! I couldn't believe Vanessa had been right! I was utterly speechless, which is a very rare occasion indeed.

"Please say something," he told me.

"Maybe," I said slowly, trying very hard to keep my emotions in check, "you should explain to *me* why you thought it would be okay to de-invite me as your date. . . ."

"See, I knew you were gonna say that."

I wanted to say, *"Then you can't be a* total *jerk,"* but again I refrained. I just raised an eyebrow and asked, "So's this just a 'friend' thing? 'Cause if it is, why can't *we* still be dates?"

"I'm sorry," he said. "But I thought it'd be fun—*we* thought it'd be fun—since Kenny missed his and everything, and . . . Oh, Madge, he's not taking advantage, and he's not my boyfriend, but can you blame me for wanting to go to prom with a *guy*?"

"I guess not," I said softly, sorta seeing his point, even though it hurt a little and I still couldn't truly trust Kenny. "And I was fine two weeks ago when I wasn't going with anybody, so . . ." But, really. I mean, could it *be* any more obvious? Animal-cracker lunches at school? Taking someone to the mall? Having them buy you shirts? And then probably having Lucas *pay* for the tuxes?!

"What's wrong?" Lucas asked.

"Nothing," I said, shaking my head. "Shit—I—I . . . forgot. I was supposed to call Vanessa about something."

Lucas just looked at me.

"I'm serious," I lied. "Look, don't worry—I'm totally fine

about you and Kenny," I fibbed again. "You *should* go with a guy to your senior prom. I just gotta— I'm gonna— Just . . . 'scuse me a second."

I took my phone out and pretended to call up Vanessa (yup, they call me Smoothie Queen) as I headed across the yard and into the house. Once I was sure that Lucas wasn't following me, I found myself an empty bedroom and closed the door.

I plopped down on the bed, wrapping my mind around everything that'd just happened. So I guess I was *pretty much* okay with not going to prom with Lucas as my date. I'd been okay before, so I had to be okay now. Then again, what *choice* did I have? I suppose we'd still go together *technically*, and we'd totally have fun, but now I just had to get some more people to go, so I could have Kenny-buffers.

But what I *really* wasn't okay with was Lucas having Kenny as his date. I don't think I can stress enough how bad-news-y Kenny seemed, and how different Lucas had been acting lately (friends-with-benefits stuff, sugar-daddying himself out to losers, not returning phone calls, backing out on plans). If Lucas had latched on to someone as sub-par as Kenny, he really needed to know that there were actual *good* guys out there as well. And if Zach was out of the picture now, there had to be someone else to bring Lucas around. I didn't care if Lucas had simply turned into an eighteen-year-old hornball who just wanted someone to do on prom night. He needed to know there were better options out there, so he wouldn't allow himself to be taken advantage of.

The problem was that there was a pretty limited pool of available gay boys for Lucas. I mean, there were a few, but no one was really popping into mind. Todd Gak had a weird name and even weirder Jew-'fro hair. Chris McNair was freakishly into Liza with a *Z* (and that wasn't Lucas's style). I was drawing a blank, until I thought back to Lucas's most recent jeans purchase.

I actually have an ass in them! It's, like, a miracle! he'd said.

And no one deserved greater ass-worship than my old pal Jonathan Parish. Ol' Jonathan had a tooshy that was simply *sabroso*, and he was totally Lucas's type. Dark hair, blue eyes, sparkling personality. And except for that weird thing last year when he slept with one of his girlfriends—and dated the Then–Top Bitch Laura Schulberg!—he was pretty much perfect.

Worst-case scenario, the boy was bi, and that isn't even a big deal. Lucas wasn't at Winter Park last year, so he'd be none the wiser.

Okay, Problem #1 was Jonathan's girl history. (Able to be dealt with . . . or not mentioned.)

Problem #2 was that the boy lived in Gainesville. (A mere two-hour drive . . . not the end of the world.)

Problem #3. Hmmm . . . why would I call Jonathan out of the blue? It could seem weird. We'd been totally bad about keeping in touch, and we hadn't talked recently. I mean, I'd need a real reason for calling him, so it wouldn't seem too random. I didn't wanna try to set them up too obviously. I think that ruins things—and come to think of it further, I really *did* like Jonathan for Lucas. He was a super-interesting guy, and *so* much fun (not to mention hotty-hot-hot!), and I was so bummed we hadn't talked in forever.

Well . . . the girl he had dated . . . Laura. She was kind of the Bridget Benson of the class before mine, minus the TV stuff. Laura was just fucking loadedd-with-two-*d*'s to start with. And *such* perfect looks and clothes and house—all that shit. Laura never had anything against me, though. I always thought she was all right—didn't know her as well as I knew Jonathan. Oh my God, you should've been at that Halloween party where he puked on Laura's ex-boyfriend. That night was fucking *epic*. I'd gone in a pink zebra-print dress (which was *so* short and *so tight* that it made my ass and thighs hang out all over the place), these hooker heels that hurt like an eighteenth-birthday-hangover, and a scraggly severe-bob wig, though it wasn't the perfect color, but who can keep up with her hair anyway? Being Victoria Beckham's fat twin was hard work, but was well worth it that night.

Anyway. So, Laura. Now that I thought of it, Laura *had* been prom queen. And I could tell Jonathan about all the crazy shit that'd been going on here lately, then tell him I'm looking to get some prom-queen advice from Laura, if he still talked to her. It was a long shot that he even still kept up with her, but that was okay. I'd just call him, get him talkin', see if maybe I could finagle my way into a weekend invite. It would have to be, like, *next* weekend, though. Prom was still a couple weeks away, but the sooner Lucas was off his Kenny kick, the better. I could tell

Jonathan I wanted to look for apartments or something, which me and Lucas had to do anyway. . . .

Brilliant! I was fucking *brilliant*! (And a little conniving, I know . . . but this is *so* not like me. Desperate times call for desperate measures.)

No time to waste.

Jonathan picked up on the third ring. "Is this my Not-So-Virgin Margarita?" he asked as he picked up the phone.

"*Oh my God*, you still have my number!" I screamed, sounding kinda gurgly from my latest sip of Heineken. He was so happy to hear from me—this was gonna be great.

After talking with Jonathan and giving him the big, ridiculous update that my life had become, I made it to my: "So that's one of the reasons I called. I was wondering if you still talked to Laura. I need some prom-queen advice. . . ."

"Oh! Well, she still lives in Orlando, but yeah, we talk all the time," he said easily.

This was kind of a surprise, frankly. They'd broken up around Homecoming *last* school year, and I never really saw them together much afterward. . . .

"Actually," he continued, "she's gonna visit me next weekend!"

Craziness! Okay, Madgie, new plan: Use Visa, get hotel room, get some free prom-queen advice, hook up my mens.

"Yeah, me and my friend Lucas were gonna come up there and look for apartments anyway," I said casually. "That's part of the reason I called."

"Oh," he said. "Well, I'm sorry, but my place is kinda small. I share it with these three meatheads—" He broke off. "Fuck, don't *ever* sign up for random roommates, Margarita," he said, sighing. "I'm so serious. Anyway, the place is tiny, so I can only have two people at a time. I share a bedroom with one of these freaks, so it's basically one guest in the tiny single bed with me, one on the floor between my and my roommate's bed, and one out on the couch. And I'd stick your friend on the *floor* next to the couch, but the *other* roommate's slutty *girlfriend* is gonna be up from Tampa for the weekend so he kicks *his* roommate out into the living room—" He paused for a breath. And then another. "I'm sorry," he said finally. "I've been doing a lot of studying for final exams, so I'm kind of at wit's end here, and I tend to ramble when I'm this crazy-busy."

"No problem," I said. *Wow.* I was *so* glad it was just gonna be me and Lucas in our fabulous apartment.

"Anyway, so if you could stay at another friend's or get a hotel or something—"

"Oh, yeah," I cut him off. "Hotel. Yeah. I can use my . . . Y'know, *Lucas* can afford anything. He'll just use his mom's . . . American. Express. Black. Card," I said purposefully. "So, *Lucas* and I will come up and stay in a hotel. We could have a hotel party!"

Loving it. Too good. Too good!

"No, let's go to this gay bar!" Jonathan said excitedly. "The resident drag queen will blow your fucking *mind*— Wait. Is Lucas gay?"

"As Anderson Cooper, baby."

"Fun! Okay, we'll talk later?"

"Yeah, I gotta go," I said.

And I did. I had to go convince Lucas to go to Gainesville in a week.

Jonathan and I said our good-byes and promised to talk later in the week about everything. I closed up my phone and left the bedroom to find Lucas. Might as well ask Lucas *now* about Gainesville. Maybe I could work the whole guilt thing and then bring it up. He'd be a *monster* to deny me then!

Plus, I think he'd wanna go. He was always up for a road trip.

"Hey, Lucas," I said when I'd returned outside. "Sorry about that."

"No problem. Look, I have to make sure: you're *sure* everything's cool with me and Kenny and you?"

"It *is*," I told him, then immediately continued with, "So after I talked to Vanessa, I had this crazy brainstorm for the prom-queen thing." I gave him a sly little grin.

"Really?" he asked excitedly. He seemed relieved that I'd changed the subject.

"Yeah. I just realized that I know this guy who was pretty good friends with our prom queen last year. Maybe he could hook us up with her, and I could get some real . . . y'know, insight from her."

"Okay . . . ?" he said, motioning for me to finish.

"Anyway," I said, plowing right ahead, "so I call him up, and it turns out this old prom queen—Laura—is gonna be in Gainesville next weekend. So if you're up for a little random adventure, we should take that trip we've been meaning to take, and go up there to look for apartments, and I can talk prom-queen strategy with this girl."

"Actually . . ." He furrowed his brow, then broke into a big grin. "I *love* it! Where do we stay? Should I get us a hotel? It'll get my mom points on her card. And she can use the car service that weekend so we can get the Beemer!"

Wow. That was almost *too* easy. I guess I'd underestimated my beloved Lucas's fly-by-the-seat-of-his-Sevens-ness. But all the more reason to get excited! Having Lucas up there, *not* against his will, and spending like a little gay Rockefeller? This was win-win, kids. He and Jonathan were gonna fall in love and have picked out the names of their Chinese babies by the end of the night. I was still mourning the loss of Zach, despite the jerkiness toward Lucas, but what can you do?

I started to tell Lucas, "Oh my God, *of course* let's get a hotel!" but was thrown off when I noticed Randy emerging from the kitchen, Bridget was right behind him, her arm around his waist. Oh, *hell* no!

"So?" Lucas asked. "How does that sound?"

"Great," I said absentmindedly as the two of them headed toward us.

"Hey, y'all," Randy called, getting free of Bridget's grasp and shaking Lucas's hand. "Good to see y'again, man, thanks for comin'."

"Oh, no . . . no problem," Lucas said, his eyes darting toward me quickly. He'd totally seen Bridget all over the man, too. "You here to play some Beer Pong?"

"Ohhh," Bridget whined. "I dunno *how* to play." She put her arm back around Randy, eyeing me icily. "Randy, will you teach me how?"

Why not shake your bare vagina in his face? I thought angrily.

Again, Randy shook himself politely free (points!), and said, "Naw, we'll do all that later. For now, I've been talkin' with some of the guys, and they all wanna get to tonight's main event."

Here we go. What was it gonna be this year?

"And they were all thinkin'—and it's all right if you don't want to—but they were thinkin' that since the two of you are here right now"—he looked at me and Bridget—"we could have a lil' contest."

"What kind of contest?" Bridget asked, looking slightly worried and uncomfortable.

"Just somethin' to determine who we're all gonna vote for on prom night," he said. "'Cause . . . no offense, y'all, but we don't really give a rat's ass about this prom-queen shit. And we figured we'd have a little fun with it. You guys in?"

Like we even had a choice . . .

So despite growing up in Central Florida—a place with basically one river and 849 lakes—I'd never been water-skiing in my life. I get seasick, you see. And I *seriously* doubt I could ever have the coordination to stay balanced while being tugged at forty miles per hour across a wavy lake.

But here I found myself, standing in water skis and holding a rope.

But on dry land.

Well, *muddy* land.

And at the other end of the rope was Randy's pickup truck.

Bridget waited her turn behind me.

"All right, ladies, here are the rules," Randy called out to us and the rest of the party. "On the count of three, I'm firin' up the truck and drivin' down toward the lake. By the time we get to that there ramp"—he pointed off into the distance, down by the small pond at the far end of the property—"we'll be goin' fast enough for you to get some real air time. I'll drive the truck around the ramp, and if you hold on and time it just right, you'll fly up the ramp, into the air, and into the water."

Shit. These damn rednecks sure loved a dose of danger. I guess I *had* been wondering how they were gonna top last year's infamous trampoline-diving competition.

"Now, we'll be timing y'all. If neither of you makes it to the ramp, whoever's able to hold on the longest wins. If one of you makes it to the ramp and the other doesn't, the ramp girl wins. If you *both* make it to the ramp, then your jump will be judged by its originality, grace, and overall awesomeness. Any questions?"

"Don't you think judging the jump might be a little too subjective?" Bridget asks.

"You're talking like you're actually gonna *make* it to the ramp, *mami*," I said.

"Still."

Randy gave this a little thought, and said, "Bridget, like we said earlier, we don't give a care about who wins prom queen. I'm a gentleman, and I'm gonna stay a gentleman. We're gonna be fair, all right?"

"Okay," Bridget said unsurely.

"All right, let's *do* it, people!" Randy yelled, and everyone headed down toward the pond to watch the spectacle.

Randy got into his truck and fired up the ignition. My muscles tensed immediately, my knuckles turning white gripping the rope handle. I was trying to maintain my composure, but I was a little worried about this. I mean, staying upright on *skis* while being pulled through a muddy, rutty acre of land? This was not something a big girl like me was built to do. I'd been hoping for an keg-stand or karaoke contest, or even mud wrestling, but this is what Randy and his pals wanted, so this is what I'd have to do.

I heard Randy's engine rev. He leaned out the driver's-side window, looked back at me, and winked.

Tasty-tasty! *Damn*, Randy looked good in that pickup truck, his hat slightly crooked on that thick head of curls.

"You ready, sugar?" he called back to me.

Ready for you to ravage *me? Yes, sir.*

"Sure!" I finally responded, balancing myself. I looked back at Bridget and said, "Get ready to lose."

She narrowed her eyes. "Have fun muddying up those last-season jeans and your little handmade outfit."

"It'll all wash out in the pond, when I land my triple-lutz." Or whatever a fancy pickup-truck-mud-skiing acrobatic move is called.

All of a sudden, there was a "One! Two! *Three!*" and I was off!

Right off the bat, my body swung hard to the right, and I nearly toppled over. But I shifted my body a bit to the left, and soon I was back and standing, centered perfectly behind the truck. The ground was surprisingly soft and flat this soon after a heavy rain, so nothing threw my feet off track as we raced toward the ramp, the air (and bits of mud) blowing fiercely through my hair.

Suddenly a loose branch appeared right in front of me but, miracle of miracles, my adrenaline pumping furiously, I was able to hop up a tiny bit and clear it with no trouble. The ramp was coming fast into view, though, so I brought my skis closer together and crouched down, getting my body centered and prepared for the jump.

Randy swung his truck a bit to go around the ramp and quickly righted himself. I veered slightly off course, but by the time the ramp was upon me, I was right back to where I needed to be.

Suddenly, I thought, where I *needed* to be was back at the party, having a beer and sucking barbecue sauce off my fingers. What the hell was I doing this for? Who cared if Bridget won these people's votes? What's the good in winning prom queen and humiliating a nearly unflappable teenage celebrity if I can't be alive to enjoy it? I was gonna bust right through this flimsy slat of wood. I mean, who was I kidding? I'm fat! I was gonna hit that ramp doing thirty-five, shatter it into a pile of splinters, and wind up unconscious—or *worse!*—in a pile of mud.

But just as my skis hit the bottom of the ramp, and I felt myself being pulled safely up it, I hit a little moment of Zen, realizing that I was already on my way up the ramp and not *through* it, and that the pond was literally *right* on the other side of it. I'd be fine—just *wet* . . . and Lord knows camouflage hunting material is water-resistant!

Next thing I know, I'm flying through the air to the sound-track of enthusiastic cheers, screams, and Lucas yelling *"Twirl, baby, twirrrl!"* and my own voice screaming an all-out-terrified *"Fuuuaaaarrrrruuuuuck!!!!!"* I definitely was not concerned with form at that point—I was only trying *not* to crap my pants as I made my descent into the pond, landing with a resounding can-nonball-contest-winning splash in the water.

I sank the six or so feet to the bottom, feeling my skis sink to the thick muck at the bottom of the pond. My overactive imagination instantly flashed to alligators and water moccasins, so I kicked them off and paddled furiously till I was at the shore, emerging all in one piece, energized, victorious.

Wait, scratch that "victorious" until later. No need to get cocky.

Oh, who am I kidding, of *course* I was gonna win! Bridget had a strange mix of annoyed, terrified, and surprised expres-sions running across her face as I made my way into the crowd to receive my high fives, chest thumps, and booty pinches. It felt great.

But having Randy run out from his pickup to wrap me in a big-strong-man bear hug and give me a peck on the cheek felt even better.

Eat *that*, Bridget!

But nothing (sorry, Randy) beat watching Bridget nearly wipe out on her attempt a few minutes later.

Nearly.

At first I couldn't *believe* that she'd made it past the ramp, but when she did that flip in the air and landed with a tiny pencil-dive *sploosh*, I flashed back to a horrible summer movie she'd had a minor role in, which pretty much entailed fifteen lines of cutesy dialogue . . . and one five-minute-long water-skiing scene.

Crap.

Maybe I needed Laura's prom-queen advice more than I thought I did, because I just lost a shit-ton of votes.

Visine Up, Baby!

The week flew by in a flurry of campaigning—shake some hands, kiss some babies, that whole thing. I helped the Environmental Club install those eco-friendly lightbulbs all over the school (Bridget was noticeably absent from this event), I volunteered to sell tickets for the Drama Club's latest production, and I even helped run the SADD (Students Against Destructive Decisions) Club's drunk-driving car. (That was a highlight—you put in your weight and how many drinks you've had, and the car adjusts itself to drive how you would be driving if you were that drunk. Let's just say it was a good thing Lucas and I had the car service from Randy's place, because there were quite a few dead or seriously injured cardboard people strewn about that driving course.)

I'd even happened upon Bridget schmoozy-schmoozing with

the Debate Team one afternoon. She must have been doing her own fair share of getting around the school to have made it as far as the *Debate* Team. (For that matter, so had I—I had to make up some lost ground.) I don't know why I was surprised when the president of the club had suggested we have a presidential-style prom-queen debate at their next meeting, to be filmed in its entirety and posted on each of our Web sites.

Oh, yeah. The Web sites. Bridget and I had been outfitted with our own "Vote for Us" MySpace pages. Lucas had created mine one night in response to one he saw that had been created for Bridget. I was glad to have nothing to do with it, since everything else was so busy. I wondered who was running Bridget's, because she said hers had been a surprise. *Hmph,* I say. *Hmph!*

I hadn't spent much time with Lucas at lunch, thanks to my prom-queen-hopeful duties, so he was apparently spending a lot more time with his new prom date. This worried me a bit, but it was nothing that a little meeting with Jonathan Parish couldn't fix. I hoped.

But happily, Lucas was psyched beyond all expectations about our information-gathering trip to UF. As was I. It was gonna be great to get out of Orlando for a couple days.

By eight P.M., I'd packed a stunning going-out outfit (as well as the usual boring odds and ends), MapQuested our Mitsy-funded hotel in Gainesville ("executive suite," meaning kitchenette, at the hotel on the UF campus), created a super-fantastical travel playlist on my iPod (Madonna! The Gossip! Kylie! Goldfrapp! M.I.A.! and *more*!), and been to the penthouse to meet up with my gay-life-partner-in-crime and stock up on some mini liquor bottles ("Time for a Grey Goose restock, Mitsy!"). Lucas and I did our little "Promiscuous" dance (yeah, it'd been overplayed and was super-old, but we were lifelong devotees) as we zoomed up the on-ramp to I-4, our hair whipping around almost violently in the wind.

Oh. Maybe now's the time to mention that Mitsy *had* indeed lent us her BMW convertible. She was hardly ever sober enough to drive it anyway ("That's why I have the car service!"), so she gave it to us for the weekend. She even let me drive it, since Lucas wasn't so good with the stick (which was almost *too easy* to tease him about). "Just be careful with it, Madgie," she'd said to me before we'd left. "It's got a little kick to it—goes up to about forty in first gear. . . ." *"Forty?"* I'd asked. "Okay, fifty," she'd answered, smirking. "But don't take it that high."

As the speedometer approached forty-eight and we were fully merged onto the interstate, I shifted to second and sped us through the luminous downtown towers toward the East-West Expressway.

"Holy shit, Madge!" Lucas yelled over the rushing air and drumbeats of the song. "You're crazy!"

"Don't worry, Lucas, I'm only doing, like, sixty—this is just what it's like to drive in a convertible! Don't you fucking *love it*?!"

"I do!" he laughed as we slowed for the East-West interchange.

Once on the expressway, I gunned it again, heading westbound toward the Citrus Bowl. The sheer power this car pos-

sessed was intoxicating . . . and a little sexy. I might just have
to marry this car. Is it a boy or a girl? Do I have to become a
lesbian? And drive us to Canada for the ceremony? Oh, I'd *so*
do it. Let's just say the revving engine under my seat was doing
things for me.

"Wipe that sex look off your face!" Lucas scolded. "You're as
transparent as . . . as your face!"

"Good one!" I laughed, getting some quarters out for the toll
as we slowed to a stop in the line of cars at the tollbooth.

Kelis's nasty-trashy anthem "Blindfold Me" came blasting
through the speakers, and Lucas practically jumped three feet in
the air in excitement. A second later, his seat belt was off and he
was kneeling on his seat, shaking his tiny ass in my face and waving his arms up in the air in that über-gay dance-y way.

I giggled and put a dollar from my toll stash into his back
pocket. "Now, sit down," I said. "You're freaking out the locals."

"How *can* I?" he cried into the night. "Kelis is my Hussy
Goddess!"

All of a sudden, we heard that oh-so-original call of "Faggot!"
from some douchebag in a beat-up, dusty truck one line of cars
over. Oh, you've gotta love Florida. You never knew when you were
gonna get slapped in the face with some nasty-smelling, subhu-
manly stupid, I-wave-my-Confederate-flag-with-pride ignorance.

"How you know that AHM not doin' 'im?" I screamed back in
my best Southern hillbilly accent.

"'Cause yer a fat bitch—ain't no one gonna hit *thayat*!"

Ugh. Put this guy up next to Randy, and you'll see why there's a difference between rednecks and stupid white trash.

By now we were next in line for the toll, so I revved my engine and was about to yell back something nasty when Lucas beat me to the punch and screamed back, "You're just jealous of our car, breeder . . . *in*breeder! Go home and screw your sister!" Then up went his out-and-proud middle fingers and his triumphant "Woooooo!!!!!!" and we were speeding out the tollbooth at seventy within seconds. Billy-Bob didn't even know what hit 'im.

Lucas and I erupted in laughter as we sped our way out of Orlando and toward the Turnpike, the tract-housing developments and super–shopping centers whooshing by in a blur. Fall Out Boy got us dance-dancing; Destiny's Child kept us jumpin', jumpin'; Madonna made us repentant in about ten different languages; Goldfrapp flew us away; and Rihanna told us to shut up and drive as the landscape changed from urban to suburban to wild, and a while later we were driving through a huge, open prairie on the approach into Gainesville.

Lucas got about forty-eight (okay, maybe less) mysterious texts during the ninety-minute drive, and anytime I'd ask who he was talking to, he'd just reply with a "Nobody" or a "My mom's tipsy and text-happy" or simply pretend he didn't hear me over the blaring vintage Whitney Houston vocals.

Part of me wanted to know what was going on, if anything.

The other part of me was freaked out that Lucas was secretly inviting his new best bud, Kenny, to come up and join us and thus ruin everything, and sometimes I liked to simply be oblivious to bad news like that.

But my Lucas wouldn't do that to me, would he? If he were texting secretly with Kenny, wouldn't that tip him off that it wasn't exactly the cool thing to do? Maybe Kenny had brainwashed him in my weeklong absence from lunch. . . .

I decided to chill out for the time being, and see what the night brought.

We found the UF campus pretty easily, and soon we were checked in to our hotel at the student union and getting changed to go out.

I put on my Sevens and a black tank top encrusted with the slogan GO BIG FOR QUEEN in rhinestones—seriously, BeDazzler, what would we do without you?—and over the tank top I draped a pink-and-black-feathered shawl my sister had made for me this spring. Once I brushed out and styled my hair—two-hour car rides in convertibles apparently *do* have a negative side effect—glopped on all my eye makeup, and wedged my feet into my glittery purple pumps (which were surprisingly easy to dance in), I was looking erect-statues-in-this-bitch's-honor *amazing*.

Lucas had played his skinny-gay-boy cards expertly with his outfit, and he was looking pretty scrumptious, too: the pair of eighteenth-birthday Prada shoes Mitsy had bought him at Millenia Mall (Madgie hungry . . . Madgie *hungry for Italian leather*!), ass-hugging (more like ass-clutching-on-for-dear-life) dark-blue Diesel jeans, his favorite scuffed-and-studded-up white belt from Zara, and a teeny-tiny Armani Exchange stretchy red shirt (one of those numbers with the zippers that serve no real purpose but to look gay) that Zach had doctored up into a makeshift Kylie Minogue shirt for Lucas in the fall. His hair was sculpted to perfection in an impossibly cute faux-hawk, and his blue eyes sparkled, even when set against the red of his shirt.

"Fabulous," Lucas said when he saw me.

"Tight," I said when I saw him.

"Drink?" Lucas asked, unzipping the toiletries bag we'd filled with Grey Goose bottles.

"No. I'm gonna walk the streets of Gainesville, Florida, clad in feathers *sober*!"

"Uh . . . you *would*," Lucas told me.

"Yeah. I would. But I'd also like a drink first."

Matchmaking was thirsty work, ladies.

"You want a Bloody Mary or a screwdriver?" he asked, unpacking the bags of groceries we'd bought on the way into campus.

I looked into the mirror over the sink in the kitchenette as Lucas bustled about. *"Bloody Mary, Bloody Mary, Bloody Mary, Bloody Mary, Bloody Mary!"* I said demonically to my reflection.

"Here you go," Lucas said, producing the drink for me.

"It worked!" I joked. "Hand me a celery stalk, will you?"

He did, and then mixed himself some orange juice and vodka. "So, where're we going again?" he asked me.

"University Club," I said. "Or UC. It's this gay bar downtown—about a twenty-minute walk from here. Or we can take the Later Gator."

"Um . . . what?"

"It's some bus that goes from campus to downtown and back till, like, three A.M. It's only a buck, and it stops right outside the student union."

"So we're not driving?"

"Not unless you want to pour out your drink and learn to drive stick, 'cause I'm sure not!"

"Then maybe it's time I told you what Kenny slipped into my backpack before you came and picked me up."

"Um . . . yeah, now I'm scared."

"It's just pot."

Hmm. Did I want to be that stupid when I met up with Jonathan and Laura?

Um . . . why the hell not?

"Yeeeee*aaaay*!!!" I cried. "I *love* college!"

"Do you think we could just live in this hotel room when we move up here?" Lucas asked. "It's so nice!"

I started laughing my ass off at that. We'd started out in the bathroom, with the air vent turned on high and a towel stuffed in the crack between the bottom of the closed door and the tile floor. We'd figured it'd be pretty bad to get busted for smoking pot on campus before even registering for classes. Kenny had rolled us a joint of his finest, apparently—it was totally giggly and fun.

All right, maybe I was being a little hard on Kenny before. . . .

All those awful rumors about him missing prom last year because he got arrested with meth in his car out in *Bithlo* (where no self-respecting Orlandoan would venture) must be just that: rumors. Oooh, damn, I could be bought faster than a two-dollar whore when I was this happy! Good stuff, Kenny. Good stuff.

Lucas and I were marveling at how wonderful everything was: The orange-and-blue sheets on our beds (Go, Gators!); the view from the balcony onto the campus, the Century Tower rising in the distance; the compact and conveniently laid out kitchenette. We were kinda just dancing around the room, checking everything out, with Madonna's *Confessions on a Dance Floor* (the best pre–going out album on the planet!) thumping out of Lucas's portable iPod dock. After bopping around to the all-over-the-place beats of "Get Together" for a couple minutes, I realized Lucas was staring at me. He had a sort of crazed look in his eye, and he looked like he was concentrating really hard.

"What?!" I laughed. "Why are you looking crazy? *Crazy* Lucas! I *hate* Crazy Lucas!"

"Because I'm trying to remember that I just asked you a question," he said, his eyes narrowing and his face scrunching up all funnily, like he was trying to prevent something from oozing out of his head.

"Well, what . . . ? Wait. You asked me a question?"

"Yes! God!" He threw his arms up in the air, and two seconds later was twirling around and dancing to the song.

"Well, what was the *question*?" I asked anxiously.

"I don't remember." And then he fell on his bed laughing. *"Get me another screwdriver, wench!"*

I stumbled over to the kitchenette and then got the sudden urge to pee. I guess I *had* had a few Bloody Marys, in addition to that Super Big Gulp from 7-Eleven I'd guzzled on the drive up.

"Lucas, I have to take a whiz, I'll—"

"Did you just say *whiz?*" Lucas laughed from the bed. *"Whiz* is so middle school, Madge."

"How 'bout *piss*, homo?" I screamed dramatically. "Or is it just soooooo last season?"

"Shut up and take your whiz!" he yelled back at me, cackling.

I laughed and shuffled into the bathroom. After closing and locking the door with a little difficulty—my sense of touch was having a weird delayed-reaction thing going on—I shimmied down my jeans and plopped onto the toilet. Just before I broke the beer seal, I heard a little snippet of Lucas answering his phone with an annoyed, *"What?"*

I wish I could've heard the rest, since any conversation that starts out that bitchily is bound to be a good one, but then I started peeing and literally *could not stop*. How had I held it *in* this long? How much longer could this conceivably go *on* for? I was paying *way* too much attention to my urine stream that by the time I stopped, I realized I'd missed out on the whole scandalous phone conversation. Lucas whispered, *"I gotta go—don't call me any more tonight,"* I flushed and washed up, and that was the end of it.

I was itching with curiosity when I went back into the room.

Was that the same caller as the mysterious text-messager from the drive up? Was it someone else? Could it have been Kenny, and why was Lucas so mad-sounding at him? I was dying to know, but since Lucas had been acting a little weird about the texting on the drive up here, I really wanted him to come to me about it. . . .

"Who called you?" I asked him flat out.

. . . (But not without a little prodding, of course.)

"Oh! No one. Just . . . Mitsy checking up on us. Outta the way, Diaz! I'm about to *whiz* my pants!" And he ran into the bathroom and shut the door, oblivious to the fact that I'd heard the intriguing beginning and end to his last conversation.

Okay, I was totally checking his incoming calls. Sue me!

That's when I saw it: ZACH.

Huh?!

Why would *Zach* be calling Lucas? Lucas said Zach didn't want anything to do with him anymore.

Hearing Lucas's peeing continuing into record time, I decided to go through Lucas's other incoming calls and texts.

Mind-fuck!

Okay, I'm exaggerating a little, but: ZACH, ZACH, ZACH, ZACH, ZACH, ZACH, ZACH, ZACH, ZACH, ZACH, ZACH, ZACH, ZACH, ZACH, ZACH.

I flipped the phone shut and threw it back on the bed just as Lucas popped out of the bathroom, face splashed with water, hair touched up, and looking ready to go.

Looking genuinely excited, he cried, "Let's Visine up and tear this mother *out*, baby!"

10

Pearls of Wisdom

● ●

The only thing more annoying than just realizing your best friend is keeping things from you is being with said best friend all night and not wanting to bring it up because he's *so. damn. happy.*

But being as tipsy and stoned as Lucas was, I was actually in such a fun going-out mood that I decided all the drama could wait till another time. A few last-minute primps later, we were out of our room, through the hotel, and at the Later Gator bus stop. The Later Gator, which was filled up with a couple dozen fucked-up-out-of-their-minds college kids—quite a few of the frat-boy variety, which made Lucas very happy—took only about fifteen minutes to get to the University Club.

Jonathan had told me yesterday to find him inside during the drag show, which he thought started at around twelve. Luckily he'd also told me that you had to use this funny back entrance to get into the UC. The club had a window facing University Avenue, like a storefront, and I could see people dancing around inside, but you had to walk around the block and into a little parking lot behind the club, then up a set of wooden stairs to this deck to get *into* the club.

He'd also warned me that they were pretty serious about keeping the underagers from drinking—which really just sounded like a challenge to me—so I told Lucas to hold his shit together while we paid to get in. I hoped our recently re-Visine'd glassy eyes and feverish chewing of multiple sticks of gum didn't give us away. For a split second, when they took our IDs and stashed them in a little flash-card box, I thought they were confiscating our licenses and were about to turn us in for public drunkenness or something. But then we got wristbands and hand stamps.

"We cut your wristbands off and give back the IDs at the end of the night," the cashier said, taking our cover charge. "Have fun."

Wow. Tight system.

But I was still determined to get me a drink at some point. This was *college*, baby.

The club was cool. Lucas and I'd been to bigger places—like Parliament House and Pulse in Orlando—but this was totally cute. Almost homey. The level we were on became a sort of bar area, which then stretched into a kind of balcony overlooking a packed dance floor one level below us. And there were also stairs leading up a third level.

I turned to Lucas and said giddily, "Let's explore!" I started for the stairs without turning back around and ran right into someone, spilling her drink all over her.

"Oh my God, I am *so sorry!*" I cried, turning around to face my unfortunate drink victim, a short but formidable, tough-as-all-shit-looking hot black woman. If I'd been gay and into hot butch lesbians with sexy cornrows, I would've been way hard up for this lady. I started for the bar. "I'm so sorry, let me get some napkins from the—"

"Girl, please," she interrupted, grabbing hold of my wrist, all suave. "Fine-ass lady like yourself should be downstairs dancin' and havin' fun, not cleanin' me up."

"Oh, well . . . how sweet. Thanks, mama," I said, all flattered and flustered. Smiling, I decided to press my luck. "Uh . . . hey . . . how 'bout I pay you to replace that drink and then you can buy me one?" There was a pause. "Look, I'm batting my eyelashes." And I was.

Hot Black Dyke just chuckled. "Since you're new here and you're so damn fine, I'll let that one slide." Then she reached into her back pocket and produced a flashlight, shining it to my wrist and then in my face. My world went white for a second. "But next time, I'll have to kick you out for that." She smiled and patted me on the back and was on her way.

I turned to Lucas, saying, "Legal Drinking Age, one; Madge Diaz, zero," which gave him a good hard laugh.

When he was able to get his breath again, he said, "Um, how

'bout you get a point for getting *hit on* before me!" He slapped my arm. "Biz-atch!"

"Now, Lucas, play nice. Hey—let's find my friend so I can talk to that old prom queen!"

First we walked to the upstairs bar, where the air was thick with smoke and distinctly Jonathan-less.

"Let's go downstairs, baby," I said to Lucas, who had just spotted a particularly attractive hipster-looking boy in cutoff denim and a Metric concert T-shirt. Too bad (for me) that the boy was clearly gay. I was gonna have to drag Lucas to some *straight* clubs when we moved here, because I could not *handle* this sexual *torture* every weekend. I know the gay boys are unavailable, but that doesn't stop some of them from being so foxy!

We headed down another set of stairs that bypassed the entire entry level and went down to the street level, where the big dance floor was. I couldn't spot Jonathan or Laura anywhere, so I kept my eyes peeled as Lucas and I danced to a couple of songs together.

Suddenly, the song cut out and was replaced with some show-tunes-y-sounding music, and the DJ announced the start of the drag show. Everyone immediately cleared the central dance floor and formed a circle along its periphery. Before I knew what was going on, Lucas and I were corralled over to the far end of the dance floor, near the base of the stairs that led up to the middle level where we'd entered and paid our cover.

Just as Lucas and I finally stopped and situated ourselves with a decent view of the cleared-out dance floor, I felt a two-handed squeeze on my ass. I whipped around, smiling knowingly, to see none other than my boy Jonathan Parish, looking *so good* in his black collared shirt and tight little jeans.

"*Dios mio*, baby, you look *hot!*" I cried, picking him up in a hearty hug. "It's so good to see you!"

"It's so good to see *you!*" he replied, playing with my shawl. "Ohmigod, those feathers? A-*maz*-ing!"

"Thanks! Jonathan, this is my friend Lucas," I said, pulling Lucas over to us.

After a brief moment of stunned silence, Lucas said awkwardly, "Uh . . . hi," and shook Jonathan's hand. Yeah, Jonathan *was* a cutie. I could see how Lucas would get a little tongue-tied.

This is a situation I'd characterize as *in the bag*.

"Oh my God, is that Kylie on your shirt?" Jonathan asked excitedly, feeling up Lucas's doctored-up shirt. Zach had made the shirt for him a couple months back. Like I said before, it was one of those unnecessarily zippered shirts from Armani Exchange, but Zach had somehow done a little silkscreen of a singing Kylie Minogue silhouette onto the front of it. He'd even pressed on a few glittery stars here and there, thus adding to its sheer gayness . . . and awesomeness.

"Um . . ." Lucas glanced down at his shirt bashfully. "Yeah . . . yeah, it is."

"I *adore* her," Jonathan gushed giddily. "I even got to see her last summer."

"No way!" Lucas said, all of a sudden less shy and more excited. "How?"

Ah, Kylie Minogue. Bringing gay boys together for twenty-odd years.

"Oh." He paused and looked behind him for a second. "Long story . . . Anyway, did you make that yourself?" Jonathan continued. "I *want* it!"

"Oh, uh . . . just . . ." Lucas paused uncomfortably and looked back down at his shirt. "Just this . . . friend of mine."

Smooth, Lucas, I thought to myself. *Way to throw him off the trail.*

As if on cue to end the awkwardness, the DJ announced the arrival of "The One, The Only, The Lady Pearl." Some Disco Era ballad kicked in on the speakers, and out she came.

"Whoa," was pretty much what Lucas and I said the second we got a good look at her. Jonathan just smiled.

The Lady Pearl, I have to admit, was *quite* the sight to behold. Bitch was seriously, like, *seven feet tall* in heels—big, clunky, clear stiletto heels, to be precise—and was definitely a proud plus-size *whoa*-man. Her floor-length sparkling gown was skin-tight and white with glittery tassels all over. When the song's tempo sped up, so did she, spinning so fast that she became a blur of shimmering, flying fabric. Her blonde helmet-hair wig was done up about a foot off her head, and her heavily made-up face was big and expressive, her mouth moving almost perfectly in sync with the vocals of the song. Every few seconds, someone from the crowd—even that hot-for-me bouncer—came up to Pearl and placed a dollar in her hand or her cleavage, and would be rewarded with a dark-lipsticked kiss on the cheek.

At one point, this old nasty guy stumbled out of the crowd and into Pearl's spotlight and handed her, like, ten bucks, one Mr. Washington at a time. After a while, Pearl seemed bored of fanning herself and acting all hot and bothered, and just grabbed the fistful of money he'd been tipping her from. Then the bouncer (Flashlight Lady) led the old geezer back into the crowd and Pearl continued with her performance.

When she finished the number, the crowd went wild, cheering loudly and proudly and drunkenly, and Pearl took a bow and headed briefly offstage.

"Hey, Jonathan," I said, "what's an eighteen-year-old gotta do to get a drink in here? Can you hook us up?"

"Oh, hell no, I'm sorry, guys," Jonathan said, his eyes wide. "Star would beat my ass if she caught me."

"Who's Star?"

"She's the bouncer here. She kicked a friend of mine out one time when he bought some kid a drink."

"Dammit!" I cried. "Can't a girl get a break around here?!"

Still offstage, Pearl (who'd now been given a mike) brayed like a big gay horse: *"Heeeeey!"*

"Heeeeey!" the crowd called back.

Pearl shuffled back onto the dance floor she'd just performed on and the crowd cheered. "How the *fuck* are you crazy motherfuckers?" she yelled to the audience.

Cheers went up all around, and Pearl said, "Bitches, I'm just hungry, y'all." Her voice was booming and low and tinged with a Southern accent. Or maybe it was just the accent of the Crude Floridian Drag Queen—I *had* heard it before, after all, back home at Parliament House. It was also was kind of how I talked sometimes when I was really, really trashed. "Any of y'all skinny faggots got a Krystal burger for Mama?"

(Mmm . . . that sounded yums. I wondered where the nearest Krystal was.)

"I got somethin' for ya!" this hot Latino boy called from the front row of the standing audience, grabbing his crotch.

"Shit," Jonathan laughed, putting his arms around me and Lucas. "Watch this."

Lucas and I just looked at each other, our eyebrows raised in anticipation.

"Oooh," Pearl said, seeming intrigued as she regarded the dude. "No, bitch, I got somethin' for *you*! You ever had a taste of the Pearl Jam?"

The audience laughed, and the dude called out, "Hell no!"

Then all of a sudden Pearl's microphone was in her mouth and halfway down her throat and she was humming "The Star-Spangled Banner." The audience went wild for this, and Lucas, Jonathan, and I cheered along. This drag queen had skills. Then out came the microphone, and Pearl called the Hispanic guy up to her and asked, "Wha's yo' name, baby?"

"Pedro."

"You a straight boy, Pedro?"

"Hell yeah!"

"Bool-shit!" Pearl spat into the mike. "If you straight, boy, what the *fuck* you doin' here?"

"I came here to see you, baby!" he answered, grabbing Pearl's ass.

"Get yo' hands off me, Mary!" Pearl yelled. "Take that shirt off, straight boy."

Pedro put his arms up in a what-can-you-do? sort of way and was suddenly acting all coy.

"You wanna interrupt my show, bitch, you better gimme *somethin'*!" And with that, Pearl stuffed the mike in her cleavage, grabbed Pedro, and had his shirt off in five seconds, the crowd hooting and catcalling the whole time.

Pedro had a mean six-pack, and a *really* nice, lick-able chest (I was liking this town so far), and the reaction from the crowd was pretty high-pitched and pleased, to say the least. I know *I* was screeching. And Lucas was cheering louder than anyone.

"Mmm," Pearl said again, stepping back and checking him out. "Shit, bitch, I'd feed you a Snickers and eat the peanuts out yo' *ass!*"

What the freaking hell was happening tonight? Where was I? This was hilarious shit.

"Bartender, get this ho-mo-sex-sh'll a cocktail. Pedro, baby, you bring me some reefer after the show, and I'll bring the Snickers. Now get the *fuck* off my stage!"

The crowd cheered more as Pedro laughed and headed to the bar, where the bartender asked him for ID. When Pearl saw this, she just yelled, "Bitch, he's twenty-one, I ate his ass!"

This Lady Pearl was a freaking *lunatic*, and I was lovin' it! I looked over at Lucas, who was doubled over laughing. Then I turned my attention to the staircase behind us and saw ol' Laura Schulberg approaching us.

She looked beautiful. I always remember Laura looking beautiful, with her impeccable wardrobe, shimmery jet-black hair, and perfect figure. And this girl's tan was putting my *own* Puerto Rican complexion to shame.

"Hey, Margarita," she said, coming up and giving me a hug. "Jonathan told me you were coming tonight. How fun!"

We said our hellos and went through the introductions for Lucas as Lady Pearl lectured the crowd. "Now, I know it's finals week for y'all, and y'all need to blow off some steam," she said to the crowd, "but if any of y'all bitches get fucked up and get behind the wheel, I will fuck you up *way* more than any goddamn car accident will. I want all y'all back here in one piece next school year, you hear me?"

Everyone clapped and cheered.

"Studyin' fryin' y'all's brains, cocksuckers? I said, *'You hear me?!'*" The crowd screamed and cheered more loudly in response.

"Good," Pearl said, satisfied. "Don't drive drunk. And if you have to, just make sure you hit *my* car. 'Cause I need the insurance money, baby."

By this point, Lucas and Jonathan were off to the side getting to know each other, so it was just me and Laura, with not much to talk about but the obvious.

"Can *you* get me a drink?" I asked.

Laura laughed. "No, I'm still only nineteen—but we can go out to the car. Me and Jonathan packed little to-go bottles, and he didn't even touch his."

"Yeah?" A little alone-time for the boys might be perfect. "Sure, let's go."

"Lemme just tell Jonathan," she said, and went over to the guys.

I turned my attention back to Pearl, who was introducing the next performer. "Now, I want you to give a good Gainesville welcome for our next performer. I want y'all to *clap yo' hands!*"

Everyone around me clapped once, I guess fulfilling some kind of UC ritual.

"Clap yo' hands!"

This time I smiled and clapped along.

"Stomp yo' hooves!"

Stomp.

"Now, all you straight, pussy-lovin' boys scream."

There were a few—more than I expected, actually—very manly-sounding hoots.

"Shut the *fuck* up, y'all ain't straight!" Pearl yelled as she headed offstage. "Now, I wanna hear you welcome Gainesville's very finest . . . Miss Juwana Jackson!"

The spotlight went out, and a loud house beat came on, and the club was nothing but swirling blue and pink pulsating lights. After a few seconds of buildup, the song exploded with some fierce, guttural vocals, and Juwana Jackson came tearing out onto the dance floor, giving *new* meaning to the word *fierce* in this purple-tasseled leotard that she was totally rockin'. Juwana was putting my own big-girl dance moves to shame, working her big-boned frame into such a frenzy of movement—high kicks, full splits (SPLITS!), and almost hula dancer–esque booty shakes—that I wondered how she could maintain the energy level.

I was sad to leave the performance when Laura came back to me, but I guess I had a job to do here.

"Here—Jonathan's car," Laura said, clicking a set of car keys and unlocking the doors of a Nissan in the distance. "He upgraded, thank *God*, from that *beast* of a Volvo he used to drive. That thing was an embarrassment."

Huh. I also remembered Laura being kinda snobbish. Guess not too much changes from high school to college.

We walked through the filled-up parking lot to the car. When we got to it, Laura opened up a back door and waited for me to get in.

"The backseat?" I asked, laughing. "What, are we makin' out or something?"

"Not unless you want to," she said cheekily. "No, I just don't think we should be sitting in the front of the car while we're suspiciously drinking out of Gatorade bottles at twelve thirty at night."

"Point taken." I took a look around us, saw no signs of authority (except the fact that it appeared Jonathan had parked in City Hall's lot), and ducked into the car. Laura followed.

We settled into the Nissan's cozy rear, ducking down as far as we could without actually lying *horizontally* on our seats. Oh, the joys of underage drinking. Laura reached under the driver's seat and produced two Gatorade bottles.

"Vodka with Lemon-Lime . . . or vodka with"—she looked closely at the label in the dark—"Frost?"

"Lemon-Lime somehow seems safer," I said, and she handed it to me.

"Here's to awkward conversations to come," she said, holding up her bottle of blue liquid in a toast.

I couldn't help but laugh as I clinked plastic bottles with her. "Right," I said.

We took a sip from our drinks—mine was a little nasty, but it would do for a few swigs—and sighed simultaneously. It seemed almost rehearsed.

"So, fire away, Margarita," Laura said, turning to look at me in the dark as she sipped from her bottle. "Tell me about this prom-queen wisdom you seek."

I was still a little stoned, so this actually sounded pretty deep to me. I searched within myself, *deep* within my deep-thinking self, and came up with . . .

Nothing.

"Margarita?"

"Just call me 'Madge'—it has less syllables."

"Sure, okay . . . So? *Madge?*" She poked me.

"Huh?"

"Jonathan told me all about this crazy prom-queen thing you've got going on. So, do you mind if I ask . . . I dunno . . . why you care?"

"You're not offended by it or anything, are you?" I asked her. "Y'know, since you *were* prom queen and all."

"Madge? Truly? I *couldn't* care less."

"Wait . . . Really?" I'd sort of had her pegged as someone who *would* care. I mean, she *was* Top Bitch of Winter Park last year and was all sorts of popular and powerful. It just seemed like a natural fit.

"Last year was weird for me, Madge. I was just over all that bullshit by the time prom rolled around. It's not like I *asked* to be elected prom queen. It just sort of happened. And I wasn't about to go onstage and be, like, 'No thanks, because I'm beyond all this.'"

"No way!" I cried. "That's kind of how *I* feel about it."

"Yeah? Then why are you here talking to me? Why do what you're doing in the first place?"

"Didn't Jonathan tell you? She freakin' *dishonored* me, dude! Plus, she *dared* me. What'm I gonna say to that?"

"'Dishonored' you? What are you, a samurai?" She laughed, wincing as she took another sip of Frost-vodka.

"Well, it's not just that. Did Jonathan tell you about the whole deal with my sister and the clothes she makes?"

"Yeah, he mentioned that. It just seems kinda . . . I dunno, don't take this the wrong way, but it seems . . . weak."

"Weak?"

"Totally. Here," she said, handing me her bottle. "We're switching. You're the guest and all, but I can't drink this weirdness anymore."

"Luckily for you, I'll drink any weirdness," I said, taking the Frost, which actually tasted okay to me. "So what do you mean by 'weak'?"

"It just seems like there's something more in it for you; otherwise, why go to all this trouble? Something *major* must've made that fight turn so ugly. . . ." She looked at me almost analytically. "What's your deal with Bridget Benson?" she asked all of a sudden.

"Where'd *that* come from?" I asked, feeling defensive. "You don't even know me."

"Listen," Laura said calmly, "I've got a pretty good idea of what you must think about *me*. I'll admit it—I was kind of a bitch for most of high school. I didn't bother, y'know, *consorting* with people who couldn't do anything for me . . . and I was friends with the people who would keep me on top and popular." She paused for a second and stretched her legs out, burping delicately and smirking. "But I've definitely changed. I mean, I'm still a bitch to whoever deserves it—and it sounds like *Bridget* deserves it after the awful shit she said to you—but all that other stuff kind of seems meaningless now. Prom, prom queen, tiaras . . . all that crap."

"Okay . . ." I said, not sure where exactly this was going. Laura must've had a *couple* of Gatorade-tinis tonight.

"Look, I'm tellin' you this because I like you, Madge," she said, shifting her body so she was facing me head-on. "I always admired you in high school, even if I never really showed it. I guess I just didn't know *how* to. You with me?"

"Yeah."

"And I can tell you don't care about the prom stuff. And up to a point, I'm not even sure you care that much about your sister's stuff—"

"Hey, now, wait a min—"

"No, *you* wait a minute. Why, when I asked you why you cared so much about this prom-queen stuff, did you say it was 'cause she dishonored you? Someone dishonors you, you slap 'em across the face. You don't run for *prom queen* against them unless there's something else going on. So go on—spill. This is just girl talk— we're all friends here."

Damn. I couldn't believe she'd figured it all out, everything I'd been trying to ignore myself. I felt like such a shit, because I really *hadn't* been thinking of Vanessa most of this time. It was all about making Bridget look bad. Making her *pay* for what she'd said and done to me two weeks ago—and ten years ago.

I spilled it all to Laura, swearing her to pinky-swear secrecy because I was so embarrassed, and she just sat there and listened to it all. I told her about our friendship, the audition, the unreturned phone calls, my inexplicable need to show her up and make her respect me . . . everything.

"I don't even know if I can win this thing anymore," I finally said, noticing how heavy with tears my eyes were. I blinked, and a couple of big salty ones rolled down my cheek. "As much as I've been doing, it's like she's doing twice as much, and doing it twice as well."

"But do you *really* wanna win it?" Laura asked me. "I mean, don't you see how petty it all seems?"

"I know it's petty, Laura. It's just . . . I just . . . I want her to feel a little disappointment in her life. For once. All she does is get what she wants, and I don't think she deserves it. I just saw this as an opportunity to take something away from her that she really, really wanted. And now I'm not even sure I can do it."

"Okay, stop your cryin', baby," she said, leaning over and giving me a quick little hug. "We're gonna do something fun. An exercise. I want you to picture something."

"All right."

"I want you to picture what it'd be like . . . to be named the prom queen. What that *exact moment* is gonna feel like. Okay? Now close your eyes. . . . Can you see it?"

Well, my highness considered, the first thing I saw when I shut my eyes was a Baja Chicken Chalupa from Taco Bell. But after telling my brain that the Bell's drive-through was open till four, my mind eventually wandered off to that wonderful world of make-believe, deep in my head. There I was, at prom. All I could see was the stage, right in front of me. Everything around me was black. Just me, and the stage. My curly black hair was straightened and sculpted up elaborately, into an almost upside-down-tornado shape, and I was in a glittering silver dress, looking like a fabulously busty disco-ball. When I heard my name called—from where I don't know—I walked onto the stage to accept that all-important Holy Grail of high-school achievements: the prom-queen tiara. It was floating in midair magically, a cloud of stars and glitter swirling around it. The room erupted into deafening applause and cheers. All of a sudden, I could see the crowd of students. Hundreds of them. *Thousands.* People were showering me with gifts—flowers, chocolates, *boxers!*—as the crown was placed delicately onto my head by an invisible, Almighty hand (God's? Madonna's? Beth Ditto's?). I smiled radiantly and bowed, but then the lights came on, and no one was in the crowd. It was just . . .

Empty.

"That's *it!*" I said, snapping my eyes open.

"What's it?"

"The best way for me to get back at Bridget . . . is to take the prom *away* from her."

A Grinch-like grin spread across Laura's face. "That's *completely* brilliant! 'Cause you know what my mantra always was?" she asked, leaning forward so we were almost nose to nose. "If someone you hate is throwing a party," she whispered, "then you just have to throw a *better* one."

"Totally!" I cried, slapping her arm. "I'm totally throwing the kick-assiest anti-prom party in the history of the world! I mean, what am I *really* missing if I don't go to prom?"

"Sugary punch and a crappy DJ is pretty much it. The only thing that you'll miss is seeing Bridget with nothing but her cheap plastic crown and an empty room." She leaned back to her side of the car, crossing her arms and raising an eyebrow, looking every bit the proud mama. "You totally figured it out, Madge. Nice job. But what about your sister?"

"I dunno," I said, my mind racing. "Maybe . . . maybe I could get someone to film the anti-prom and someone to film the *real* prom and then sell the footage to someone. Maybe Lucas's dad! *He's* a producer! And I can have my sister redesign my prom dress and I'll look crazy-dazzling. . . . It's perfect!"

"See?" Laura said, downing the rest of her drink. "Aren't you glad you came up here this weekend?"

"*That's* the understatement of the century! Wait," I said, grabbing hold of Laura's wrist. "Do me a favor. Don't tell Lucas or Jonathan about all that stuff I said earlier . . . y'know, about my . . . issues with Bridget."

"Um, okay?"

"It's just that I don't wanna look all weak to them. It's embarrassing."

"Sure," she said. "I swear." She punched me playfully on the shoulder. "Now let's get back in there and stuff some dollar bills into some surgically-created cleavage!"

11

In Liquid Cocaine *Veritas*

• •

Back in the club, some other drag queen (I later found out her name was Jasmine) was dancing to Janet Jackson's classic "If," mimicking the look and the moves perfectly. It took me a few minutes get through the thick crowd of people, but I finally made it to Lucas, giving him a big hug from behind. He immediately turned around and just started dancing with me—riding my knee all nasty-like, shakin' his lil' toosh like a saltshaker—obviously in a really good mood. He was gonna be so excited about my new prom plan!

"I am having *so* much fun!" he yelled into my ear. The music had gotten louder.

"Yeah? Isn't Jonathan great?"

"Oh, totally! We're all gonna hang out next time he's back in Orlando."

"Sweet!" I said. *Everything* was peachy-keen! But just as I was about to tell Lucas about the fabulous anti-prom party, a deep, nasal voice cut through our happy little dance-bubble with a pointed, "*Don't* fuckin' dance while I'm onstage, *bitches!*"

And that's when we realized that the music had stopped and the spotlight was back on the hostess Lady Pearl. Actually, Pearl was facing us, her formidable seven-foot silhouette towering over us, backlit by the blinding spotlight.

Everyone around us took a small step back, the whole thing very movielike.

"Sorry!" Lucas said gaily.

"I'm guessin' this in't yo' girlfriend, baby?" Pearl asked Lucas, coming closer to us. "This bitch in the pink feathers?"

"No, she's my faghag," he called out in response, putting his arm around me. A few people laughed and clapped. Some girls would be put off by the term. I really couldn't care less. 'Cause I know I ain't no hag!

Pearl turned to me. "Hmm," she grunted, tilting her head. "This fruit fly's more like a big ol' fruit *beetle* if you ask me." The crowd laughed at that, and without missing a beat, Pearl barked at me, "What's that say on yo' tight-ass shirt?"

"'Go big for queen,'" I replied. "It's hard to explain."

"Mmm. Looks like you go big for the *Dairy* Queen, baby,"

Pearl deadpanned. "Now I know why all them Ethiopian mothafuckas're starvin'! *Get* up here, ya chunky bitch—let's get a good look at that ass!"

I figured I had no issues with my ass, so I sauntered up into the spotlight, toward the imposing figure of Lady Pearl. Up close, once I'd turned so I could see more of her in the light, I noticed how much makeup she had caked on her face. And when she asked me, "What's your name, baby?" and thrust her lipstick-encrusted microphone in my face, I saw even *more* clearly how much makeup she used.

"Madge," I said, staring at the thick flakes of pink an inch from my mouth.

"Madge, huh?" Pearl asked. "We got Madonna in the house, ladies and gentlemen!" she called to the audience, which elicited some laughs, even from me.

"*What* you laughing at, *bitch*?" she barked at me. "Don't come up onto my stage and interrupt me!"

"I'm sorry!" I guess those Gatorade cocktails had really renewed my buzz, because I couldn't seem to stop laughing. "I'm sorry—"

"Don't be singin' your songs to me, Miss Madonna—*Pearl* asks the questions up here." She paused and looked at me quizzically. "You got any reefer, honey?"

This made me laugh even more.

"I'll trade you some Trim Spa for some reefer," she continued. "I'll fuckin' Anna-*Nicole* yo' ass!"

"I—don't—e-e-even know what that m-mea—"

"You like Krystal burgers, flightless bird?" Pearl interrupted me.

"Hell yeah!" I screamed, still in my laughing fit.

"I thought so. How you like 'em?"

"Um . . . with onions?"

"Bitch, you nasty, get the hell off my stage!" I turned around, giggling idiotically, when I heard Pearl yell out, "Bartender, get this funny fat faghag a drink!"

Whoa!

Success!

I practically *flew* to the bar, the pink feathers of my shawl billowing in the breeze as I rushed through the crowd of people surrounding the bar. I couldn't *wait* to taste the sweetness of the Crown and Coke I was gonna order. Mmmm. Like candy. Or maybe just a glass of Ketel on the rocks. Enough with the mixers, already. Let's keep this party *going*!

Finally, the bartender finished with the two drinks he was mixing for the cute dyke-y couple next to me and came up to me, and just as my lips were forming a nice, delicious *V* for *vodka*, he asked me, "Got ID?"

Fuck.

Enough of this.

Soon after that—after Pearl closed out her show with a heartfelt lecture on safe sex ("Wrap it up, 'cause no injection is worth the infection of dyin' over!")—the music switched from gay-gay-gay to gangsta rap, so the four of us had had enough.

Plus, thankfully, Jonathan told us there was a party we were going to.

"First we're parking at my shithole apartment complex, then we're walking to this party a coupla visual-arts friends of mine are throwing in the Student Ghetto," he told us as he fired up the car.

"Uh . . . 'scuse me?" I asked. "*Walk? Ghetto?* These are words I don't like to hear together."

"Yeah," Lucas said, "kind of like *moist* and . . . anything."

"It *is* a dirty-sounding word," Jonathan agreed, turning onto University Avenue and heading back toward campus. "But don't worry—it's only a few blocks from my place, and it's only really called the Student Ghetto 'cause it's so cheap. It's just a bunch of houses and cheap apartments near campus. I mean, your bike might get stolen, but it's not that scary. I just don't wanna have to drive home. And you guys can walk back to your hotel on campus after."

Ten minutes later, we were parked at Jonathan's apartment complex, The Courtyards. He got out of the car and told us to wait for him while he went into his apartment to get some liquor. "It's scary in there—it's all macho meatheads and drunk sluts. God, I can't *wait* to move outta here in the fall."

A short while later, Jonathan ran back to the car to beckon us to the Student Ghetto. He had a double-bagged Wal-Mart bag stuffed with a bottle each of Jägermeister, Goldschläger, and Bacardi 151.

Damn.

Boy wasn't messin' around.

◆ ◆ ◆

The Student Ghetto wasn't as bad as I'd pictured it. I guess when I heard the word *ghetto*, I pictured burned-out crack houses and liquor stores with barred-up doors and windows. But the little area just a couple blocks north of campus, a ten-minute walk from Jonathan's apartment, was pretty cool. The streets were narrow and not too busy with traffic, and there was nothing but lots of little houses with moss- and twig-covered yards and small two-story apartment buildings. And the best part of it all was—are you ready for it?—there was a Krispy Kreme and a McDonald's within spittin' distance!

The only sort of weird thing about the neighborhood was that it wasn't all that well lit, and there were a couple of random drunk people wandering around on our way to the party. But I was getting the impression that there were drunk people wandering around all over Gainesville, so I wasn't too put off.

Laura and I were telling the boys all about our talk in the car.

"Really," Lucas said flatly, when I'd told him about the anti-prom plan. "You *really* wanna do that?"

"Why not?!" I said enthusiastically. "It'd be so much fun!"

"But where would you *have* it?" Jonathan asked. He seemed less than thrilled with the idea, too. What was *with* these boys?!

"I have a pretty big penthouse," Laura told us. "I could fit a *bunch* of people in there."

"Wait," Lucas said, "*where* do you live?"

No shit.

Turned out Laura and Lucas were next-door neighbors!

"Do you think Mitsy would let us have it at your place, too?" I asked, the smile on my face practically giving me a headache. "Think how *incredible* that'd be. Views out both sides of the building!"

"Yeah," Lucas said, "she'd probably let you. . . ."

"I love it!"

"Madge," Jonathan said (he was hip to the "Madge" now, too), "are you sure you wanna skip out on prom? It's kind of a rite of passage. . . ."

"Eh, I went last year. And *this* year I have a purpose."

"To defend her honor," Laura said reverently, which made me laugh. I crossed my fingers that Lucas wouldn't ask about Vanessa yet—I wasn't ready to ask about the possible Lucas-dad favor—and luckily he didn't. In fact, he barely spoke at all after that.

As we approached the party house, I couldn't help but notice two things: 1) I was about one no-longer-mysterious text message away from slapping Lucas silly, and 2) the house was *literally* across a fence from the Krispy Kreme. Which Jonathan assured me was open very late.

I noted this, as an aromatic glaze-haze cloud wafted our way.

"Okay," Jonathan said to us all, "the guys that're throwing the party are in the visual-arts program. The guy I know is Travis, and he's got two roommates." Now he jumped in front of us and turned to face us, putting his hands in the air to stop us from walking. "And one more thing: *please* don't judge the guys based on their art. They're total sweeties, and they mean well."

"Oh, I'm looking forward to *this*," Laura said, smiling big.

"Be nice," Jonathan told her, and led us up to the front door.

I didn't really know what to expect, till I opened the door and heard Ladytron blasting from some speakers and was faced with a short hallway full of painted mannequins staring at me. Along the two walls of the foyer, a couple feet off the ground, a shelf painted in swirling colors had been nailed in on each side. On top of each shelf stood two male mannequins. Each was dressed in a simple white muumuu, but all four were painted different colors—one black, one white, one yellow, and one brown.

"Oh, puh-*leese*," Laura moaned in my ear. "So tell me," she continued, getting all serious, "what does this piece mean to you?" I was starting to really like this girl.

"Um . . . well, *piece* is the right word, but . . ." I pretended to think about it a second. "Do you think all these colors represent races of people, and so this is saying that all are welcome in this house? And the simple yet functional clothing tells us that we're all equal?"

"I think you hit the nail on the head there, Miss Diaz."

"Yeah, but where's my *fat* mannequin?" I asked. "I don't feel welcome in this house."

"Behave, or we crash a lame kegger back at The Courtyards," Jonathan said, leading us into the living room, where a bunch of people were milling about, drinking imported beer and smoking

Dunhills and cloves. We went to the kitchen to drop off the liquor and meet our hosts, got hooked up with bottles of Newcastle, and then I sort of wandered off to explore the place on my own. The house was small, but really decent—nice-sized living room and bedrooms, and even a backyard. And the kitchen, dining room, and living room were all one continuous space, which was really nice, especially for a party. In one of the corners of the living room stood a six-foot-tall floor lamp, composed entirely of green and blue and yellow Lite Brite pegs.

On one of their living-room walls, I spotted another lovely little piece of art—this one was a stuffed bunny rabbit stuck into the wall by a knife through its chest, and under it ran a thick area of red paint dripping down the wall. Oh, you think this is bad, but wait'll you hear what came next—in the swirls of dark red paint were the finger-painted words: MEAT IS MURDER. I guess our hosts didn't make much use of that McDonald's across the street.

Mmm . . . McDonald's.

I hung out for a while, talked to Laura and a few new people—about what I can't really tell you (there was a pretty inexhaustible supply of beer at this party, and I was fairly convinced I was getting a contact buzz from all the weed being smoked), but it was fun. I was liking it. It was different from a high-school party. I wouldn't say it was more grown up or anything like that. I mean, I spent a good deal of time playing drinking games like Asshole and Kings, and at one point was belting out my own special rendition of "Baby Got Back" to a karaoke machine, so I definitely wasn't feeling too . . . sophisticated. And it *definitely* wasn't sophisticated when I brought out one of the mannequins to help me sing a duet of "Love Shack" by the B-52's. But it just felt cool—less supervised, less worried that a parent might show up, less fake people who were thrown into the same room out of basic necessity. Because I guess in a college town with fifty-odd thousand students, people hung out with each other because they *wanted* to—not 'cause it was the only thing to do.

There were no Bridget Bensons at this party. No cokehead slutty sidekicks like Lindsay Taylor.

I mean, they were definitely around—just not at this party.

Probably back at The Courtyards.

Just then I heard Jonathan calling for me, so I left the living room and headed into the kitchen, where I spied him pouring out some shots of brown liquid, Lucas observing intently. He kept pouring till the cocktail shaker was empty, and by then, he'd made seven shots and they all got passed around.

"Okay," Jonathan said, "this is called a Liquid Cocaine. So, on three—one . . . two—"

"Wait!" I interrupted. "A Liquid . . . *Cocaine?*"

"Uh-huh."

"What the hell is that? Is this gonna kill me?"

"Um . . . yeah, Madge," Lucas said, "that's *sort of* the point."

"What's in it?" I asked.

"Well . . . all the stuff we got out of my liquor cabinet."

Jonathan shrugged and smiled coyly. "It'll fuck you up, Margarita—beware."

That was all I needed to hear. "Three!" I yelled, and slammed back the shot. "Holyshittingfuckingmotherof*god*!" I screamed, literally feeling a fire of licorice and rubbing alcohol and spiciness shooting out of my mouth. "That was freaking *ridiculous*!" I burped and actually tasted a trace amount of vomit, so I quickly poured myself a cup of water at the sink.

"I told you!" Jonathan laughed.

Lucas was looking a little green in the face, now that I noticed, so I went back to the sink to get him some water, too.

Some people requested more shots, and as everyone in the kitchen started moving around again, Lucas got another call on his cell. I looked back from the sink and saw him regard the display screen and sigh. Then he flipped the phone open and said, "Hel-*lo*?" much in the same way he did back at the hotel room.

"Yeah," he continued into the phone. "Yeah . . . I'm in Gainesville and I'm *drunk*, okay? What the fuck do *you* care?" Then he noticed me looking at him and took his conversation into the backyard.

I'd pretty much had enough of playing it safe, and I figured that since I'd just downed something called a Liquid Cocaine, I could live dangerously and find out exactly what was happening. And I was all geared up to do it, but then the doorbell rang and there was pizza. Pokey Stix from Gumby's, to be exact.

Gainesville was a true stoner's paradise, I realized, as I dug into the pizza-shaped lump of cheesy, seasoned dough. I would have to really focus here to get anything done. But tonight, I was on "vacation" and it was a weekend, so I continued to indulge myself. The disk of Pokey Stix was cut into long, thin strips, and the box they came in was filled with all sorts of dipping sauces—ranch, blue cheese, garlic butter, marinara . . . it was a box of pure happiness.

Luckily, they'd ordered three of them.

But by the time Lucas came back inside, they were all but gone.

"Here," I said, giving Lucas his long-overdue cup of water. "Drink this now. And take the last Pokey Stix—you need the dough in your stomach."

"Okay," Lucas said sulkily, and like a petulant little child, he scarfed it down. He paused a moment while he chewed, then exclaimed, "Shit! *That* hit the spot!"

"I know, right?" I said, glad to see him smile, but still determined to find out what the hell was going on. "Hey, let's go back outside and get some air."

"All right."

We headed out the door and found a couple of lawn chairs on the small concrete-slab back porch.

"So . . ." I said. "Fun night?"

"Totally fun night." Lucas burped. "I can't wait to move here."

"Are you spinning right now, too?" I asked. "I'm kind of messed up."

"I second that. I actually puked a little just before I came back in the house."

"You okay?"

"Yeah, I'll be okay."

"You could stay with Jonathan tonight. . . ." I ventured.

"Why would I do that?" he asked, a little edge to his voice. "We're staying right on campus."

"Oh . . . no reason."

"Madge." Lucas looked at me dead-on. Well, his head was bobbing around a little, but I gave him an A for effort. "Are you trying to set me and Jonathan up?"

"No . . ." Shit.

"Madge, I *know* you. I *know* you hate Kenny . . . and wasn't it your idea that I pack this shirt?"

"Well . . . kinda—"

"*Jesus!*" Lucas shouted all of a sudden. "*Dammit*, Madge, why can't you just *butt out*?!" He stood up suddenly from his lawn chair and stumbled down to me, putting his hands on either side of my lawn chair and leaning over me. "Did you know that Jonathan has a *boyfriend*? Huh? Did you bother *asking* him that before you brought me up here?"

"No, I—"

"I mean, what's your *deal*?" he asked, cutting me off. "Is it that you're pissed that you don't have a *prom date anymore*? Is *that* why you want to throw prom in my *fucking condo*?! Because I've got news for you, Madge: I *want* to go to prom—*real* prom—

whether you're prom queen or not! And what the fuck about Vanessa and her clothes? How does *that* fit into your anti-prom extravaganza?"

"Well . . . I didn't wanna say anything, but I kinda thought if we got someone to document the party, we could . . . I dunno . . ."

"Spit it out!"

"Maybe your dad would be interested in it," I said quickly, bracing for the shit-storm.

"Oh, *that's* perfect, Madge. 'Cause you *know* how close I am with my dear old dad!"

"You wanna answer *me* a couple questions?" I blurted out, jumping up from my chair and knocking him off balance. Enough of this—I know I was being kind of a jerk, but it was time for *me* to go on the offensive and get some answers. "Who was that on the phone earlier?"

"Just . . . just Kenny calling to say hi," he answered unsurely, looking a little surprised to be on the other end of the yelling.

"Yeah? Well, you know what, Lucas? I know you're full of crap."

"What . . . what do you *mean*?"

"You and Kenny have been too buddy-buddy for you to answer the phone like that. I *know* it was someone else. Who was it?" I tried to focus on the backlit figure of Lucas to combat the swirling of the surrounding landscape.

"Why should I have to tell *you*?" he asked, backing up shakily.

"Why *wouldn't* you tell me?! I thought I was your *best fucking friend*!" I tried to ignore all the spinning, but it wasn't really stopping. "Why is Zach calling you all the time, Lucas? I thought you said he was ignoring you."

"How the hell do you know it was Zach?"

"It's not like I've been bugging your house or something—all I did was check your incoming calls list on your cell. I'm an investigative *genius*."

"You had no right to *do* that!"

"Yeah, well, *you* have no right to be lying to me like you've been doing! And *while* we're on the subject, all I've been trying to do with this Kenny shit is save you from getting hurt! I don't understand how you can't see as clearly as I do that he's just using you! *Who* paid for the tuxes?"

"Me."

"*Who* suggested the trip to Millenia?"

"Kenny."

"Who suggested the *second* trip to Mil—?"

"Okay, I *get* it!" he screamed, cutting me off. "But *you* don't get it. You're not the one who hangs out with him. You just need to stop being so self-righteous, okay? You're starting to sound like your *mother*."

Suddenly it felt like the air—no, make that my *life force*—had been sucked out of my body. My *mother*?! I could *kill* him! "That . . . that was a low blow, Lucas," I said slowly when I could finally speak. "I'll see you at the hotel," I growled angrily, and walked back inside.

I hurried through the house before Lucas could have a chance to stop me—if he even *wanted* to stop me, the selfish little lying *prick*! Seriously—what the fucking hell?! Luckily, I didn't see Jonathan or Laura as I raced out the front door and into the dark side streets of the Student Ghetto. I'd let *Lucas* explain why I'd left. Let that be his prize. Despite the pleasant weather outside, I felt my body overheating, pumping out sweat—I guess I was going into shock over what'd just happened.

Fuck this.

It'd all been such a *waste*. I hadn't even found out why Zach was calling Lucas!

Now I realized that it was four in the morning. And there was something that I'd been meaning to do that I hadn't done yet . . . but what was it . . . ?

Ohhh, yeah . . .

In my short amount of wandering (along the driveway and down the street, really), I'd come face-to-face with the glorious red, white, and green neon lights of Krispy Kreme. The tears that I hadn't even noticed were flowing dried up in glaze-anticipatory elation.

Ten minutes later—after a bum told me that I looked "like shit run over twice" and I let some inebriated gay boys give my cleavage a motorboat with their shaking faces—I was back to stumbling around aimlessly, but this time with a dozen of the finest, flakiest, glaziest doughnuts on earth.

I decided to give my wandering something of an aim, and set myself on course for the hotel on campus. And when I say "on course," I pretty much mean just walking across University Avenue onto the campus and then following bright lights like a bug. Like a fruit fly. Or a fruit *beetle*, as Pearl had called me.

Not that it really bothered me, I thought as I wound my way among the beautiful redbrick buildings and plazas of the UF campus. I guess I *never* let much get to me. And it truly wasn't in a fake, oh-look-at-me-I'm-so-fucking-confident way. Yeah—I didn't *used* to be this confident. It took time to get here—and to get over the old embarrassments and disappointments of childhood—but I *was* here. And I had pretty much all I wanted—friends, a fun reputation, a fantastic social life. Where my own parents lacked, dear ol' Mitsy picked up the slack. But even though Lucas was far from my *only* friend, we'd totally clicked this year, and I considered him my *best* friend . . . and having your best friend lie to you, and not give a shit about what you had to say, hurts—no matter how many other friends you have.

Wow, these were deep thoughts for someone to have after having ingested three Bloody Marys, a couple swigs of Gatorade and vodka, a few beers, a Liquid Cocaine, and a bunch of weed. But I guess my extra weight, the six or seven Pokey Stix, and my . . . six—yeah, six—doughnuts had worked well for me in counteracting all the drunkifying substances *just enough* to keep me moving and thinking.

I saw a lot of stuff going on for four in the morning. I saw people out for a smoke, talking on cell phones. I saw a couple having "a moment" outside a dorm building. I saw a kid throwing up in a garbage can. I even saw a jogger. And there were kids walking around with bookbags slung over their shoulders—I guess Pearl *had* said it was exams week.

Oh, that Lady Pearl—so concerned for everyone's welfare, telling the students to return back to school safe and sound. Maybe I could get her and my mom to trade places. That'd be pretty sweet. I popped another doughnut in my mouth and let the crispy glaze dissolve on my tongue, and I laughed, thinking about Lady Pearl in my mom's rooster apron (I can imagine only too well what Mom-Pearl would say when she put it on), standing a foot and a half taller than my dad, cooking up some *tostones* or home fries, or walking through the front door with a big bag of Krystal burgers and a smile spread across her heavily made-up face. If Pearl were my mom, I could laugh at home a little more often, be myself more of the time. If Pearl were my mom, she wouldn't insist on making my prom dress, and even if she *did*, it'd be super-fab. If Pearl were my mom, she and Mitsy would get along so well. Lucas and I could set up play-and-drink dates for them at one of our houses, and then Lucas and I could have the other house to ourselves to hang out in, staging dramatic reinterpretations of key moments in *America's Next Top Model*, or cooking up our favorite snacks. Assuming the fact that Lucas and I were still friends.

But I guess in a world where my mom is a drag queen with a linebacker's build, anything is possible.

Yeah. Okay.

Now I had no idea where I was. Who knew a school could be so fucking massive?

Next thing I knew, I was sitting down on some lovely patch of grass, enjoying myself a doughnut and fighting off sleep. And this is right around when I blacked out, weird flashes of light pulsing behind my eyelids.

12

Everything Looks Better
(or at Least More Interesting)
in the Morning

•••

The first thing I tasted when I came to was glaze on my lips.

Well, it wasn't blood, so at least I wasn't bludgeoned or anything.

The second thing I tasted was grass, and not the fun kind.

Funny that I tasted Krispy Kreme residue before I noticed that I was lying on the fifty-yard line in the middle of an 88,000-capacity football stadium. (Hey, it was in a brochure, and okay, yeah—I read the fucking brochures! Don't make fun.)

With crazy people running up and down the bleachers.

Up and across and down, then across and up and across . . .

Couldn't these people use a treadmill?! Insanity.

Okay, so the mildly obese and stinking-of-alcohol eighteen-year-old shrouded in a pink-feather shawl and lying in the grass next to an empty Krispy Kreme box *probably* shouldn't be judging these dedicated, sweaty, and (mmm!) drool-worthy athletes so much.

A quick body check revealed that I was okay. No one had taken my shoes. I still had my little purse—phone, wallet, money, ID, keys, and all. But it looked like the heel on the right shoe had broken.

It was just after sunrise, so I guess I must've wandered in a few hours ago. I probably found an entrance to the stadium, ambled in, walked down the stairs—how I'd managed *that* without break-ing my neck I have no idea—and plopped down on the fifty-yard line (actually, it was more like the forty-second—guess I didn't quite make it after all those stairs) and had myself some delicious sugary doughnuts before passing out cold.

Just like the end of any of my other Saturday nights.

Um, *no*!!!!

What the hell had I *done* to myself last night? Note to self: Don't ever, *ever* wander off alone while that fucked up *ever* again, considering the last thing I remember of my evening was Lady Pearl, as my mother, asking me if I liked my eggs scrambled or full of sperm. (Ha-ha, Drag Mother!—wouldn't that make a fantastic *Leave It to Beaver*–style family comedy show?)

Who knows *what* could've happened to me, had the partying deities not granted me this reprieve.

Okay. Glad to be alive and still flush with cash—done with that.

Time to check phone messages . . .

And surprisingly, I had multiple missed calls from my no-good liar of a best friend.

I could've just not called him back, since I didn't necessarily want to speak to him at the moment, but I *was* missing my favorite peach-flavored lip gloss, and though I doubted that a thief had scoured through my purse and decided to steal only that item, I thought I'd clarify that Lucas had borrowed it the night before and simply forgotten to give it back.

Rather than listen to the voice mails, I called him directly, and he answered on the first ring.

"*Please* tell me this isn't Margarita Diaz's murderer!" he said without even saying hello first.

"No, it's *your* murderer," I said. "What the fuck was *wrong* with you last night?"

"Look, Madge, I wanna talk. I'm an asshole. Where are you?"

"Did you borrow my lip gloss last night?"

"Yeah, it's . . . it's in my pocket. Where *are* you?"

"I'm . . . uh . . . I'm in the stadium."

"*In* the st—?!"

"Yeah, let's skip this whole part. Yeah. I'm in the stadium. I just woke up." I glanced at the Krispy Kreme box next to me, practically licked clean of dried glaze. "And I can't believe I'm saying this, but I need breakfast. I'm massively hungover."

"Okay, we'll go to a McDonald's drive-through. My treat. Why don't you walk down to the hotel, and—"

"I need food way too badly. Let's just meet at the car. But

I'm gonna need directions to find it," I told him honestly.

So after some online mapping of the UF campus, Lucas gave me directions to follow down to where we'd parked the car the night before. I have to say, I'd been looking rather praise-worthy and amazing the night before, but that kind of outfit—no matter how divine—didn't fare as well in direct sunlight, especially after a night of heavy partying, eating, crying, and . . . sleeping on dewy grass. I couldn't help but feel just a *bit* self-conscious and ridiculous as I groggily trudged along—past people doing last-minute cramming, through crowds of kids filing into auditoriums for final exams (on a *Saturday*, how brutal!)—at one point nearly falling from surprise as a jogging club thundered past me.

Finally, I made it to Mitsy's BMW, where Lucas was eagerly waiting. As soon as we saw each other, he ran up to me, a look of pure relief on his sweet face. As he embraced me happily, saying, "I was so scared, I'm so glad you're okay, I'm so sorry," I couldn't help but think what a funny-looking sort of leap-into-each-other's-arms reunion this was.

"Hey, yeah, I'm fine," I said, glad that I could sense his complete and utter genuineness. "I'm sorry about our fight . . . and for trying to set you up. And I'm sorry I didn't save you any Krispy Kremes."

He pulled back for a second and looked at me curiously. "What?" he finally asked, laughing.

"Oh," I said. "Long story. Okay, at least I'm not drunk anymore, so I can totally drive. Let's get to this drive-through, like *stat,* and then we're gonna have a nice, long talk." There was no point in talking to Lucas about anything serious before I'd eaten breakfast. Breakfast was my morning coffee—I wasn't any good without it. We're talking major evil, crabbypants situation.

Sitting in the grassy amphitheater outside the Student Union with the warm sun on our backs—and with some breakfast burritos and sausage-egg McMuffins in our systems—Lucas and I finally began "our talk."

We'd already covered what the rest of Lucas's night had been like—throwing up more and being practically carried home by the very sweet Jonathan and Laura. Lucas had slept in Jonathan's bed, with Jonathan on the floor and Laura on the couch, till he woke up at six A.M., hangover headache splitting his skull in two, and pure, sickening embarrassment tearing at his insides. Jonathan had heard him get up to leave and insisted that there was nothing to be embarrassed about, and even forced Lucas to exchange numbers. "And tell Madge to drink plenty of liquids so she doesn't dehydrate!" he'd called out.

Yeah.

That so-called "punishment" I'd given Lucas—the one where *he* would have to explain my flight from the party to Laura and Jonathan? Well, Lucas had told them that I'd had to run 'cause of impending explosive diarrhea. Touché, Lucas. Touché, indeed.

"So can we talk about Zach?" I asked now.

"Oh, God . . . Zach." He sighed. "I'm such a prick. Okay. We *did* break up. But then he started calling me to apologize. All the time. And eventually, he was even taking it all back, and saying he was gonna change and come out to his parents and take me to my prom. And it was really sweet . . . but by then, I was all set to do the single thing, plus I was already going to prom with Kenny."

"So that day he was all mean to you on the phone . . . ?"

"Yeah . . ." he said bashfully. "I fibbed a little on that one."

"So Zach *really* wants you back?" I asked hopefully.

"So he says . . ."

"Then why continue with the whole man-ho thing? You gotta admit, most people've got *nothin'* on Zach. I love Zach."

"Yeah . . . I think I do, too," Lucas admitted. "But I just can't get hurt again. He says he's gonna change, but he's said that before. I don't want to risk it." He sighed. "Plus, I think Kenny's really excited about going to prom . . ."

". . . since he missed it last year for reasons that will forever remain a secret."

"Yeah," Lucas said. "Y'know, even Jonathan and Laura didn't know for sure. . . ."

"And that doesn't *scare* you?"

"Do *you* believe every rumor you hear at Winter Park? Please! It was probably nothing."

"I guess so." I took a long swig of Coke, then burped up all sorts of memories from the night before. I shuddered. "So Kenny's *really* excited to go? Somehow I don't see that coming from him."

"Yeah, well . . . okay, this is embarrassing," Lucas said, avoiding eye contact.

"What? C'mon, tell me."

"Nothing! . . . Well . . . just that the whole prom-date thing was *my* idea that day at the mall," he said. "I just *really* wanted to go with a boy. And Kenny *is* cute. But when I said we should go, he got all weird with me, and it took, like, *twenty minutes* to convince him it was only a friends thing. Which I'm *sure* made me look supersexy."

"Babydoll, you're supersexy *all* the time."

Lucas cracked a little smile at this. (Success!) "Thanks, Madge. I just feel like a total loser. And for the record? All that stuff about Kenny being excited?" He sighed heavily. "Total lie. Or, at the very least, conjecture."

"What about Zach? You said he's willing to go with you now," I said hopefully.

"I know. I'm just not in the mood for any more potential drama right now. I still don't fully believe him."

"That's kinda sad."

"It is." Lucas propped himself up on his elbows and looked at me, squinting at the bright sunlight. "But Kenny did say yes, so we'll see what happens afterward. I might get back with Zach, but I'm not gonna risk anything right now."

"What about my anti-prom?" I asked. "And by the way, forget I even said *anything* about your dad. That was way outta line. Blame it on the Liquid Cocaine," I said jokingly.

"*Or* I could blame it on your assiness."

"Yeah. You're right."

"Well, we'll have to talk about the whole anti-prom thing, too. I wanna do both, Madge. I'm sorry."

"I'll figure something out," I said, pausing for a moment.

"You know," Lucas said, smiling big, "you *could* just ask that Randy guy to go with you. I wouldn't be surprised if he said yes."

I felt a few butterflies take flight—or try to, anyway—in my messed-up stomach. "Yeah," I said a little dreamily, "maybe."

"You *love* him!" he teased.

"Shush." I was smiling big now, too—I couldn't help it. "Look. I'm sorry I was such a psycho last night. I passed out on a football field after eating a dozen doughnuts, so I obviously wasn't at my best."

Lucas laughed. "It's okay, Madge—I shouldn't have lied to you. I just didn't want you telling me to get back with Zach this whole time. And you *know* you would've."

"Yeah?" I asked. "Yeah, I guess I would've."

"Are you kidding? Madge, I love you, but you're one of the most opinionated people I know—and that can be good sometimes, but other times it's a little . . . tiring. I just knew I wanted to do my whole single thing for a while, but if I told you about Zach calling me, you would've flipped your shit."

"All right, all right," I said, putting my hands up. "I *swear* I'll be better in the future. Okay?"

"Loves it."

"And while I'm at it," I said reluctantly, though I knew I had to make things right, "I'm sorry I'm always so hard on Kenny. I guess I'm just . . . opinionated, like you said. And the whole Jonathan thing? Totally harmless intentions, for real. I wanted to introduce you to another Zach-like amazing guy. I only wanted you to see what you were worth."

"It's okay. I know you were only looking out for me. But at least now you know how you get."

I smiled. "Yeah. Thanks. And I'll try to be better from now on."

"Same here."

We hugged on it and finished our breakfasts.

A short time later, as we headed back up to our hotel room for a much-needed nap, Lucas was telling me about how Travis and his roommates were leaving their house in the Student Ghetto at the end of the summer.

"They said they can't afford to stay there, so they're moving into a place with more bedrooms and more roommates."

"Sounds like hell." I remember being told last night what the ridiculously cheap rent was. "How can they not afford it anymore?" I asked.

"I dunno, actually . . ."

"Too much money on drugs and bad art." I laughed. "Though that Lite Brite lamp was pretty cool."

"And there was the room with all the baseboards and moldings painted in blacklight-sensitive paint," he added, slipping our keycard into the hotel-room door.

"Yeah, that was an entirely new brand of kitsch."

"Maybe we should just move in there," Lucas said as he stripped off his shoes and socks, then collapsed onto his bed.

"Maybe we should look at the apartments we found online first—after a nap." It was literally impossible to keep my eyelids from closing. I wish I could fall asleep this easily all the time. . . .

After our beauty rest, we did the good-kids thing, and pushed through our headaches and sleepiness, and went on tours of three apartment complexes around town. Maybe we'd picked the wrong places to tour, but what we found was a little discouraging.

First off, all the apartment buildings were totally cookie-cutter. Well, maybe if *one* of these buildings was by itself in the Student Ghetto, it might look unique—but we're talking apartment *complexes* where there were, like, twenty or thirty buildings that looked exactly the same. And maybe one of the complexes—with their clubhouses, pools, hot tubs, workout rooms, cable-and-Internet-ready-ness, and ample parking—would've caught our eye, had it not been for how shoddy their construction looked. Some of the places looked like they'd be wiped the fuck *out* if a category-four hurricane blew across the state. This was confirmed when I saw that one of the complexes had a building under construction, and it seriously looked like the thing was being built out of nails and graham crackers.

Finally, as we parked the car and headed back into the hotel for yet another nap (it'd been a long, long night and day), we started talking seriously about renting out the three-bedroom house. It *was* in our price range, after all. As we rode the elevator up, we entertained ourselves with ideas of how to use the spare, blacklit room.

"We could buy one of those doggie fences," Lucas began, "and fill the room with those balls that you see in McDonald's PlayPlaces!"

"Only *you* would want a room full of balls."

"Or what if we put some really powerful fans in there and constantly had Monopoly money flying around inside?"

"Like one of those money rooms they have on game shows?" I thought about it for a second. "That I could get behind."

"Or we could make it our workout-and-get-sexy room," Lucas added.

"Don't push it, boy," I said. "'Cause I was gonna suggest just covering the floor with cushy beanbag chairs and cheap faux-fur rugs and tacky furniture from Ikea. And pillows! *Lots* of pillows!"

So it was settled. Lucas and I got Travis's number from Jonathan, and in a few minutes, we had the landlord's information and everything. Since it was so early in the game, Travis was almost positive we'd have no trouble taking over the lease.

That night, Lucas and I decided to have a date night of sorts. We were a little done in from the night before, so drinking and partying wasn't really in order. We had an awesome dinner at this Pan-Asian restaurant that overlooked an alligator-filled lake, we saw an art-house movie at this theater downtown called the Hippodrome, and we explored the campus, which was way more fun and beautiful now that I was sober and could fully take it all in.

Over ice cream near campus, Lucas and I discussed our strategy for anti-prom night. Since I was dead-set on having it, and *he* was dead-set on experiencing *real* prom, we decided that we'd find out when prom queen was going to be announced at the dance. If it was going to be announced at, say, ten o'clock, we'd have our anti-prom party stop admitting guests promptly at ten. That way, if people wanted to experience real prom, they could, but they'd have to be at anti-prom by ten, to ensure a nice, empty room for when Bridget—or I, for that matter (though that wasn't so much the point anymore)—was announced as prom queen.

We also decided *not* to tell people about this new plan until the very last minute. No need to give Bridget an opportunity to plan a counterattack. I wanted to catch her off guard. Plus, the longer I campaigned as if for prom queen, the more and more people I'd have on my side. My campaign friend list online had gotten pretty large, and was growing by the day—though Bridget's was around twice my size. But, come on! The girl was a freaking celebrity! I think I was doing a-okay.

Feeling good on so many levels, Lucas and I turned in early, and got ten hours of blissful sleep.

13

A Soft Spot
for Bearded Ladies

· ·

"*Coño*, Mami, watch where you stick those pins!" I cried, swatting my mom's hand away.

"Margarita, if you don't stand still, we're never going to get this done," my mom scolded.

"You need to let it out about an inch," my grandmother instructed my mom in Spanish. She picked up a *tostone* from a plate on the kitchen counter and took a bite.

"*Abuela, yo quieeero,*" I whined in my best bratty-girl voice, pointing at the plate.

"You get nothing until we're done with these adjustments, *amor*," she answered me, smiling.

Such tricky bribery from these mean old birds. They'd been

waiting for me when I'd walked in the door Sunday morning after driving back from Gainesville.

The food was a trap.

My mom *never* made good food like this except for my dad, and for when family visited. In addition to the *tostones*, she'd whipped up a batch of lobster *empanadas* and a huge pot of *arroz con pollo*. But I had to suffer through this fitting—and endless prom talk—to get my first bite. I was standing on a foot-stool, being held hostage by about two dozen pins all over my body. There was nothing to do but comply. Apparently, taking my measurements in the previous weeks wasn't enough—they wanted to put the newly made dress on my body afterward, to make even *further* adjustments. I understood the need for per-fection, but this was ridic! Just let it go, ladies!

"So, Margarita," my *abuela* asked, "you going with anyone to the prom?"

As excited as I was for the anti-prom penthouse party (Mitsy had agreed, by the way!), I couldn't bring myself to break it to my grandma, or even to my mom (yes, I had a heart), that I wasn't going to prom this year. So I said, "Just a couple of friends."

"And she doesn't seem at *all* excited about it," my mother said, taking a lap around my body and checking stuff out. "I don't even know why we're doing this."

"Hey, I didn't ask for this, Mami," I said. "All I want is an *empanada* and to stop feeling like a pin cushion." She and my grandma worked in silence a little longer, pinching here, pulling there, pinning *all over*. "Hey," I finally asked. "Where's Papa?"

"Where is he always, Margarita?" my grandma asked me.

"Work?"

She nodded.

I poked my mom. "But it's Sunday."

"He said it was just for a few hours," she said, defending him. "He's been very busy lately, *mija*."

I'll say. I felt like I never *saw* the guy. And I gotta say, with my *abuela* visiting and my mom being decent to me—going easy on the nitpicking and promising me fried foods, which, as I've said, very rarely happens—I couldn't help but miss him a little. Like this Sunday-afternoon gathering would've made a cute family portrait, if only he didn't work himself to death. . . .

"Okay," my mother said, leading me down off the stool. "Let's take a look." We all walked to the full-length mirror in the master bedroom, my feet shuffling tiny bits at a time, so as not to get pricked.

I stood before the mirror, taking it all in. *"Bella,"* my grandma whispered happily into my ear. *"Como una princesa."*

And she was right. I did look like a princess. The floor-length gown was made of lavender satin, and it had a semi-deep V-cut in the front, to show off my chest (but in a more understated way than I was used to doing), thick shoulder straps to hold it all up, and the entire dress was free of bows and ruffles, as requested.

"You look beautiful," my mom said. I could've sworn there was a tear in her eye. It was nice to hear her say that—and to see her so emotional—considering that it felt like she was constantly judging me, trying to change me. But now I could feel genuine love coming from her, and I realized suddenly that all that dietary stuff she tried to force on me really did come from a place of genuine concern. My dad and I weren't exactly the healthiest people around (See Figure 1-A: "The Way I Woke Up Yesterday Morning"), and I guess she just figured it was too late to change my dad's ways but that she could still take care of me. Like she still takes care of Vanessa, as I'd found out last weekend.

I vowed that from this day forward, I would eat my kale without giving any grief.

And that I *wouldn't* tell my mom about anti-prom. I'd give her her pre-prom photo shoot, then go to Mitsy's condo, and she'd be none the wiser. No need to hurt her feelings.

"Thanks, Mom," I said. "I *feel* beautiful." I gave her a peck on the cheek and tried to contain my emotions. I didn't want this turning into some over-tender scene straight out of a bad *telenovela*.

"You want an *empanada*?" she asked me, dabbing at her eye with the back of her hand.

"Hell yes," I said, smiling.

I still hadn't broken the anti-prom news to my sister yet, so after an hour or so of eating and hanging out with my mom and grandma, I snuck off into my room to call her.

"Listen," I said, after we'd been speaking for a few minutes.

"I have some sorta bad, but could be sorta good news about the prom-queen thing. . . ."

"Yeah?"

"Yeah. There's . . . been a slight change of plans."

"Tell me," she said. "Just get to the point."

"I'm not running for prom queen anymore," I said. "Well, I *am*, but I'm *not*. It's complicated."

My sister took a deep breath on the other end of the line. "You're gonna have to *try* and explain, then."

"*Claro.*" And so I did. I told her about my conversation with Laura, about my Gatorade-tini realizations in Jonathan's Nissan, about everything.

"But I still want you to design my anti-prom dress," I said. "We'll try and get some kind of exposure for it or something. I dunno how, but . . . we'll see."

There was silence on the other end. But I know my sister very well, and I could tell it was disappointed silence rather than I'm-going-to-kill-you silence.

"Say something?" I said pleadingly.

"I'll do the dress. As long as you admit that I was right."

"Right about what?"

"When you were over here last weekend and I said you weren't over Bridget stuff."

"V, *c'mon*—"

"I wanna hear you say it, *hermana*," she teased.

"Fine! I'm *obviously* not okay with everything. I still have this

ridiculous ten-year-old rivalry with her that can only be satisfied when I know she's been deflated! She makes me *loca*! You
happy?"

"Very. One more thing."

"I can't wait."

"You sure you wanna skip your prom?" she asked me.

"Yes! Why is *everyone* asking me that? Look, you think you can
make me an anti-prom dress that'll bring 'em to their knees?"

"You know I can make you anything, Rita," she said. "Just do
not tell Mom. I know she can be a pain sometimes, but you don't
want to destroy her."

"I already thought about that, so don't wor— Oh, wait," I
said, "Lucas is calling me on my other line."

"Just call me later, and we'll talk concept."

"Got it. Thanks, V." I clicked over to Lucas. "*Why* are you so
obsessed with me, man?" I joked.

"Madge, I think you should go to Bridget's campaign page
now."

"Why?"

"Just look at her newest friend comment."

I was right by my laptop, so I was there in seconds. I'd been
expecting that someone had posted some sickeningly perfect
photo of Bridget on the page, but I was wrong. It *wasn't* some
gorgeous, airbrushed-and-Photoshopped-to-perfection Glamour
Shot of Bridget. It wasn't even her with a clipboard and a plaque
at Lake Cleanup Day. And, by God, it wasn't even a sparkling ver-

tical shot of her in her Homecoming Queen crown from earlier this year.

Nope.

Someone had posted a picture of *me* on Bridget's page—a picture of me . . . passed out on the UF football field, with an empty box of Krispy Kremes on my stomach, and a caption under it reading, IS THIS WHO YOU WANT TO REMEMBER AS YOUR PROM QUEEN?

"Oh. My. *GOD!*" I shrieked. "Who the fuck *took* that picture?!"

"I don't know, the profile is private," Lucas said. "I already tried."

"Somebody's been fucking *following* me, Lucas!" Now I remembered those weird flashes from just before I'd passed out that night. "Oh, come *on!*"

"You think Bridget sent a *spy?*" Lucas asked.

"Well, what else, boy genius?"

"How did she even know we'd be up there?"

"I dunno . . ." I thought about it for a second, moving around Bridget's page to see if there were any *more* photos of me posted. "I—I must've mentioned it to her at Randy's party or something. Or she could've overheard us talking. . . . She could've paid someone to follow us. It could be fucking *anybody*. . . ."

"It's kind of cool."

"*Cool?* It's not *cool*, Lucas! There're pictures of my fat ass shrouded in *pink feathers* passed out drunk in the biggest football stadium in Florida!"

"I guess. But any publicity is good publicity."

"Lucas, I'm okay with my body and all, but I'm not stupid. This mound of feathers and glaze does *not* look like someone who people are gonna want to be their prom queen."

"But it *does* look like someone that people are gonna want to celebrate anti-prom with. . . ."

That stopped me for a second. "Okay, maybe you're right. But that doesn't make it any less creepy."

"What, you think she's sending people to knife you in your sleep?" Lucas asked, chuckling. "No—they're just douche bags with cameras. It's probably some other kid in our class—maybe Lindsay. We all know the girl needs the money."

"Yeah . . ."

"Look, I'm gonna post something on your page in response to this—it'll all be in good taste. You'll just keep doin' what you were doin' last week, and don't worry about this stuff."

"Whatever. I'm exhausted just thinking about it."

And I was right to have been. The next couple weeks were horrendous. When I wasn't working my ass off writing papers or studying for AP exams and finals, I was at as many major parties or social/academic events as was physically possible. Pulling all-nighters was becoming almost routine for me, and I was fairly certain that my blood was about 50 percent caffeine. . . .

Bridget, by the end of that first Sunday night, had deleted the football-field photo from her page and posted a notice for everyone, saying, "Oh my God! I am so sorry about that mean picture, guys. I have NO IDEA who posted it, but be warned: If anyone does ANYTHING so mean-spirited and unsavory in the future, I'm deleting your comment, like, PRONTO!" I guess she *thought* this exonerated her, but it didn't at all—at least as far as my own deductive reasoning went. I realized that all Bridget had to do to keep these "unsavory" pictures off her page was change her account settings so she had to preapprove everything that was posted in her comments section.

But did she?

No.

She just posted that very stern "warning."

And as the weeks went by, it became obvious to me that Bridget was *letting* these things be posted on her page. A nice little comment, followed by a picture. Some highlights for me were:

- **"I don't want a SCARY prom queen."** Below was a picture of me covered in long brown fur and bearing a mouthful of fake fangs. Oh, yeah, and I'm in a basketball jersey. So what?! It was from the Senior Class Homecoming Float, and the theme was eighties movies—and, hello! *Teen Wolf*! So the hell what?!

- **"This girl has NO TASTE."** A picture of me taken that Monday morning, running out of my car, and wearing my new THAT'S JUST HOW I ROLL T-shirt (from Madison Whiteman's house party) with a pair of eggs-and-bacon flannel pajama bottoms and Homer Simpson slippers. Okay, "no taste," I'll give them that one—but I'd overslept, and I was coming into school early for a makeup exam! I wonder what invisible creep took that picture. Probably the same one who snapped me in Gainesville.

● **"Should this FAT HOOCHIE be my prom queen?"** First of all, I'm not nearly as offended by the term "hoochie" as one would assume. I actually like the sound of it—it's fun to say, and I say it's time that the ladies reclaim the word as our own! Anyway, this picture was of me laughing as I shoved two guys' faces into my cleavage. Again . . . and I care about this because . . . ? It was a party, I was drunk, they're just breasts, and *the guys were gay!* It's not like I was straddling someone's face in the middle of a church.

Bridget would leave these pictures up for a few hours—so that a bunch of people could see them, and subsequently gossip about them—then delete them, so it seemed like she cared about running a clean campaign.

Please! How transparent can you *be*?!

But at least—as Lucas had pointed out—she was inadvertently helping me reach my ultimate goal, which made me feel pretty good.

And the response that Lucas cooked up for the posting of all the "mean" pictures of me? It was the sweetest thing on earth, I could have just *bitten* him! He'd posted a little Flickr slide show on my campaign page—set to Madonna's "Die Another Day"—of a bunch of photos of me, I guess submitted by all the friends on the page. The lyrics about breaking the cycle and shaking up the system worked rather well, I thought. Many kudos to my little Madge-ophile.

There was one of me and Environmental Club Annabelle in our pajamas, green facial masks on, giving each other French manicures. It was from my girls'-night fifteenth-birthday party sleepover. My mom had caved and made me and my friends ungodly amounts of amazing food and then stayed in her side of the house for the whole night. I remember it being one of the best nights of my life. Just me, ten of my closest friends, a stack of John Cusack movies (from the eighties only!), and pounds and pounds of *empanadas, tostones,* green mint chocolate chip ice cream, and Red Bull. We'd been off the wall that night—I even remember Annabelle getting so hyper that she organized a diving contest in our pool at two in the morning. My mom and dad—I guess just glad that I didn't want a multi-thousand-dollar *quinceañera*— were supercool and just chilled in their room all through it.

Dozens more pictures made the cut—pictures of me with friends at parties, at restaurants, at Homecoming dances. There was a picture of me making mango margaritas at a Fourth of July party last summer, a bright hibiscus in my hair. There was one of me and my friend George Gordon, chomping away at opposite ends of a six-foot sub (though we came close, we couldn't quite finish it). Then one of me at the Homecoming game this year, my face completely covered in orange-and-black face paint, scream- ing my head off for the team. (Actually, I didn't care much about football, but the pink Tab energy drink and the Pop Rocks may've had something to do with my hyperness!)

And then my favorite of all, which had no doubt been

submitted by my dear Lucasito himself. It was from one of my and Lucas's first "friendship dates" in the beginning of the school year. I had convinced him to go with me to see electro shock-rocker Peaches play at Firestone. He'd been a little reluctant at first, but when I showed up at his place to hang out before the show (since the show was downtown, all we had to do was walk ten minutes from his condo), I offered him a way to hide his fears: a disguise!

Yes, in homage to the cover of Peaches' second album cover, on which she's pictured with a big black beard on her face, Lucas and I did shots of Mitsy's gin (which tasted like pine needles, blech) and walked to the show wearing fake long black beards I'd bought from a costume shop. We looked *so* not sexy, but it was a true bonding experience. Actually, I kinda looked like my dad, but in drag.

The picture was classic: me and Lucas, front and center on the barricades, jumping up and down and screaming like maniacs, as Peaches—all curvy and skank-tastic in her silver coochie-cutters, thigh-high hot-pink boots, and a bikini top—poured a bottle of champagne on us from the stage.

It made me happy.

So despite my exhaustion, everything was actually going pretty well. Bridget's friends kept posting stupid pictures that hardly affected me at all, people kept posting *sweet* pictures on *my* page to be added to the slide show, I was getting around big-time, my crazy dress was coming along swimmingly (oh, you'll hear about that later!), and the debate was tomorrow. . . .

Which was where I was planning on announcing that people should stay tuned to my Web page for a big announcement in the coming days. . . .

Then, a few days later—just before prom—I was going to post details of the anti-prom penthouse event, which was being planned furiously by Mitsy. (What can I say? The lady liked to throw a party, and what else was she doing with all her free time and expendable income? We're talking gourmet catering, ice sculptures, mood lighting—the whole nine yards. And set four hundred feet over the city, it was going to be *quite* the swankety-swank affair.)

It was just around then—at the peak of all this awesomeness—that I got a call during lunch period.

My father had had a heart attack.

14

New Course of Action

• •

The heart attack hadn't killed him (thank God!). He had a major blockage in his arteries, though, and he was due in for an angioplasty early the next morning. But we had until the end of visiting hours that evening to be with him.

My papa looked weak, I realized as I entered the hospital room. I wasn't used to *seeing* him in the first place, but to see him here, in the light of day, looking so tired and helpless, was really difficult. He was a big guy, with a full belly and a big, thick beard. But somehow, lying motionless in that hospital bed with his hand in my mom's, he looked so small. I tried to keep it together. If my dad had to be the weak one in this situation, I'd be the strong one.

"Hey, Papi," I said when I walked through the door. "Hell of a week you must be having, huh?"

He opened his eyes slowly and chuckled. "The worst."

The limited interaction I had with my workaholic father was usually of the joking and sarcastic variety. So I didn't want to go against our normal father–daughter rule set. Didn't want him to see how worried I was.

"Margarita," he said. "Thanks for coming. I'm . . . I'm so sorry."

"What the hell for?" I asked. "This isn't your fault."

"It's *my* fault," my mom piped up, taking her hand away from my dad and crossing her arms. Or was she hugging herself? "I should never have started making two dinners for the family. *Ridículo.* I should have had us *all* eating the healthy dinners—"

"Gabriela, please," my dad interrupted her. "*I'm* the stubborn one—you couldn't force-feed me that whitefish to save your life."

"Well, maybe you'll change your mind after all this, Paulo," she said, lovingly and hatefully at the same time. I didn't know that was possible.

"Maybe," he said.

"And maybe you shouldn't work so damn hard," I said suddenly, surprising myself. I figured now was the time, if any, to press my luck. The guy doesn't like to be told what to do. "I don't want a hospital room to be the only place I see you before nine o'clock at night," I continued.

"Maybe," he repeated.

Hey, that was *something* for my father. I smiled and bent down to give him a kiss on the cheek.

"Thank you, *mi amor*." He looked at my blouse. It was this amazingly bright yellow number with diagonal strips of thin orange velour fabric cutting across it in all directions. "This is nice," he said, feeling the material between his fingers. "Vanessa make this one?"

"Yeah," I choked out, all of a sudden exponentially more emotional. "Where is she anyway?" I asked, taking a deep breath to stave off the threatening onslaught of tears.

"About twenty minutes away," my mom answered.

"You look beautiful in it," Papa said.

"Th-thanks," I managed. This was brutal.

My mom got up from her chair. "Now that you're here," she said to me, "I need to use the ladies' room and make some calls." She bent down and kissed my dad on the head, then told us she'd be right back.

"You know, *amor*," my dad said, motioning for me to take my mom's place, "I hate to say it, but I haven't seen much of you lately, either."

"Yeah, I know," I said, sitting down in the chair and folding my hands in my lap. "It's been a busy time."

"You look tired."

"And you're just the spitting image of health today," I said defensively.

He just chuckled. "I know, I know, I have no room to talk about being too busy or not treating my body right. . . . But I haven't seen you in a long time. Why don't you tell me what's been going on with you."

I didn't know even *where* to start, so I just sat there in silence a minute.

"Aha! Now I *know* something's going on." He appeared almost animated now. "Come on, *mija*. Tell me. I won't tell your mother. *Te promeso*."

And so I told him. For one thing, it felt good to tell him what I'd been *doing* the last few weeks. For another thing, it was a way for me to talk to him without wanting to break down in tears. I just wondered how he'd take all the news. The last thing I wanted was for him to try and convince me I wanted to go to real prom, like everyone else had initially done, even if only for a minute.

But what else could I expect him to say?

"I think this party sounds like an amazing idea," he said.

Whoa! Well, not *that*!

"Seriously?" I asked. "I thought you were gonna try to convince me I wanted to go to the real prom."

"Why would I do that? *You* know what you want to do." He winked. "But if you thought I was gonna try to convince you, maybe you *wanted* me to."

"Nice try, Papa."

He laughed a little. "*Oye*, Margarita, *en serio*, if you think people would want to go to this party, and *you* want to give them this party, I think that's a very nice thing."

Huh, I thought. "I gotta say," I told him, "I hadn't really thought about it like that before. . . ."

"You mean you just wanted to throw this party for spite?"

"Um . . . maybe?" I said, realizing that what I was saying was kind of true.

"Now, Margarita, you can't just think of yourself. You should realize that by throwing this party, and by putting yourself out there, you're giving people something to look up to. To look forward to." He shook his head slightly, smiling at me admiringly. "I wish I'd had your confidence when I was in high school. You have a real gift with people, *amor*—don't waste it by being petty. If you're throwing this party, throw it for the right reasons."

Suddenly, it was all too much. All the Bridget Benson drama seemed minuscule in comparison to the fact that my dad had had a fucking *heart attack*. I started sobbing then, realizing that my dad was going under the knife in a matter of hours to have his overclogged, overfed arteries cleared of all their gunk.

My father reached over and took my hand in his, trying his best to soothe me. "I'm sorry," he said. "You don't have to worry about me, okay? After this, I'm a new man. I swear. They say the whole thing's minimally invasive, and I'll be out of here before I know it."

But I couldn't stop the crying! I don't know why your brain does this, but when you're already all choked up about something and then the tears start, you just have these mind-flashes of everything that make you even *more* emotional. I had visions of my dad driving me to my first audition, the one that landed me my first real part. He took us to my favorite ice-cream parlor, at the Yacht & Beach Club Resort at EPCOT, for gigantic sundaes afterward, and told me how proud he was of me. And when I became this big sad sack after everything went wrong with Bridget, my one and only friend, he was the sweetest man alive. He'd take off from work and organize fun little day trips for me, him, and my mom—to Blue Spring to look at the manatees, to Kennedy Space Center, down to Tampa to the Florida Aquarium. . . . And when he saw I'd never recover, he was the first to suggest I drop the whole acting thing, saying it wasn't worth my happiness, which turned out to be completely true.

Finally, though, I was all cried out, the tears wrung out of me like water from a sopping-wet towel.

"So have your party," he said, patting my hand. "And do me a favor, okay?"

"Sure," I said, wiping my eyes.

"Go easy on your mom. She only wants the best for you. You do know that, right?"

"I do, I guess." I took a deep, shuddering breath. "No. I do know."

"Good. *Te quiero.*"

"I know. I love you, too."

I hardly slept at all that night. Vanessa and my grandmother arrived shortly after that talk with my dad, and we'd all hung around the hospital till the absolute end of visiting hours. Finally, my mom and I dragged our exhausted selves back home. It wasn't even that late, but the events of the day had taken a toll on us. Too tired to cook, we actually hit up a drive-through and feasted on a Boston Market family meal before passing out in bed.

Well, *trying* to pass out. It's not exactly easy to sleep when you know your dad's gonna be in surgery by the time you wake up.

I talked to Lucas on the phone for a long time—that helped calm me down. He was being a total sweetie. The whole time we were talking, he was making me one of our favorite snacks in his kitchen. It was a multilayered chip dip: one layer refried beans, one layer sour cream with taco seasoning, one layer salsa, then shredded cheese, chopped tomatoes, and cilantro on top.

"I'm gonna bring it in for lunch tomorrow," he told me. "*Think* of how nice it'll taste once it's had a night to cool! You think Mrs. Kellerman'll let you store it in the office fridge till lunch?"

"Um, I hate to sound like some sort of born-again, but this whole heart-attack thing has got me thinking . . . that maybe I should cut back on the nastiness."

"I *thought* you might have had one of those epiphanies," he said cheerfully. I could hear him chopping something on his cutting board. "So it's all low- and nonfat."

Trying not to break out sobbing again, I choked out, "I love you, little man."

"I love you, too."

He was very supportive, along with my father, about the debate the next morning before first period, and about the party.

"Yeah," Lucas said, "your dad has a nice way of thinking about it. I'm so excited now!"

I hung up with him around one in the morning, and tried my hardest to fall asleep. Hardly worked—I'd have to caffeine-up in the morning, big-time—but I guess I *did* nod off eventually, because at one point, I found myself on a sort of game show, with some strange cross between Tyra Banks and Alex Trebek as the host(ess). I had to choose between eating the last deep-fried turkey on earth, having necessary open-heart surgery in front of the entire school with Bridget wielding the scalpel, or taking an all-expenses paid trip to a Sandals resort in Jamaica. (Freud would have such interesting things to say.) Sadly, since the surgery was *necessary*, it was the natural choice (even though it'd be a shame to let the earth's last deep-fried turkey go to waste), but when I didn't answer quickly enough, "Tyrex Trebanks" started getting impatient and got the countdown clock ticking and beeping, and finally I woke up to the beeping of my 5:30 A.M. alarm, telling me to get up and ready for school.

After slowly showering and dressing, I zombie-walked into the kitchen, where my mother was waiting with breakfast for me: eggs over easy, toast, orange juice, and coffee.

"Wow," I said. "Quite the far cry from Grape Nuts and grapefruit."

"Enjoy it while my mood lasts, *mi amor*," she said tiredly. "You're going to school today?"

"I really have to be in first and second periods today," I lied. "Plus, Papa's surgery's not done for a while, right?"

"Actually," she said, smiling, "I just got a call. They fit him in earlier, and the angioplasty was a complete success. He's doing great. We can go in and see him in a few hours. I already wrote you a note to get out of school."

I breathed—*heaved!*—a sigh of relief and ran to my mom, kneeling down and knocking the wind out of her with my sudden hug. She tensed up for a second, like she didn't know what to do, then relaxed into my embrace, and hugged me back.

"I love you, Mami," I said. "I'm sorry I'm such a brat sometimes. I'm gonna try to be better from now on."

"You're not a brat, *mi amor*," she replied softly. "You're just my Margarita. And I love you, too."

"And thanks for the eggs," I told her, standing back up. "But I actually have to do something before first period, and I'm late, so I'll grab something on the way. But, hey—*you* enjoy that breakfast, okay?"

"Okay," she said, dabbing at her eyes with a napkin. "I'm actually going to try to sleep a couple hours."

"I love you," I said again, and headed to my room to grab my bag. Just as I hoisted it over my shoulder, I heard my cell phone ringing inside. I reached in and grabbed it, wondering who'd be calling me so early.

Lucas.

"Morning, sunshine," I answered. "Wanna meet me at Starbucks and get a Red Eye?"

"Madge, don't shoot the messenger, but you have to look at the comments on Bridget's page, like, *now*."

"Why?" I asked groggily. "Can't this wait till after I've had my caffeine? Hey, my dad's okay, I just found out!"

"That's great, sweetie!" he said happily. "*Oh* my God, that was just so *scary*, wasn't it?"

"Yeah, you're tellin' me. I'm getting out after second period to visit him."

"Well, the fact that he's okay might make this thing a little less awful, but still . . . I think you should see what's on her page. The same profile that posted the picture of you on the football field has struck again."

I flipped open my laptop and quickly made my way to Bridget's page, where I found it:

The famous football-field photo of me lying flat on my back, but with my fake-bearded, Peaches-concert face Photoshopped on top. I guess Bridget—or whoever her hired photographic thug might've been—had noticed the similarities between me and my dad in that photo, too, because I was Photoshopped further into a hospital room, with my passed-out body hooked up to all sorts of machines and IVs. A caption under it read: HEART DISEASE RUNS IN THE FAMILY, PROM QUEEN! YOU DON'T WANNA END UP LIKE YOUR DADDY.

I was actually too shocked to speak for a moment.

"Shit," Lucas said. "This is fucking *war*! Madge, hit REFRESH and look at this!"

I did, and then saw a new blog entry from Bridget. She must've just posted it:

Hi, everybody! Beautiful morning, right? Anyway, I wanted to post a response to that awful picture of my prom-queen opponent that was just put on my page—which will now be DELETED, btw! While I don't agree with the mean-spirited motives behind posting such a terrible picture, I do agree that Margarita Diaz is an unhealthy individual. She needs to realize that treating herself like crap can eventually land her in the hospital, just like what happened to her dad yesterday. And plus, I mean, if presidential candidates have to be given physicals, shouldn't prom queens, too? Ha-ha! Kidding! (Sorta.)

Toodles, kidz!

"Is this really happening?" I asked Lucas. I could actually *feel* my blood pressure rising, my heartbeat quickening, my sleep-deprived vision blurring around the edges. "Did she really just say all that?"

"She did," Lucas said solemnly. "Look, don't listen to a thing she says—"

"Lucas!" I cut him off. "Just hold on a second while I think."

I could not *believe* she'd gone this far. Like I'd said before, it was obvious she was completely responsible for what was posted on her page. There was no "surprise" person behind her page—it was all *totally* her, and all she was doing was manipulating people. And to suggest that I'm not *fit* to be prom queen . . . *literally*! And to exploit my poor, heart-attack-victim father! *Over* the line! *WAY over!!*

I wanted to fight fire with fire. Eye for an eye, tooth for a tooth—all that crap. If she was gonna have pictures of me taken on a football field, or outsource some Photoshop job to be done on me, I was gonna get something on *her*. I didn't know *what*, but I knew I had to try.

Prom was still a little while away. I could get her class schedule from the front office. Trail her. Eavesdrop. Ask around. It wasn't *that* hard to dig up dirt at our school. Up until now, I hadn't been playing that dirty. I hadn't gotten too personal.

Well, things were different now, and Bridget was gonna pay for what she'd done. Big-time.

"There's a new game plan," I said to Lucas.

"There is?"

"*Oh*, yeah."

I strutted into the studio room the debate team had secured for the morning's main event, caffeinated to the point of danger. At the sight of Bridget, I nearly went into an all-out anger-fit, but I had to keep myself under control to do what I'd come to do.

I have to say, though, the Debate Team had really gone all out with this thing. At the front of the room were two podiums, each with its own lil' microphone and glass of water, and one of the TV-production-class cameras was set up opposite them. It was a shame the show was gonna be so short.

Bridget, predictably, had gotten all cuted up for the occasion. She wore some pearly-white-and-fake-wood sandal-heels; a little skirt that was just on the acceptable side of short and slutty; a tight, collared, three-quarter-length-sleeved crisp aqua blouse to accentuate her Waspy blue eyes (and blood); and her hair was done up into an impossibly tight bun, in all its painstakingly streaked-to-perfection glory.

When Bridget saw me in my outfit—pink disco-ball-looking blazer and the GO BIG FOR QUEEN T-shirt—I swear she shivered, just a little bit.

I said my hellos pretty quickly, studiously ignoring Bridget—who was definitely returning the favor—and made my way up to the podium. The whole Debate Team had shown up, so the room was packed to the gills—six whole people. At the last minute, Lucas ran in the studio, his own camcorder in hand. I didn't want there to be a chance this footage wouldn't be posted on my site.

At the "Three . . . two . . . one," we were filming.

"Welcome, ladies, to the first-ever Prom-Queen Debate," moderator and Debate Team President Charles Loomis said. "We'll be speaking with the lovely prom-royalty hopefuls Margarita Diaz and Bridget Benson. As moderator, I will ask each candidate a question, and one at a time, with a two-minute limit, each candidate will respond. Each candidate will also have time for a one-minute rebuttal. I'm going to flip a coin to determine who will have her three-minute opening statement first." He produced a penny from his pocket. "Heads for Bridget, tails for Margarita." He flipped the coin and said, "Miss Benson, you may begin your opening statement now."

"Thanks, Charlie!" Bridget chirped fakely. Like they were just the best buddies in the world. "Hi, everyone. I'm sure you all know, but I'm Bridget Benson, and I *really* want to be your prom queen. I've known many of you for years now, and when I come to school each morning, I feel almost like I'm coming home. You *all* are my family, and I'm proud to be a member of that family along with you."

It was like a deluge of nice-sounding words, all strung together to sound meaningful but that really just sounded like nonsensical, insincere bullshit. I wondered how people could believe a word out of her mouth.

"I've been an active member of this family for years now," she continued, "spending many hours practicing to cheer on our teams, keeping the student government running smoothly, and staying on top of my studies—all while maintaining a grueling filming schedule for my current TV show." (She *had* to throw it in, didn't she? And call me crazy, but didn't she only shoot when school was *not* in session?) "I'm personally responsible for fund-raisers that have generated enough money to repair our bleachers after tornado damage, repaint our *drab* old cafeterias, and plant more shade- and oxygen-giving trees around our campus. I am *also* responsible for helping the Environmental Club pull together Lake Cleanup Day last month, which—along with a *super*-fun pool party afterward—was a total success.

"So," she said hurriedly (thank *God* her time was almost up!), "I hope that everyone will agree with me that I'm the most qualified and hardworking candidate for prom queen. I thank you all for your love and support."

"Thank you," Charles said. "Miss Diaz? Your opening statement?"

Okay.

This was it.

I took a deep breath and got started.

"Hi, everyone. I'm Margarita Diaz, but a lot of people call me 'Madge.' I actually wanted to ask Bridget why she didn't feel the need to bring up her perfect appearance as a reason to elect her prom queen."

There was a short moment of silence before Bridget turned to Charles and asked, "Am I supposed to say something?"

"Yeah, say something, I just asked you a question," I said matter-of-factly.

"Well, this is highly unorthod—" Charles began.

"Yeah, well, so is a *prom-queen* election," I interrupted him. "It's part of my three-minute opening statement," I said, regarding Bridget. "Why feel the burning need to blog about how a prom queen shouldn't be fat and unhealthy, and then not bring it up in your opening statement?"

"Well, I . . . uh—"

"It was important enough to say earlier this morning, but it isn't now?"

"I guess I—"

"Forget it. So now, whoever goes to Bridget's campaign site will see a blog entry, posted early this morning. In it, if should you possess the powers of observation equivalent to that of a ten-year-old, you'll see the one major reason Bridget doesn't think I should be prom queen: I'm fat. I'm a fat, tacky bitch who passed out on a football field while eating doughnuts, and Bridget doesn't think this makes me dignified enough to be given the all-important honor of prom queen."

I paused, leaning forward over my podium and looking the camera *right* in the eye (or is it lens?). "Well, I have news for you, Winter Park," I continued. "I'm *not* going to engage in this debate. It's not worth it to me. Prom queen isn't some sort of almighty diplomatic position, and I don't feel the need to debate about who gets to *be* queen. And I find it sad that Bridget has to resort to such cheap tactics and name-calling to get her point across.

"Ladies and gents," I went on, "I have my *own* reason for why *Bridget Benson* shouldn't be prom queen. But you'll have to wait for it. In the next week or so before prom, stay tuned to my site for an announcement . . . that will destroy your worlds. Thank you."

And with that, I was off, much to the general confusion of everyone in the room.

I reached Lucas at the back of the room quickly, and he was beaming.

"That was *brill*," he said excitedly as we walked out of the room together.

"Thanks, baby. Did you get it all on tape?"

"Lens cap was off and *everything*," he said proudly, leading us out to his car in the parking lot, where we could talk in private.

We got there, sat down in the front seats, and closed the doors, and Lucas asked me, "So, what's this new plan?"

"You're meeting me after my first period in the office, and I'm handing off Bridget's class schedule. Then I'm visiting my dad at the hospital after second. Maybe you and Kenny can sort of . . . I dunno . . . trail her today. I mean, it's a long shot, but you never know what might happen or what you might overhear."

"Sure, I can try that for a day or two," he said willingly, hiding his camera under a pile of shirts in front of the passenger seat. "But you know, you still haven't really told me the point of all this."

"The point? Lucas, considering how low she just went on *me*, I figured it was time I return the favor. So I'm not taking prom away from her anymore." I smiled.

"So . . . how is that returning the favor?" Lucas asked, raising an eyebrow.

"Well, I'm giving her the *prom* . . . but I'm back on for prom queen."

"You wanna win now?"

"I really just want her to lose. But winning would be pretty sweet."

"What about anti-prom . . . and all those people who were gonna be so psyched about it?"

"Oh, the party's still on," I said. "Once Bridget's world collapses at the dance, I'm leading prom back to the penthouses."

"Except what if we don't find anything on Bridget in the next week or so?" He seemed worried.

I put my arm on Lucas's shoulder. "We will cross that bridge when we get to it, my friend," I said in my best wise-man voice. "So, you gonna help me?"

He sighed. "Of course I will. You know I will."

"And that's why I love you," I said.

"No," Lucas said, pointing to the backseat. "*That's* why you love me."

"The dip! Oh, Lucas. You are *too* good to me. Truly."

"Don't I know it," he said. "Well, store it in the fridge till second period, then take it home with you. I'll never finish it by myself. You can share it with your mom! I'm sure she'll love it," he joked.

I thought back to the uncharacteristic breakfast my mom had made me this morning and smiled. "You know what?" I said. "She just might."

15

Stakeout Sisters

∙∙∙

My dad looked *so* much better today than he did yesterday. I mean, still—the man had been through surgery and a heart attack all in the last twenty-four hours, so he wasn't looking his greatest. But he was certainly looking a lot happier.

My whole family was in a light, buoyant mood. Even my *mom* was cracking jokes with him about how he'd better start liking the taste of rice cakes, because that was all he was getting for a while. And I gotta say, I was surprised he wasn't saying "No way in hell"—in fact, it seemed like he was really ready to change his ways. Working less, eating better, being around more . . . guess all it takes is a near-death experience for some people!

But I wasn't gonna give him grief. I was just glad he was back with us, wholly and completely.

I still couldn't *believe* how Bridget had used this sore spot in my life against me so carelessly. It actually hurt any time I thought of it—especially while I was spending time with my dad—but then I'd add a little seasoning of vengeance to counteract the hurt, and I'd have a delicious snack! I was not going to let her get to me. I was gonna get to *her*.

Lucas called after school let out, telling me he and Kenny hadn't found out anything useful about Bridget. Then he invited me over for dinner, to sort of unwind after all the events in the last couple of days. It was Friday night, and I'd already decided to clear the social calendar for the weekend. I needed a rest.

"And I have a small surprise for you," he said.

"I thought you didn't find anything today."

"That's why I'm calling it a 'small surprise,'" he said, giggling conspiratorially. "You'll see when you get here."

So after making sure my mom was okay with me leaving for dinner, I headed downtown, and rode up the thirty-five floors to the Ellisons'. As soon as the elevator doors opened, Mitsy, who'd been waiting by the front door with Lucas, came out and gave me a big bear hug. Well, as big a bear hug as a 110-pound woman can give a girl like me. While holding an empty wineglass.

"I'm so glad he's okay," was the first thing she said. "And I hope *you're* okay."

"Thanks," I said. "I am okay. I'm actually *better* than okay."

"Well, I have to say that despite the circumstances, you look quite stunning today."

"Oh, thanks," I said. I still hadn't changed out of my debate outfit from earlier that day, but at least now I knew I didn't look so tore up and tired.

"So, when does your dad come home?" Lucas asked, giving me a hug and kissing me on the cheek.

"In the next coupla days . . ."

"That's *wonderful* news," Mitsy said, raising her empty glass in a toast. "Hey, come in, come in—I ordered Thai. I just couldn't be bothered to cook anything, what with all the work I've been putting into this . . . *party* of yours!"

"Yeah?" I asked excitedly, following Mitsy and Lucas to the kitchen. "What's the latest?"

"Well," she said proudly, opening the fridge and extracting a chilled bottle of chardonnay, "the final drag queen is confirmed. You, my friend, are going to have a full-out performance of Destiny's Child's 'Bootylicious' here at the party, at midnight."

"My theme song!"

"That it is," she said, winking and pouring herself another glass.

"So is that my small surprise?" I asked Lucas.

"Actually . . . no," he said, looking at his mom. "Mom, you want to tell her or can I?"

"The floor is yours, dear," she said, taking a dainty sip of wine.

"So Kenny and I found out, like, *nothing* today. But then I come home and update *this* crazy lady on all the happenings, and what do I discover?"

"What?" I asked, the anticipation killing me.

"Mom's going to the Bensons' for a cocktail party tomorrow night."

"They do it every spring," Mitsy added, shaking her head and raising one expertly tweezed eyebrow. "It's the new money's way of trying to get folks like me to stop thinking so little of them."

"Really?!"

"Yes. And if they want me to take them even the *least* bit seriously, they'll have to stop serving Smirnoff at their bar." She snorted slightly, raising an eyebrow. "Top shelf or *no* shelf. Really. Where were they raised, a cave?"

"So we're gonna have Mom be our little spy," Lucas continued. "'Cause you *know* Bridget's going to Lindsay's big party tomorrow night, so we can have Mom, you know . . . snoop around, poke her head in rooms—*all* that stuff!"

"*Really?!*" I asked again. "You don't mind doing this?"

"What else is there to do for me on a Saturday night?" she asked matter-of-factly. "Except going downstairs to Mrs. Brinkley's and looking at her ex's newest wife's latest cosmetic-surgery debacles."

"You're not worried about . . . I dunno . . . being caught?"

"What could they *possibly* do to me?" she laughed. "If anything happens, I'll just act tipsy and say I was looking for the bathroom," she said simply. "Now. Who's hungry?"

The next night, after visiting hours were over at the hospital, I went back to Mitsy and Lucas's. I wanted to see Mitsy off before the party, and I was gonna chill with Lucas and Kenny, watching movies and making snacks, in case Mitsy had any news from the Bensons'.

(Please kindly note how I have nothing vile to say about Mr. Daniels. . . .)

Why stay in on a night like this? Well . . . Spies! Espionage! Upper-crust soirees! Plus, there was no *way* I was going to Lindsay's party. I mean, yeah—that might've been a good place for me to go and do some dirt-digging of my own on Bridget, but I *seriously* doubted that I'd even get in. Lindsay hires security for her parties to make sure no one gets in with any cameras or camera phones—we've discussed Lindsay's nasty illegal habit, have we not?—and I'm *sure* she'd have a "not allowed to pass under any circumstances" list in addition to that, with my name right below the Winter Park Police Department and Mandy Moore.

The last few weeks had really taken it out of me, anyway, and I needed nothing more than to chill the fuck out. So a night of PG fun sounded all right to me.

When I got there, Mitsy was modeling her vintage cocktail dress—bright sea-green satin and utterly *stunning*—and Kenny was nowhere to be seen.

"He had somewhere to be," Lucas grumbled, obviously not wanting to discuss it further. "Anyway, you're just in time to see Mom off!"

"You kiddies don't have any bugs or tiny cameras for me to slip anywhere?" she asked us jokingly. "You don't want me to put one of those teddy-bear cameras in her room?"

Shit. If only there'd been *time* for a teddy cam! Oh, well.

"Nope," I said, "nothing that high tech. I guess just call if you think you find anything."

"Oh, I will." She went to the foyer and dropped a couple of Grey Goose minis into her purse. "In case it's Smirnoff again."

I laughed. "Thanks again, Mitsy."

"For you, darling, *anything*." She gave us each a hug and a kiss and was off.

I looked at Lucas and shrugged my shoulders. "So what now?" I asked.

"I guess we just wait. Kinda like a stakeout."

"Right, stakeout," I said. "Well, except that this stakeout is in a penthouse with a gourmet kitchen. . . ."

"Yeah, let's make some food!" Lucas said excitedly. "You got the stuff?"

"Oh, I got the stuff," I told him, holding up the plastic bag full of groceries I'd bought on my way over.

I'd gotten ingredients to make our favorite low-fat snack, the recipe of which I'd actually picked up from one of my mom's zero-calorie WeightBuster cookbooks. It consisted of low-fat Cool Whip spread between two graham crackers and then frozen. (Well, my usual *slight* modification to this virtuous recipe was dipping the little frozen sandwiches into melted dark chocolate and then refreezing them, but not tonight. I was on a slight health kick—or at least a don't-overdo-it-all-the-time kick—so this time we were doing it *sans chocolat*.)

We set up our waxed-paper stations and got to work making the sandwiches.

"So what'd Kenny have to do tonight?" I asked Lucas casually.

"I don't really know . . . just some errands, he said."

"That sucks," I said. "I was finally getting used to the guy. I was hoping that by the end of tonight, we'd have our heart-to-heart and be best friends!"

"Oh, shut up, Madge, you know you hate him."

"Not true!" I cried.

"Yeah. Well . . . I'm starting to have my own suspicions. . . ."

"Yeah?"

"Well . . . he hasn't exactly been around much at lunch lately. He was eating with me for a while there, like, every *day*."

"So why the sudden change?"

"I dunno. Maybe he thinks I want him to be my boyfriend or something. Then again, maybe he just has the attention span of a grasshopper."

"Do grasshoppers have especially short attention spans?"

"Well, they can't be that *long*, if you wanna get all technical."

"Damn, girl!" I said, stepping back. "Testy, testy."

He laughed a little. "Sorry. I'm just a little bit down. I'm starting to wonder if I should've even asked him. I feel like a big, wide-eyed idiot."

"Lucas, *darling*," I said, going into my purse and extracting my iPod. "Stop talking like you've made this be-all, end-all decision that you're gonna have to live with for the rest of your life."

I walked over to the Bose deck in the living room and placed my iPod into the portal. "Zach obviously still cares about you, and if you decide to give it another chance, he might just say yes. And if you made the wrong decision with Kenny, you'll just have a shitty time at prom, a *great* time at the anti-prom, and that'll be that!"

And with that, I pressed PLAY, and the Bose kicked into life, blasting out the opening chords to "Bootylicious." When I say it's my theme song, I don't just mean because of my own bootyliciousness. I'm saying I know every single word and note, and even have a *dance*. A dance that truly cheers Lucas up no matter what shade of blue he might be.

And this time was no different, with Lucas breaking into a big smile as I jiggled my way over to him. When I'd reached him in the kitchen, I turned my back and rode him dirty-dancing style, then flipped my big head of hair backward, swatting him in the face. He laughed and playfully pushed me off.

"Things'll turn out fine," I panted as I continued my violent body-shaking dance. "And just think—soon—you're gonna be host—to the most *delicious* party—Winter Park has ever seen. Do you love it?!"

"I love it!" he said, exasperated. "Now help me *finish* these, please!"

"Pushy boy," I said, shaking my head and cutting my routine short. "But I love you anyway."

"You, too."

"I'm glad I'm not being a total bitch to you anymore," I said suddenly, thinking back to the Gainesville weekend.

"The feeling is mutual, Your Madgesty," he assured me.

Best friends should really have a gigantic fight at *least* once a year. It truly does wonders.

Before our sandwiches even had a chance to freeze, we got a call from Mitsy's cell.

"You're on speaker phone, *mamasita*," Lucas greeted.

"Dears!" Mitsy said into the phone. "I was just poking around the house, and Bridget's still here."

"She's not at Lindsay's?" I asked.

"Well, I happened to be walking by her room, and I heard some snippets of a pretty heated exchange between her and her father."

"Just spill it, woman!" Lucas cried.

"He's sending her off on some sort of errand. He's telling her she has to go somewhere tonight; she's saying she doesn't want to."

"Well, do you have any idea *where*?" I pleaded. "I mean, he could be telling her to . . . go out for ice or something."

"Madgie-pie, the Bensons don't have to 'go out for ice,' no matter *how* new money they are," Mitsy said. "I can try to find out, but if you really want to know, I'd suggest you get your butt down here quickly! She looked like she was about to— Oh, no, she's leaving now."

"Mits— Mitsy, where *are* you?" I asked.

"Calm yourself, love, I'm not hiding in the girl's trunk or

anything, I'm just out front. And Bridget is getting in her car to leave *right now*."

"Well . . . well, Mitsy, can you . . . can *you* follow her or something?"

"You think I drove my*self* to this party? With the promise of middle-class vodka?!"

"Mom!" Lucas cried.

"I took the car service, sillies. They need more than a minute's notice to get here, you know. Look, the valets *packed* this driveway. Bridget's not making it out of here for at least fifteen minutes. But she *is* outside, and she is *fuming*. There must be something up."

"What's she wearing?" I asked.

"Sweats."

Holy Mother of *God*!

"Something *is* up. *Thank* you, Mitsy."

"I think I might poke around her room later tonight, too," Mitsy said. "Depends on how much duller this party gets."

"Just call me on my cell if you find anything," I said. "I *love* you." I hung up the phone. "Lucas, we are so *on* this shit!"

"What? Oh, you don't think—"

"Lucas!" I screamed. "Sweatpants! She's missing Lindsay's party, and her dad is sending her on a mysterious errand where Bridget will not be seen by anyone. Why else wouldn't she do herself up? *Especially* when she has fifteen minutes while the valets move the cars." I was in full-on crazy mode, barking orders at Lucas. "Okay, I want you to grab your digital camera, that little recordy-thing you use to tape lectures, and a black hoodie for yoursel— Do you think you have a *big* black hoodie for me?"

"Um . . . I have a black *sheet.*"

"Grab that, too!" I was pulling my shoes on as fast as I could. "Well, *go!*" I cried.

"You're really forcing me to do th—?"

"*Lucas*, there is *no time* for this. I *need* you. Now, come on!"

It seemed a shame to go following Bridget around town without big cups of strong coffee—the possibility of the evening turning into an *actual* stakeout weighed considerably on my mind. So on our way to Bridget's house in Mitsy's convertible, top and tinted windows up ('cause Bridget would *totally* recognize my car), I gave Mitsy a ring and asked about the valets' progress.

"Let me just go out there and see. . . . Oh, yeah. You have at least another ten minutes."

"Sweet."

So after a Dunkin' Donuts run (two large iced coffees with shots of espresso—and a marble-frosted and a Boston Kreme, because really, how could I say no?), Lucas and I were ready. Caffeinated and sugar-rushing. Powered up. Ready for the chase. Stakeout Sisters . . . with iced coffees.

We made it to Bridget's block just in time to see her turning that big fat Escalade out of the neighborhood.

"Badass," I said, sipping on my straw.

"You're an idiot," Lucas mumbled.

16

Some Serious
Scary-Movie Stuff

The idea of the rough-and-tumble, rock-'em-sock-'em Stakeout Sisters quickly lost its cachet when Lucas and I spent the next half hour in a strip-mall parking lot, waiting for Bridget to finish her dinner at Panera. Then a visit to the ATM.

It wasn't until we were headed east—*way* east—on Colonial Drive that I started to suspect something truly interesting was gonna happen. Because when you're coming from Winter Park, the farthest east you'd wanna go on Colonial would be to Alafaya, the street that Waterford Lakes (and my sister's apartment) was off of. Beyond that, there's not much of anything besides a couple of podunk towns—Chuluota, where Randy's party was, being one of them—and then the Atlantic coast.

When Bridget passed Alafaya, and then the very end of the

East-West Expressway, I started getting concerned. When she didn't turn off for Chuluota, the last street in my comfort zone, I was officially weirded out.

"You're following too close," Lucas scolded. "Slow down and let another car or two get between you."

"Well, I don't wanna *lose* her, since I have no idea where the fuck we *are* now," I said frantically, the caffeine in my jumbo-sized coffee all of a sudden kicking in full force. "Where is she *taking* us?"

"I dunno, *Bithlo*?"

"Oh, *God* no. Not Bithlo."

I might've mentioned Bithlo a few times already. But Bithlo really requires a bit of explanation. You know how every family has that one person in it—the black sheep, the ingrate, the one who's just a little bit *off* in comparison to the rest of the family? Well, Bithlo (pretty much just a small collection of trailer parks, convenience stores, and gas stations) is kind of like Orlando's red-headed bastard stepchild. Although to put it more accurately, it's the classless, trailer-trashy, Confederate flag–waving, *toothless* red-headed bastard stepchild of Orlando.

Come to think of it, that hiccup of evolution who called Lucas a faggot on our way to Gainesville could've been from Bithlo.

Point is, it's not the coolest place to be on a Saturday night at ten o'clock.

"Madge, if Bridget is leading us into Bithlo, we are so outta here. No *way* are we driving my mom's car into Bithlo."

"Um . . . Lucas, darling," I said as sweetly as I could manage, "this thing goes from zero to sixty in, like, half a second. We'll be fine."

"But they shoot fags on *sight* out here!" he cried. "Please, let's turn around."

"Lucas, did we come this far and drink this much coffee to just turn around at the first sign of danger?"

"I didn't know there was gonna *be* any danger!"

"Where's your sense of adventure?"

"Way back in Orlando—with the streetlights and the tall buildings and the theme parks with their carefully maintained rides! Civilized people don't *need* a sense of adventure, Madge. Our foreheads aren't sloped at forty-five-degree angles, okay? We've evolved *past* Bithlonians! Now take me back to my safe and secure penthouse so I can live through the night, please!"

"No can do."

"Kidnapper!"

"Look, Lucas. Why don't we just follow her a little farther?" I suggested calmly, trying not to grind my teeth too hard as we passed the Bithlo city limits sign. "We'll kill the headlights when we pull off the highway and just see where she's going. We don't even have to get outta the car."

Lucas took a hugely deep breath and exhaled slowly, trying to get ahold of himself. "As long as you *promise* not to get outside to investigate some *strange noise* in a cornfield or something, I'll go along with it. This is how every scary movie starts, you know."

"But none of us are black, so who's gonna die first?"

"Shut up! *No one's* going to die!"

"I'm just messing with you." I laughed. "Oh, shit—she's turning off the road."

"No!"

"What, you expected her to just keep driving?"

"I was hoping we'd end up at the beach. . . ." Lucas peered out the window, looking shell-shocked as he took in the surroundings: dense scrub forest on one side, dark and ominous junkyard on the other.

I couldn't help but want to be at the beach right now, either, as we passed a group of Olde English–swilling mulleted men in wife-beaters who were eyeing our luxury car suspiciously from their lawn chairs. "It's almost ten o'clock," I said. "The beach was wishful thinking."

"Like you *even* have to point that out to me." He followed the group of guys with his eyes until we were well clear of the trailer they were hanging out in front of.

"Lucas, they're not *animals*—they're not gonna chase us down or anything."

"Yeah, 'cause they're too drunk on malt liquor and too stuffed with cans of Vienna sausages to move!"

"Lucas, I had no idea what a classist little pig you were."

"Shut up, Madge, it's just my gay-boy defense mechanism going up," he said, looking at himself in the mirror. "I have to insult them before they insult me."

"Maybe your first line of defense should be taking off that pair of hot-pink sunglasses."

"Fine." He pulled his favorite pair of ginormous Paris Hilton–style shades off his face and tossed them into the backseat. "I was thinking they'd look good with this hoodie," he said, flipping his mirror back up. "Hey, maybe your sister can cook up something creative to do with that *black sheet* you've got wrapped around yourself!"

"*Hey*, the darker a figure I am in this car, the better. I don't need Bridget looking in her rearview and recognizing me."

As we got farther away from the state highway and the town became more sparsely settled, I was finally comfortable enough to turn out my headlights. Bridget was a way's ahead of us, but her rear lights were still in sight. A few minutes later, the road took a sharp turn to the right, onto a street called Amityville Drive.

"Are you *kidding* me?" Lucas said spastically. "We're following her onto a street named after a horror movie?!"

"The horror movie was named after a town in—"

"Yeah, a town on Long Island where this guy totally slaughtered his famil—!"

"*Shush,*" I interrupted him. "She's pulling up to that trailer."

Shit. Having a picture of Bridget at this *trailer* would probably almost be enough to sully her name forever. I mean, we're talking trash-*ayyy*. Like, this is where Britney Spears would have been if not for her "talent." Pink flamingos, hubcaps, busted tires, beer cans, and all sorts of indecipherable junk littered the lawn surrounding the rickety old trailer, which was half puke-green and half rusted-over. It was like this particular trailer, on the outskirts of the town, had become the unofficial dumping ground for anyone who didn't want to drive all the way to the other side of town—ten minutes!—to dump their shit.

I drove past, hoping Bridget hadn't noticed us following her, and headed down another street.

"*Ho*-kay," Lucas gasped, seeming out of breath. "*Now* we can go home."

"*Home?!*" I cried.

"Yeah. Bridget has a secret redneck lover in Bithlo. She likes to get it on to Kid Rock and Limp Bizkit, and she really prefers Natty Light to cosmos. Now let's just get *outta* here!"

"Whoa, whoa, *even* if that was her Bithlonian boyfriend's trailer, we still wouldn't have any *proof*, so we're going back anyway. Plus, her *dad* sent her here, so that's probably not even what it is," I said as I pulled into a driveway. (I *guess* you could call it a driveway—it was more of a car-shaped area of dead grass.)

"Wait, what're you doing?"

"What do you *think* I'm doing, I'm turning around."

"Madge, *please!*" he squealed. "I'm seriously scared!"

"*Shh,*" I said, driving the car super-slowly. I was doing this not only to remain inconspicuous but because the streets weren't very well lit, and my headlights were still out. "We have to be quiet now."

"I'm gonna *kill* you later," he whispered forcefully.

"Not if the ax-murderer kills me first!"

"*I hate you,*" he spat.

I pulled as slowly as I could back onto Amityville Drive, looking for an out-of-sight place to park, trying to keep the car on the cracked-up road. I didn't want anyone driving by to spot the BMW and blow our cover. Not to mention put Mitsy's fine automobile in grave danger.

"What are you thinking, Madge? You can't drive past Bridget and *not* look suspicious in this car," Lucas said. "For all you know, she would follow *us* then!"

"She's not seeing the car, because I'm parking it somewhere," I said. "And I'm sneaking up to the trailer."

"*Madge!*" Lucas screamed.

"*Shhh!* We're really close to her, Lucas, and people can hear you screech from a mile away." I pointed to a carport coming up on our right. "Here, look. We'll park in this—there's not even a camper next to it."

"I'm not liking this. . . ."

"Too late," I said, pulling into the carport, still well out of earshot and sight from the trailer Bridget had pulled up to moments before.

The carport was almost pitch-black—only a few vague edges illuminated by distant streetlights and the half moon that was out tonight. I undid my seat belt and reached into the backseat for our backpack full of equipment.

"Lucas, honey," I whispered, "I'm gonna go out there and see what I can find."

"*What?* I am *not* going out there."

"Well, *I* am, so you can just stay here."

"I'm not staying in here alone!"

"So you have a choice to make then," I said. "It'll be *fine*—stop freaking yourself out." I eased the door open and stepped outside. Since I was in black anyway, I decided to ditch the sheet, throwing it back in the front seat and feeling my way outside the carport.

It was actually a pretty nice, comfortable night. Mid-sixties, a slight breeze in the air. Tons of stars in the sky, way more than I see back in Orlando. The mystery trailer in the distance cast a dim light.

I stood there a moment, to get my bearings, and to give Lucas a chance to join me. Just as I was about to give up and head toward the trailer solo, I heard rustling in some bushes about ten feet away. I nearly peed my *pants*, it startled me so bad.

I straightened my body, stiffening, and listened for more sounds from the bushes.

That goddamn Lucas had me totally pyched out now, 'cause all of a sudden I was really, really scared. I guess I had rushed into this kind of crazily. The last couple days of stress and sleep deprivation had made me a tad bit psychotic lately . . . but that prissy bitch Bridget Benson had shit all over my dignity, and that just *put me over the edge.* I *had* to bring her down somehow. And now here I was, scared shitless, probably with some chubby-chasing serial killer about to jump out of the bushes and chop me to pieces!

Fucking crap, something just jumped out of the bushes!

But my so-called "killer" turned out to be an armadillo that was just as scared of me as I was of it . . .

. . . but not as scared of Lucas as *Lucas* was of it.

"Mmm-ggghh-aaaah-duh!" is the best way to describe the gibberish that came out of Lucas when the armadillo ran directly across his path as Lucas made his way carefully from the carport out to the woodsy area I was standing in.

I looked quickly to the trailer to check for any sign of activity, but there wasn't any.

"Shut *up!*" I told Lucas.

"You're telling me to *shut up* after a fucking *dinosaur* ran across my feet?!"

"It's *just* an armadillo," I said, as if it hadn't scared the hell out of me a couple minutes earlier.

"*Yeah*, well, ex*cuse* me if I'm just not used to seeing the fucking things *alive*, okay?"

"Point taken." It *was* kind of weird to see an armadillo all in one piece, come to think of it. They seemed to be just as common as roadkill as they were as living, breathing, *creepy*-looking creatures.

We stayed where we were for a second, getting our bearings. I couldn't help but feel a little shaken up after that scare. My heart was absolutely *pounding* in my chest, and Lucas was shivering despite his hoodie. But we had to press on.

There was about a hundred yards of not-too-dense scrub forest separating us from the trailer Bridget was at. I could see her car from here, dimly backlit by the soft glow from within the mobile-home monstrosity.

"Come on," I whispered to Lucas. "And watch where you step."

We made our way as quietly as we could through the stretch of woods, through the sand, mud, palmettos, and pine trees. Despite the pleasant weather, I was beginning to sweat profusely, and I could feel a mosquito bite swelling on my neck. And it was almost *impossible* to see, it was so dark. Sure, the mobile home kept getting closer and closer and brighter and brighter, but it was still a little while away, and the light from its interior didn't travel all the way to where we were trudging.

I took my cell out of my pocket and opened it up, using the small amount of light from the display screen to illuminate the ground in front of us. I just hoped and prayed that some rattlesnake wasn't gonna come out of nowhere to bite and kill us. Because I didn't know if it was better to see or *not* see something like that right before it happened.

"I am gonna shit my *pants* I'm so nervous right now," Lucas said. "What about my mom's car?"

"Unless you think that armadillo's gonna hot-wire it and take off, then it's *fine*, Lucas."

"If I get killed tonight," he said, ignoring me, "tell Zach I love him."

"Don't be dramatic."

"I'm *serious*. I'm seriously scared and I seriously love the guy—"

"Then if we live, you're breaking off prom with Kenny as *soon* as we get home," I said to cut him off. "Shut up, will you—we're almost there."

The palmetto bushes and trees became less dense at the edge of the patch of forest, and the land opened up into the junkyard property surrounding this mystery trailer. Bridget's car was just fifty feet away, right next to a turned-over and out-of-commission tractor.

"Let's get to that tractor over there," I said.

"No way! There's too much open space between us and that."

"Just crouch low and move quietly," I ordered, then did so without waiting for him to argue with me further.

I could feel the caffeine/adrenaline combo pumping furiously through my veins as I hurried—stooped low and probably looking very undignified—toward the beat-up tractor. I arrived a minute later, out of breath and practically panting. I could see Lucas bounding lithely across the expanse of junkyard, like a little gay gazelle. In a hoodie.

I gave him a thumbs-up.

He gave me the finger.

I motioned to the trailer, and that I wanted to get a better look inside. Who *knows* what'd been going on in there for the last fifteen minutes!

But he shook his head no, and just as I stood to peer carefully over the tractor, there was a deafening *Beep-beep-beeeeep!*

This time *I* was the one to start screaming gibberish, but Lucas leapt up and clapped his hand over my mouth before I could give us away.

The beeping had come from a banged-up pickup truck that was quickly, clunkily approaching.

The sound of a car door opening caught our attention, and we looked and saw Bridget, just a few feet away, get out of her car and head up to the truck.

Fucking *hell*, that was a close one!

I hadn't even *seen* her in that car this whole time. Could that've meant that she'd seen us approaching all along?

Probably not, since she didn't seem to be trying to hide anything from us now.

"Where the fuck have you been?" Bridget asked, obviously pretty pissed off. "I've been waiting here, like, half an hour."

Like I said, it was more like fifteen minutes. But I wasn't about to leap up and correct her.

The truck door opened and out popped a rail-thin woman— um, I *guess* you could call her a woman—about five feet tall and looking as dried out and shriveled as a raisin. Trashy McInbred wore a faded American-flag long-sleeved shirt tucked tightly into what looked like Wrangler jeans (but they really could've been *any* brand that a Wal-Mart Supercenter carried), which were tucked into big brown work boots. She was short, but she had a big presence. Her skin was tan, leathery, and wrinkled, and she had long, frizzy, strawlike blonde hair down to her ass (*very* sexy). I couldn't see much of her face from here, but from what I could tell, she didn't have a Cro-Magnon-like slope to her face, so at least we knew she was human.

Oh. And did I mention the chewing tobacco?

Did I really even need to?

"Hey, darlin', how are ya?" this Charlize-Theron-ala-*Monster* woman said to Bridget. She stooped down, popped open the lid of a turtle-shaped sandbox in the front yard, and grabbed a can of beer. "You want one? Fridge's on the fritz—figgered I'd stash the brewskies out here. Don't wanna hafta go all the way to the kitchen for one after work."

"*Work.* Right." Bridget sighed. "And no, I don't drink beer. Look, can we just go inside and get this over with?"

"Faaahn with me," the woman drawled in response, popping open the can and downing its contents in one enormous gulp. (I wondered if she'd beat me in a funneling contest.) She belched as she walked past Bridget to the front door. "Y'coulda just gone in, ya know," she said. "Thought you had a key."

"The leather seats in my car were just fine, thanks."

And with that, they were inside the camper.

Who *was* this nasty woman? Was Bridget taking a dip in the redneck lesbian cesspool? Was she out in Bithlo buying some hillbilly heroin for Daddy? Was this woman blackmailing her or something? The possibilities were endless! I *had* to figure out what was going on. . . . Fuck the prom-queen shit—I was just morbidly curious at this point!

I immediately tiptoed out from behind the tractor, to stand

between the SUV and the outside of the trailer. I looked back to see if Lucas had followed me. He hadn't. He popped his head over the tractor and just shook his head. He wasn't coming.

Fine. At least I had the backpack.

I felt around inside. The tape recorder wouldn't work. All I could hear from the camper was muffled voices. But the digital camera would do. A couple shots of Bridget on the inside of this dingy, nasty trailer would do *something* for my reputation, for sure.

Not to mention shatter Bridget's perfect public image.

Loves it.

I pulled an old tire over, so I could stand and get a better view inside. Then, when the voices sounded far enough away—which in this tiny trailer wasn't all that easy to determine—I said a quick little prayer to the *Mission Impossible* gods, stood up delicately on the tire, and peered inside.

The inside of this rat's nest of a trailer was almost as bad as the trash-covered land surrounding it. Beer cans and a couple empty bottles of Jack, a sofa so frayed and beat up that not even the thriftiest college student would pick it up from the side of the road, a vintage 1980s-style TV with bunny ears covered in tinfoil, and piles upon piles of clothes and unopened mail.

As I looked down to turn on the camera, I heard Bridget and the woman coming back, closer to the window I was standing at. I quickly dropped down and hid, just in time. I was gonna have to be super-stealthy with this camera work. I just had to wait for the right time to jump up and snap the shots. . . .

With Bridget and Leatherhead talking right above my head, I could actually make out what they were saying better. I caught a few snippets of their conversation—"I just don't know why you always have to make things so difficult!" "It doesn't *hafta* be this way." "Why? Are you gonna get tired of taking my fucking *money* all of a sudden?" "I'm not just doin' this for the money!"—but I couldn't hear enough to really figure out what the hell was going on before they headed to the other end of the trailer again.

Then, just as I was about to try my luck and get into position to snap a good photo, Bridget rushed past the window (not even noticing me) and to the front door, screaming, *"I can't BELIEVE you're my MOTHER!"*

Holy.

Effing.

Shit!

17

Jade + Jed 4Ever!

· ·

First of all, Holy Effing Shit, this truck-stop skank was Bridget's *mom*. (For the sake of ease, I think I'll just refer to her as Trixie from now on.) And the second H.F.S. was in regard to the fact that Bridget was obviously storming back to her car, which I was now *squatting right next to*!

I scrambled frantically away, praying the noise I was surely making would be drowned out by all the mother–daughter yelling. I was so scared I'd get caught that I didn't even bother trying to listen. I had all I needed—now I just had to get away with it undiscovered.

The best option—since running all the way to the other side of the trailer was too far to go in just a few seconds—was to hide behind Bridget's car. Hopefully she didn't have anything to put in the trunk, 'cause I was *screwed* if she did. Just as I got to the Escalade and dove as low to the ground as I could, Bridget slammed the front trailer door closed and hurried toward her car. I could hear her trying very hard not to cry—that kind of gaspy, trying-to-catch-your-breath thing.

Her footsteps grew closer, getting to the front door of the car and seeming to keep going. I held my breath and prepared for the inevitable. My luck hadn't failed me yet tonight, and I felt like that was too good a streak for me. This was it. All the hours of buildup, of Mitsy's helping, of stalking, of caffeinating—all gone in a *poof!* because I was too cocky. Cockiness and self-righteousness had worked out well at Lake Cleanup Day . . . at the debate . . . even when faced with Lady Pearl at UC. But now it seemed that they would be my downfall. . . .

"*Bridget!*" Trixie yelled, coming out the front door.

Bridget stopped dead in her tracks. "What?" she said quietly. I wondered if her mom could even hear it, all the way back at the front door.

"I'm sorry," she said. "I just can't help it. I have a problem!"

"Whatever! Just stop selling it, and maybe you'll stop *using* it!" And she opened the driver's-side door and got in, turned the ignition, and drove off.

All of a sudden, I was completely vulnerable. In seconds, the car was gone, and I was left crouching on the ground, halfway between the beat-up tractor and the rusted-over trailer. I looked up quickly and saw that Trixie was too busy watching Bridget's car drive off to notice me. I quickly shuffled back to the tractor, probably making too much noise. But this woman was probably used to these sounds outside her tractor, since raccoons, opossums, and (obviously!) armadillos called Bithlo home, too.

Behind the tractor again, Lucas greeted me, eyes as wide as saucers, with, "What the fuck is *wrong* with you? Do you *want* to get caught?!" I heard the front door open and Trixie walk back into her mobile home.

"You should be more quiet—Bridget's *mom* might hear." I smiled devilishly.

"I *know*, I *heard* that!" Lucas said, still a little too loud. "*Total* scandal. What do you think all that selling stuff was ab—?"

"What do you *think*, Lucas? She's probably got some sort of meth lab in there or something! This is fucking *pricele*—"

I was suddenly cut off by the sounds of an approaching car, which tooted its horn three times. Trixie opened her door and went outside to greet the driver.

Okay, now over the last few weeks, in the ridiculous soap opera my life had become, I'd come to expect the unexpected. Since making that easy fifty bucks at Madison Whiteman's party, I'd gone pickup-truck skiing through a field of mud, I'd laughed in the face of a giant Krystal-burger-crazed drag queen, I'd done Liquid Cocaine and lived to tell about it, and my father had survived a fairly serious heart attack.

But *this* kind of unexpected, I'd never expected.

"Is—is that *Kenny* sitting in that car?" Lucas asked me.

"Looks like our boy Kenny might actually have some money of his own," I said as we watched him hand over a wad of bills, getting a brown paper bag in exchange.

"Please don't say—"

"—I told you so?" I finished for him.

"*You* shut up. I'm still pissed at you for dragging me out here. But come on! What the fuck? Is Kenny *stupid* enough to buy meth?!"

"Or whatever she sells outta here. . . ."

By now, Trixie was back in the trailer, and Kenny was firing up his ignition.

"I feel so *stupid*!" Lucas spat. "I can't believe he spends his money on this shit!"

"Look, Lucas, don't worry ab—"

But just as Kenny started to pull onto the road, Lucas leaped up and started running after the car. I guess it'd all been too much for him, and he was just so keyed up and stressed out that he wasn't thinking—but he took off like a shot. Not fast enough to catch up to Kenny's car, though. I was too shocked to move at first, and then, just as I started to get up and motion for Lucas to make his way back to the BMW with me, a gunshot rang out from the trailer—*BAM!*—and I dove down for cover.

Lucas screamed.

My body went cold.

My heart felt like it had stopped pumping.

My caffeine jitters stopped.

Even my mosquito bite stopped itching for a second.

"What the *hell're* you doin' on mah property?!" I heard Trixie yell.

Thank *God*—Trixie must've just fired a warning shot.

"Um . . . n-n-nothin' . . ." Lucas answered.

"No one comes all the way out here for *nothin'*." She paused. "Would another shot jog your memory?"

"I was just coming up here to steal a beer," Lucas said quickly. Then his voice dropped an octave and lost its frantic, squealing quality. "I heard a rumor you keep 'em in a sandbox. . . ."

Wow. Lucas had even added a slight drawl to his voice. I stood up and peeked my head over the tractor so I could see what was going on. I saw Trixie walk down the trailer steps and head over to the sandbox. The mannish swagger she'd had earlier with Bridget around had sort of morphed into a strange, almost *flirtatious* strut-lumber.

"I don't recognize you, sugar. You ain't from around here, are ya?"

"Huh? Oh, no, ma'am," Lucas said, trying to look coy with his hands in his pockets.

"Wha's yer name?"

"Uh . . . Jed."

I stifled a giggle.

"Well, I'm Jade."

Jed and Jade. It was poetry. I wonder if Jade was her real name. I was probably closer with Trixie.

"Nice to make your acquaintance."

Oooh, Lucas was charming the pants off *me* with these little Southernisms. It seemed to be working on Trixie/Jade, who had now thrown Lucas a lighter so he could spark up her Marlboro Red.

"Likewise, dollface." She took a long drag on her cancer stick, stepped back, and kicked open the sandbox. "How old're you?"

Lucas hooked his thumbs through his front two belt loops. "How old you think I am?"

"Old enough." She laughed—a heavy and labored smoker's laugh—and picked out two beers, tossing one to Lucas.

"Fuckin' A." He actually caught the beer can and tipped it at Jade in a toast.

Then Jade pulled the same move she did when she saw Bridget, popping open the beer can and chugging it all down in one pull. When I saw her body twitch a bit in anticipation of a belch, she actually *stifled* it rather than let it rip like she had in front of her daughter.

Then she gestured at him, suggesting he do the same.

Lucas laughed a little and nodded, actually smiling a tiny bit. Maybe he was reminded of me, and my adored pastime of beer-funneling. (I don't know what it is about it, but there's something so rewarding about being able to drink a beer in two seconds flat—and *nothing's* more rewarding than that post-funneling belch!)

Actually, if Lucas was reminded of me at *all* at this point, he would most certainly not be smiling. I did sort of create this—the most terrifying evening of his young life to date, I'm sure. Armadillos, gunshots, trailer trash, canned beer, and *farm equipment*—they all added up to a fairly unfriendly environment for him.

But he seemed to be doing okay now.

He actually managed to chug the beer without stopping for breath, even though I think he cheated a little bit.

"You wanna come party with me?" she asked him all of a sudden.

"Uh . . . you mean . . . in *there*?" He shot a rapid-quick look of desperation in my direction. As well as this little flirtation was going, I knew Lucas wouldn't want to take it indoors with this straw-haired VD vessel.

I gauged the distance between us. I could probably sneak up and charge the bitch before she'd get a chance to run back for her gun, which she'd thankfully left on the front steps to the trailer.

But then what? What the hell was I gonna *do* with Bridget Benson's secret trailer-trash mother when I attacked her? Would I have to knock her out for me and Lucas to get away safely? Shove her into the sandbox and jump up and down on the top of it like an overstuffed suitcase till it closed? Grab the gun myself and—?

No. Too far. Officially too far.

But if this twink-hungry Jade wanted to take Lucas inside and have her way with him, I might *have* to step over the line, to keep my friend safe (and to keep him from having to service those nasty pipes).

But then Jade said, "Naw, not in there—I wanna go *out* and party tonight. You in?"

"Sure," Lucas surprised me by saying. "Why don't you run on inside and get ready. I'm gonna take a leak."

"Oh, you can come on in for that, darlin'."

"Naw—I figgered you'd wanna get prettied up in there . . . not that you *need* to—"

"All right, all right, Casanova. I'll go put on mah face and be right back."

I ducked back down and listened as Jade went back into the house.

In a flash, Lucas was back beside me. He stood tall behind the tractor, pretending to pee and whispering quietly to me.

"Are you believing this?" he said.

"I know. Let's just get outta here. I'm *so* sorry! *Please* forgive— Wait, you don't even *have* to forgive me—"

"No, I'm totally baggin' this babe." He smiled smugly. "C'mon, you know how I always secretly want an adventure. . . ."

"Right. Okay, let's just sneak back the way we came," I said, ignoring him. "She won't even notice."

"Please. It's gonna take that freak, like, three seconds to get ready, okay?" Lucas snorted. "Plus, she's got a gun. We're not gettin' away. I think I've got this one under control."

"What?"

"Just go back to the car as soon as we leave, and I'll go to whatever shit bar she wants to go to. First opportunity I get,

I'll text you and tell you where I am, and you can come pick me up."

"Are you *sure*, Jed?" I asked.

He chuckled softly. "Yeah. But if she takes that gun with her, fucking get her license-plate number and call the cops."

"You're being so . . . so brave all of a sudden." I patted him on the leg. "It's sexy."

"If only Zach could see me now."

"I'll tell him all about it," I said. "Now, get out there and have some fun! And be careful."

"I will."

He did a fake zip-up and was back in the front yard in seconds, just in time for Jade to come out from getting all sexied out. Well, all *slutted* out, whatever you wanna call it. We're talking floral-print tube top, raggedy denim skirt so short Lucas could probably see where Bridget had emerged into the world, and clunky cork-wedge heels. Ickity-ick!

But fashion sense aside, at least she put the gun back in the house.

"Let's go, big boy," she said playfully, slapping his ass and pushing him toward the pickup. A minute later, they were gone.

I stood, stretched, and waited for five agonizing minutes, just in case Jade forgot something and needed to come back. Finally, I decided it was safe, and I started to walk toward the road. No need to return to Mitsy's car through the pitch-black patch of forest again.

But just as I made it to the street, I realized that I was leaving here with nothing, nothing at all. With this recent development, I actually wondered how badly I needed to humiliate Bridget. It seemed rather unsportsmanlike to do so, considering how potentially painful and shady her past was. Would *I* want someone to expose my deepest, darkest secrets? And further, did I want to be the kind of awful person who would do such a thing?

But then again, there was the whole laundry list of terrible things Bridget had already done to *me*. Karma was a bitch, after all, and some people just needed to be taught a lesson. Plus, there was the fact that I had a loving and supportive sister working a dead-end job who stood to benefit from a little Bridget-blackmail. I figured the *least* I could do was snap a few pictures of the inside of Jade's trailer. No telling if they'd scare Bridget into letting Vanessa dress her for that *OK* shoot, but it was worth a try.

A few minutes later, I was back in Mitsy's car and heading back into town. I drove to Waterford Lakes and parked in front of the movie theater, deciding to just sit there and wait till Lucas told me where to pick him up.

Two long-ass hours later, after a bunch of DON'T WORRY I'M FINE texts from Lucas, he finally called.

"Whuddup, Jed?" I answered. "What *took* you so long?"

"*Ho*-migod, Madge, you will not *believe* where I am!" he said breathlessly.

"Wait . . . are you okay?"

"Yeah, I snuck away for a minute."

"So what's up?"

"Um, nothing except for the fact that I'm in *love* with Bithlo!" he cried. "Hold on, you should come pick me up." And he gave me directions.

"So what's this about loving Bithlo?" I asked incredulously, starting up the car. "A few hours ago, you were—"

"I *know*, I *know*, but lemme tell you about my night, okay?"

"All right," I said skeptically.

A Brief Lucas Interlude—

"Okay. It was a really weird couple of hours. It was scary and then kind of fun but also a little depressing, too, but I'm gonna start from the beginning. All right, so at first, I was pretty terrified. But, like, exhilarated, too—'cause I hadn't ever done anything crazy like this, y'know? And Bridget's mom totally *wanted* me! It was *hot*! Even though *she* wasn't, really. And I'm not just saying that 'cause of her . . . you know, womanhood. Jade is just not a MILF in any way, shape, or form.

"*Anyway*, so we start driving through Bithlo, and she's asking me all about my life and who I am and stuff—so I told her I was visiting my aunt in Bithlo for the week and that I was from Ocala and that I grew up on an alligator farm and I just couldn't stop bullshitting her—it was so fun! Then she's all like, 'Who's your aunt?' and then I start freaking out because Bithlo isn't exactly a big town so she must know almost everyone, so I just blurt out, 'LuAnn!' because I figure it sounds safe, and she was like, 'Oh, yeah, I know LuAnn.'

"So then she starts telling me all about *her* life and about her beautiful daughter, and just as I think I'm gonna get something outta her, she drives into the Lil Champ parking lot and tells me to wait in the car. Okay, I have to admit, I was all set to jump out and hide in the woods until you or the car service could come pick me up, but I just couldn't, because I was *totally* intrigued. And she seemed harmless enough so far—almost a little nice— and I figured I could handle myself. *Plus*, I had that spray bottle of Mace in my pocket, so there was always that—"

"Wait, *Mace*? How the hell'd you get Mace?"

"From the penthouse, *duh*. Like I was gonna let you stalk Bridget without a little protection."

I was rendered speechless for the moment. I smiled big and said, "My little bodyguard man. You're a sweetie."

"Okay, there's so much more, are you ready?"

"Sure."

"So then Jade comes back with a twelve-pack of Natty Light and a bag of pork rinds and she's all like, 'Let's party, Jed,' and off we drive to this big dirt parking lot that's, like, *filled* with cars, and there's this big set of bleachers at the end of it. People are all hangin' out and stuff, drinking beer and bourbon and grilling hot dogs and hamburgers and blasting country music, and I'm seriously like, *Okay, what the fuck?* But there're so many people there that I don't wanna be asking Jade about it, because then it'll probably blow my cover, since I've been staying with my aunt for a week, and this is clearly some big event that I should know about.

"So we hop out of the truck, and Jade pops down the . . . the back flap of the pickup truck. . . . I don't even know what it's called. Oh my *God*, I can't believe I've kept up this Jed facade for so long! Anyway, so she pops down that thingamajig and then sits in the bed of the pickup truck, and lets her legs dangle off the back. So I do the same, and we drink our way through the twelve-pack—"

"*Lucas*, how much did you drink?"

"Easy, Diaz, you know my tolerance level."

"Yeah, well, *lately*—"

"Okay, I need less of this, and more of *this*. . . ."

I paused and thought for a second, and then asked Lucas, "Were you just making little talky gestures with your fingers?"

"Yeah."

"Well, I can't see you doing that, you know. You *are* drunk!"

"Okay, lemme finish. You'll be glad you did. Now, *shuh*!"

I didn't respond to show him that I understood.

"Good. Well, to answer your question, yes, I am a little drunk. But I only had three beers, and they're Natty *Light*, so it's like water anyway, all right? She pretty much guzzled her way through the rest of 'em on her own. Anyway, we're talking and talking, and passing the bag of pork rinds back and forth, and I learn a couple of juicy little nuggets: First of all, Bridget and her dad left Jade when Bridget was just four. They'd all been living in Sanford since she and Bridget's dad met and married, and to supplement their income—since Bridget's dad was barely making enough for them to get by at that point—Jade started selling drugs."

"Shit," I said.

"Yeah. Totally. Anyway, so now she starts getting all depressed and says, 'All right, baby. Let's go crash some school buses.' Which totally threw me, because . . . well, *crash some school buses?* Come on! Then I realize, once we climb onto these rickety old wooden bleachers, that that's what the main event is. We were at a freaking school-bus-racing track! So, yeah. It's this huge figure-eight racetrack, where all these crazy people drive a bunch of souped-up school buses on the loopy track, trying not to hit each other. Or maybe *trying* to hit each other, I dunno. But it's *so much fun!* It's like going to a hockey game, a boxing match, a NASCAR race, and a demolition derby all rolled into one. 'Cause people would go *nuts* when one of the buses would flip over, or when one of the buses would run another off the track, almost into the bleachers. There was this one in particular that was painted like a snarling alligator that was *really* aggressive. He ended up winning, 'cause he was basically the last one standing. It was fucking *awesome!* I'd been cheering for that one all along. . . ."

I was laughing my ass off at this point, trying not to lose control of the car.

"Anyway, the crowd was really riled up then, and they were screaming their *heads* off, and then a bunch of trucks with boats attached to them pulled out into the racetrack, and people started hollerin' even *more*, but I figured it was time for me to get going. . . . But *not* before I figured out why Bridget was visiting Jade in the first place. . . ."

"Tell!" I screamed.

"Okay, so this is kind of the sad and depressing part of the evening. . . ."

"You mean the drug-dealing wasn't the sad part?"

"No. Well, that's kind of subjective. But *I* think this is the worst part of it all. Basically, Jade started selling drugs to support the family. And then Jade started *doing* the drugs she was dealing. Crack, mostly. Now, she was a little shady on the details, but right when that happened, things started getting bad, and Bridget's dad filed for divorce and moved him and Bridget out of the house."

"Jesus!"

"So now Jade gets alimony, and is only allowed to see her daughter in the privacy of her own home, once a month—when Bridget delivers the money. And when I asked her why all the importance of it being at her trailer, she got all quiet. So I'm guessing the alimony's part hush-money, because she wasn't going into too much more detail. Maybe if I got her some more Natty Light . . ."

End Interlude—

"So she's good and drunk?" I asked him.

"Yeah, I left her back at our seats—told her I had to hit the head."

"Cut it out with the straight-guy talk, Lucas, you're hurting my ears!"

"Sorry."

"Look, I think we can use this whole Jade thing to our advantage—and to Vanessa's. So you've got to do me another favor."

"Oh, God."

"Bring Jade to the Bensons' party."

"Are *you* on crack?!"

"Nope. There's no two ways about it."

"What?!" Lucas cried. "Of *course* there's two ways about it. There's . . . *your* way, and then there's the *sane* way!"

"C'mon, Lucas, we're so close!" I begged.

"So close? Forty minutes from the Bensons' party is hardly close. And Jade's too tanked to drive, anyway. That's the other reason I called—you gotta come pick me up."

"I'm on my way, I told you. But we gotta seal the deal!"

"No way, Madge," he said sternly. "I'm sorry. I *get* it—how you have to get Bridget back for all the bad shit she's done to you. But don't you think she's had it rough enough *already*?"

"Well . . ." I thought about it a second: Bridget's dad skipped out on Jade as soon as things started going bad—*fourteen years ago*! Since then, he'd become a wildly successful attorney with a *knockout* of a trophy wife (who *didn't* smoke crack and who, now that I thought of it, looked almost *nothing* like Bridget), and Bridget was poised to become one of the biggest future has-been twentysomething stars of my generation. I'd venture to say that the girl's life had been pretty okay.

So *had* she had it that bad? I wondered.

"Um . . . no?" I said unsurely.

Now, I know that I'd put myself through the wringer for the last few weeks, and that I had enough caffeine in my system to give a Thoroughbred the twitches—and enough age-old ill will in my heart to start up my own Middle East—but I was being *totally* reasonable!

Wasn't I?

"Madge!" Lucas yelled. "*Listen* to yourself. Since when have you been this petty? And *mean*?! So what if Bridget wins? So what if she's a disrespectful bitch? Are you not already throwing the coolest anti-prom party *ever*?! Should it even matter to you?" He paused, sighing. "I'm sorry, but if you do this, you're gonna come off way worse than she is. Trust me, please? Madge? Is there really any reason to destroy her?"

When I didn't answer immediately, he continued on: "Look, you fucking dragged me out on this . . . this *mission* of yours, *totally* against my will, my life was put in danger, and now I've found out all this horrible stuff about Bridget's past, and now you want to use it against her?"

"Lucas! *Trust* me, okay?" I said frantically, my eyes filling with tears. "You don't even know the *half* of it! If you did, you'd understand. . . ."

"Would I? Well, why don't you fill me in, psycho, because I'd really love to know the reason my best friend has been such a freakish, crazy *bitch* lately!"

"Fine!" I screamed. "I'll tell you everything!" And so I did. I said "suck it" to my pride and told Lucas all about my and Bridget's pained and tainted past—the friendship, the audition gone wrong, the unreturned calls, even the stuffed-animal octopus I'd worked so hard on. "So," I finally asked, "don't you see why I *have to* do this?" Though for the first time in forever, I was starting to wonder if I was just full of shit. I mean, did I really need to be doing this? What *had* happened to me these last few weeks?

"No," he said simply. "Look, I'm glad you finally told me all about your Bridget issues, but sorry—that was ten years ago. And I had no *idea* you could be so small. And how could you believe you'd let me think—let *yourself* think—that any of this was for Vanessa in the first place? It's all for *you*! All of this! I mean, what the—?"

Lucas's voice got momentarily cut off by another incoming call. From Mitsy. Thank *God*, thank God!

"Lucas, hold on, your mom's calling me," I said, glad to have a brief reprieve to collect myself. I took a deep breath and clicked over. "Hello?"

"Madgie! How's the hunt going?"

"Um . . . fine," I said. "Yeah, fine. Fine, fine. What's up?"

"Where was Bridget going in such a huff?"

"I'll fill you in later, Mitsy—what's going on?"

"Nothing. I just thought I'd tell you I snuck into Bridget's room a little while ago, just to do a little poking around."

"You find anything?" I asked.

"No, nothing really. Just your typical girly-girl room. Except for that *hideous* stuffed octopus on her bed."

"Now hold on, that octopus is *not* hideou—"

Oh my God.

I was officially a monster.

A self-deluded, moronic monster.

"Mitsy, is the octopus purple?" I asked, my voice breaking a little.

"I believe it was, yes. How did you—?"

"I can't believe she kept it," I mumbled to myself.

"What was that?"

"Nothing, Mitsy—I have to run, but thanks for everything." I clicked back over to Lucas. "I've made a huge mistake," I said.

"*I'll* say you have!" he yelled back without missing a beat. "Now shut up and get your bitch-ass *over* here!"

18

Deep Thoughts

....

Remember what I'd said about getting into a fight with your best friend once a year?

Yeah!

That sounded lovely.

But getting in *another* fight just weeks later? Not as fun.

I felt like total crap. As I raced down Colonial Drive, I was realizing, for the first time, the full extent to which I'd psychoed out on my best friend in the world. I'd tried to "break him up" with his newest friend—and I'm sorry, even if I *hated* Kenny as much as I did (and with good reason, as it turned out), I had no reason to do that. Not only that, but I'd dragged him along on all my misadventures. Making Lucas do manual labor at a *lake*? Thrusting a class schedule at him and expecting him to follow Bridget around school? Kidnapping him for a late-night stalker mission in the outer boondocks of East Orlando? Do I not know him at all?! Sure, he'd said yes to some, but was it fair that I expected him to do it all?

And *speaking* of best friends . . .

I'd apparently misjudged my situation with Bridget from the very start. I was obviously missing something in the time line, because why else would she still have her seventh-birthday present from me? If she'd hated me as much as I'd always assumed, wouldn't all eight of its arms been amputated by now?

That was something I'd have to find out. . . .

Wrapping my mind around all these realizations, I pulled into the parking lot where Lucas was waiting. He was right—there were *tons* of cars here. It was like a big ol' block party, and I caught a whiff of grilling hot dogs. Slightly burnt. Just the way I liked them.

Focus.

I spotted Lucas and quickly pulled into a spot. But just as I was getting out, I was stopped by a hard pat on my shoulder.

"*Maaaaar*-garita!"

Redneck Randy.

"Oh!" I said, turning to jelly as I twirled around to greet him. Oh, *shit*, he looked good. Yellow-striped off-brand polo shirt, big baggy camo cargo shorts, a NASCAR hat tilted *just-so* to the side on top of his big mop of sandy curls. "Fancy meeting you here," I managed.

"What're you doin' here?"

"Just . . . picking up a friend," I said. "He lost his ride."

Lucas, in the distance, had spotted me, but wasn't coming over. In fact, he turned around and headed back toward the stands!

"Oh. Well, I won't keep you, darlin'," Randy said, starting to walk off slowly.

I felt a buzz go off in my sweatpants. It was a text from Lucas: PROMISE TO STOP BEIN A PSYCHO, AND I'LL GIVE YOU 20 MIN. WITH RANDY.

"Hold on!" I called to Randy.

He stopped in his tracks and looked at me expectantly, shooting me a killer head tilt/half smile. "What's it gonna be?" he asked easily.

I stood there in stunned silence for a few seconds, then sighed contentedly and said, "I've . . . I've got some time."

As luck would have it, Randy was the one who was cookin' up those slightly charred hot dogs. ("I can't believe you like them like this, too!" I'd said giddily.) He was taking a break from the festivities to indulge in a late-night snack, before heading back in for the main event—which was God knows what!

"You're not gettin' any ideas for next year's big bash, are you?" I asked him. "I'm not hooking my skis up to the back of some school bus."

He laughed. "No, but now that you mention it, I *should* be takin' notes!" He paused for a moment, taking a swig from his beer. "Damn. I can't believe our senior year's almost over."

"I know. It's crazy."

"Prom's soon, too," he said, nudging me.

"Mm-hmm . . ." I managed.

"Hey, I got a question for you."

"Yeah?"

Oh my God. Was Randy gonna ask me to prom?

What would I say?

What would I *do*?

Was there time for him to get a vest to match my dress?

What dress would I wear? The homemade one, or the epic drag-queen-from-space getup Vanessa was putting the finishing touches on?

Which *prom* would we—?

"What've you got up your sleeve?" is what he ended up asking.

"I . . . Wait, what do you mean?" I asked back.

"What's this big announcement you're makin' on your Web site? I saw that debate video on there yesterday. Wasn't much of a debate, though. . . ."

"Oh." I laughed nervously. "Well, you'll just have to wait and see."

"Aw, c'mon now," he said, putting his arm around me and pulling me close. (I smelled Old Spice and cigarette smoke—who *knew* it could be such a sexy combo!)

"Well, what do you *think* it is?" I asked coyly, pushing him off me flirtatiously.

"Shoot, *I* don't know," he said. "But you promised it was gonna *destroy my world*, so it better be good."

"Oh, it'll be good," I said, hoping my uncertainty wasn't too obvious.

He nodded, taking another swig from his drink. "You mind if I say somethin', though? And I mean it with the utmost of Southern-gentleman respect."

"As long as you call me 'ma'am.'"

He chuckled. "All right, ma'am. Well . . . the thing is, you didn't . . . seem like yourself on that video."

"No?"

"No way. The Margarita *I* know in't that . . . I dunno, *crazy*. What was it that Bridget had done to you? I confess, I didn't even read that blog entry you were talkin' about."

"I heard she deleted it right after the debate anyway," I said quietly. "You know what she did to me?" I said, feeling the anger rising in me. Octopus or *no* octopus, she'd still disrespected the only father I'd ever have. "I'll *tell* you what she did to me. . . ."

But then I couldn't. I didn't want to. In light of the recent developments, it didn't seem as important, and I just felt like a huge dumb-ass. Plus, I really didn't feel like messing up this moment—lounging in the back of Randy's pickup, staring up at the stars, the thunderous cacophony of cheers and engines revving in the background.

"Never mind," I finally said.

"Well, I just wanted to know, 'cause I didn't like seein' you like that. Like I said, it's not the *you* that I'm used to."

"What's the me that you're used to?" I asked, starting to feel a little bit rotten.

"Aw, you're gonna play that game with me?"

"Yes!" I said dramatically. "Tell me *everything* you like about me! *Please!*"

"There you go!" he said, putting his arm around me again. "That's what I like about you. You're funny, Margarita. And you don't let shit get to you. You're always there with a joke or some funny-ass response—or at the very least . . . a really interesting outfit that you *always* look sexy in."

I laughed, taking the plunge and putting my head on his big, broad shoulder. He didn't push me off. "You know, Randy," I said, "sometimes I *do* let shit get to me. I'm not always so strong."

"I'm sure you do," he said. "Like yesterday at that debate thing. You let shit get to you then. . . ."

"I really did," I said softly.

"Well, I wish you wouldn't. I like you better the other way."

"Yeah. Me, too."

I mean, really—what the hell was *wrong* with me? There was a *reason* I was such a happy person before this whole debacle. I was living my life—how I wanted to live it, and who I wanted to live it with. I didn't let unimportant crap get in the way of my happiness, and I had this amazing group of people in my life to keep me sustained. Even now, after my dad's heart attack, I had an even *stronger* support system. (Can anyone say "blessing in disguise"?) But somehow, with one thing leading to another, I'd lost sight of all that. I'd let my emotions—and my temper—run away with me, and I'd become a total monster.

The whole thing had just gotten way out of hand. I'd completely forgotten what my dad had said to me in the hospital that day: *If you're throwing this party, throw it for the right reasons.* He'd been so proud of me, for giving something amazing to the people who didn't *want* to go to the prom. Something they could feel comfortable and happy at, and be away from all the stupid prom-queen bullshit.

Realizing all these things I'd been so studiously—*crazily*—avoiding, I wondered if there had ever been a truly good reason to beat Bridget for prom queen. I'd had what I needed all along, so why did I even accept her stupid challenge? Clearly—and I wasn't proud of this—saying it was for Vanessa was a total lie to everyone, including myself.

I looked up to see Lucas, Jade-less, heading slowly toward us.

"Hey," Randy said, shifting his body to sit more upright and turning to face me. "You better call that friend of yours—we've been talkin' long enough."

"Yeah," I said, sitting up and stretching. "And hey, thanks."

"For what?"

"You know . . . for whatever."

"Very specific, Margarita." He smiled. "Hey, I forgot to ask you somethin'."

"What?"

"If you haven't already got your own, you wanna be my date for the prom?"

I guess I could've answered his question with a question: *Which prom?* But he didn't know about anti-prom. No one did but me and Lucas. That was the "trick up my sleeve."

But instead—in the interest of keeping the moment as wonderful as it could possibly be—I said, "Yes," and told myself I'd figure out all that other shit later.

19

How It All Shook Out

So you're probably wondering a few things.

Don't worry—that's what your benevolent narrator is here for.

For example, which prom did Randy and I go to?

And we'll get to that, after I get through the Bridget stuff.

So, despite her obvious flaws, I decided that Bridget—after all she'd been through—did deserve a bit of sympathy. And that's what I gave her. At least, that's what I *planned* on giving her at first. It ended up becoming a little more eye-opening and intense than that, though.

So that night, after Randy and I kissed good-bye (*yeah*, baby!), I gave my best friend a much-deserved and hugely self-deprecating apology and drove the two of us to the Bensons'. Lucas waited in the car while I walked up to the house. I was greeted by Bridget's mother (*step*mother, I now knew), a heavily Botoxed walking advertisement for tastelessly done plastic surgery. Ironically, she looked at *me* like I was deformed. I told her that Bridget and I were lab partners and that I needed to drop off some notes with her. She quickly led me straight to her room, and returned to her guests without even knocking on Bridget's door to announce me.

I knocked myself.

"Who is it?" I heard Bridget's strained voice ask.

"It's, uh . . . it's Madge Diaz."

"Diaz?" she said, surprised. "What the fuck're—? Get outta here!"

"Bridget," I said, taking a deep breath. "I . . . I wanna talk. About Jade?"

I heard Bridget bustling around behind the door, and soon she and I were face-to-face. I'd never seen her looking so imperfect. Her hair was all over the place, her eyes were red and glassy, and her face was lined with dried tear-trails.

"Get in here," she said simply.

I obeyed, regarding the sheer *normalness* of her room. (Mitsy had been right.) This wasn't the lair of my nemesis ice queen that I'd always pictured. Actually, I don't know *what* I'd always pictured—a "burn book"? a wall mural of herself? a heavily beaten-up voodoo doll of yours truly?—but it certainly wasn't anything as sterile and run-of-the-mill as a queen-sized bed, wall-mounted flat-screen TV, and a few framed posters of her various movies and TV shows.

"What do you know?" she asked, eyes wide.

"Everything," I told her. "Don't worry—I'm not going to tell anyone."

She looked absolutely terrified. Panicked. "How do you—?"

"Just calm down, and I'll explain." I told her the story of our scary-ass evening. Bridget went from angry to shocked, even as far as *human* (a side I'd hardly seen in the past decade), as I described in vivid detail the stakeout, the stalking, Jade's impromptu date with Lucas . . . everything.

"My mom went on a date with your gay boyfriend?" she asked, awestruck. "When will the wonders cease?" She cracked a meek smile now, sighing heavily.

"Bridget," I said. "I'm . . . I can't believe I'm saying this to you, but . . . I'm sorry. I'm really, *really* sorry . . . about everything you have to . . . deal with."

"It's not even just about my mom, Diaz," she said quietly. "It's my stepmom. I mean, she pretends to the whole world that she's my biological mother, Dad's perfect trophy wife. She throws the best parties, has the biggest house, and raised the perfect daughter. And you *know* what the perfect daughter has to be. . . ."

"Prom queen?" I ventured.

"You got it."

"I thought it was for the sororities."

"Well, that, too—but whose idea do you think it was at first?"

"Right. So why the challenge, then?" I asked. "You gotta admit, before you threw *me* into the mix, you pretty much had it in the bag."

"Maybe it was all the cosmos," she said.

"Or mixing them with beer," I suggested, which made her smile again.

Yeah. This was weird. I hadn't made Bridget smile in a non-evil way since we were kids.

"Bridget . . . do you really hate me?"

"I don't know," she said. "I think maybe I just hate that you seem to have it all, but you don't have to work for it. It just gets to me."

"You know, I might not have to work so hard for people to like me, but it *is* a little hard to correct people's misconceptions. It's not like my life has been a cakewalk from the beginning."

"I guess." She took a deep breath and released it, and ran her hands through her hair.

"Bridget?" I said quietly. "If you kept Octavian the Octopus . . . why did you dump *me*?"

"What do you mean?" she asked, quickly turning around and self-consciously regarding the stuffed animal in question.

"I *mean* that after that . . . audition—the one where you got the part and I didn't?—you never called me. I was hurt—*really* hurt—but I called and called, and never heard back from you."

"Whoa, whoa, whoa," Bridget said, holding up her hands. "You *never* called me."

"Um, yes, I did," I said. "I called you for weeks—*months*—but I could never get a hold of you."

"But my mom and dad never told me. I wanted to call you

after I got that part *so bad*, but they said your feelings were gonna be hurt, and that I needed to wait for you to call *me*. I was *eight*, so I listened to them."

"So you're saying your parents never told you about all the times I called you?"

"Not once." She thought about it for a second, then said angrily (we're talking *scary* angrily), "Those mother*fuckers*! Why would they do that?"

"Beats me," I said. "Maybe I just wasn't good enough for your family."

"What's *that* supposed to mean?" she asked, the edge back in her voice.

"Oh, c'mon, Bridget—your superrich parents all of a sudden have an excuse to keep us apart, and they're not gonna use it?"

"Please. We weren't rich back then. Maybe they just didn't like you."

"Maybe it was 'cause I'm Puerto Rican trash," I said half seriously.

Bridget looked humiliated. "I'm sorry I called you that," she said. "I wouldn't put it past my parents to think that. But for the record, *I* don't."

"It's okay," I said. Then, thinking back to the infamous audition, I asked, "Wait, so your family didn't have money when you took that part from me?"

"Took that part from you?" Bridget asked, raising an eyebrow. "Um, *no*. We didn't have as much money, and I did *not* take that part from you. I auditioned fair and square, and I got it. It had *nothing* to do with any pull my parents might've had."

"Sorry," I said, reminding myself that my judgment had been off by a good mile for the last few weeks (and apparently the past few *years*, too). "I guess I always needed the justification. I was way hurt when you got it."

"If it makes you feel any better, I think they just cast me instead of you because I looked more like the dad. My hair was a lot lighter back then, remember? And the dad they cast was practically a Swedish albino."

"I'm officially the world's biggest idiot," I confessed sadly.

"Listen, don't worry about it," Bridget said, actually putting her hand on my arm. "Look, I want you to know how sorry I am for all the shit I've said and done to you. I didn't mean the things I said, and I shouldn't have let things get so ugly—I guess I just sorta lost it. This's been a really stressful time for me."

"*Ay*, please. We *both* thought we hated each other, and it was just one big fuckup. It's forgotten." And it was. At least I wanted it to be. I was sick and tired of feeling so much hatred; it was such a waste of time. "But, hey—who'd you hire to follow me to Gainesville that night?"

"Hire?" she laughed. "Please, and pass up a chance to get out of *this house* for the weekend?"

"*Seriously?*"

"Yeah. I borrowed some of my . . ."—she lowered her voice—"*step*mom's slutty clothes and went as a guy in drag."

"No *way!*"

"Don't underestimate me, Diaz—you're not the only one who can stalk people undercover."

"Hey," I told her, "speaking of the stalking—*your* secret's safe with me. It's shitty enough that you have to hide who your real mother is without me making things even worse. . . . But do you mind if I ask you something?"

"'Kay."

"Why keep her a secret? I mean, Lucas said you guys left her when you were really little."

"What, and butcher my dad's precious career? Please," she huffed, looking down at the ground. Then she looked up and asked me suddenly, her eyes sad and pleading, "Do you think that I'm just hardwired to be an awful person?"

"Wait, what do you mean?"

"I mean, my dad abandoned my mom when she needed him most, and he wouldn't even help her get better. And *she's* a drug-dealing *crack* addict. Do you think I'm just fucked?" A few stray tears ran down her cheeks. "I mean, I was *awful* to you, and to your dad—and it just came so naturally. I didn't even have to *think* about it."

Damn. I could talk shit about my parents all I wanted, but at least they had never warped me *this* bad.

"Bridget," I said. "I think you can be whoever you want to be. We're not programmed to be who our parents are."

"Actually, I've been saving some of my money, a little at a time, so Dad won't notice. . . . Jade makes me crazy, and I want to cry every time I see her, but she is my mom, and I care about her." She sniffled, her eyes welling up a little, but she kept it together. "And once I have enough money, I'm thinking I'll send her to rehab . . . the *best* facility . . . if she'll go."

"*God,* you're stupid."

"Fuck you!" she cried shrilly.

"No!" I said, putting my hands on her shoulders. "You're stupid to even *think* that you're a bad person if you're doing something so loving."

Now she really started to cry, and when I reached for her to hug it out, it felt just like old times. . . .

Needless to say, after this tear-jerking experience, there was no way I was gonna try to empty out prom before prom queen was announced.

So after leaving the Bensons' and driving myself and Lucas—and Mitsy, who was eager to hear all the latest details—back to the penthouse, I had Lucas log me onto my campaign page, where I typed out the following announcement:

Hey, everybody. I know I told you all I had a major announcement re: Bridget Benson being ill-qualified to be your prom queen. Well, I'm changing my tune a little bit. After some soul-searching and girl talk and a duel-to-the-death pillow fight, BB and I have decided that this whole fighting-for-PQ thing is BS. We're tired of it. We let ourselves get carried

away, and really, you all should just vote for who you want to win. We'd
be honored if you voted for us, but we're done whoring ourselves out for
you people! Ha! But seriously, y'all. We're sorry we acted like such bitches
(even though it was fun at times for us, as we're sure it was for you). This
year will definitely go down in the WPHS history books.

I went on to give details of the anti-prom party, for those who
wanted to attend. It would begin at the penthouses directly after
the prom-queen vote. Dress code was strict: no open-toed foot-
wear or T-shirts for boys, and no midriffs for the ladies. (Hey,
even anti-prom-goers should have standards!) Those who wanted
to skip prom altogether could party at the anti-prom, but only
after half of the "real" prom was over. I thought that was a nice
compromise.

Plus, it gave my mom the prom pictures she always wanted.

I have to hand it to my mom and grandma—bitches knew
how to make a *dress*! Vanessa had obviously inherited her vast
store of clothing knowledge from somewhere. Me, I just knew
how to *wear* anything. Creating shit was a whole other matter.

So there we all were, posing in front of the azalea bushes in my
front yard, me in my sumptuous lavender gown, which hugged
me in all the right places—and hid me where appropriate, too—
and Randy? Mmm. I always say, *any* man looks good in a tux.
But a man who looks good in jeans and a T-shirt . . . looks *smol-*
deringly sexy in a tux. I was having some major James-Bond-ala-
Daniel-Craig fantasies running through my dirty little mind.

Lucas was there, too (looking very handsome in his tux, as well). No Kenny, though. On our way to Bridget's after leaving Bithlo that night, Lucas had called him to see what was up. There was no mention of what we'd seen, so as not to give Bridget's secret away. All Lucasito could make out on the other end of the line was a cracked-out-sounding Kenny and some very giggly gay boys. I didn't want to think the worst, but Lucas did. He prom-dumped him via text message two minutes after hanging up on his sorry ass.

(Incidentally, Kenny didn't make it to prom again this year. And surprise, surprise—nobody knows why.)

Considering the heavy doses of drama we'd all been through these last few weeks, Lucas had decided he wanted a break from boys for a while. He said the thought of calling and making up with Zach exhausted him to no end, and that he'd deal with it all after graduation.

Please.

Lucas on a boy break?

What's a nosy, all-knowing faghag to do . . . but call Zach herself?

Zach *had* been serious about coming out and facing what would come. He'd been going to the Orlando Youth Alliance, this gay youth group that helped him decide what was best for him to do. With their guidance—and impeccable taste—he'd decided it was time to win Lucas back . . . by showing up at my house, just in time for pictures, wearing a rose-colored prom dress that brought out the color in his rosy cheeks *just so*.

Lucas was floored.

"Zach," he said, looking his ex-boyfriend up and down, taking in the sight of the styled black wig and white stilettos, "you make a fucking *hot* woman."

"I did it for you," he told him. "I wanted you to *know* that I was serious about coming out. It's time."

I swear, I hadn't seen Lucas that happy since the Spice Girls announced their reunion tour. He wrapped Zach in his arms, and was just about to go in for a kiss when he said, "Zach, I love you—but *not* as a woman." Then he leaned in closer, so that none of the camera-toting parents could hear, and whispered, "Plus, I wanna do prom-night stuff with you later, so I'm lending you my suit for tonight." (How nice to be in a gay relationship with someone who wears your size!)

The dance was at Hard Rock Live, this concert venue at Universal CityWalk that was constructed to look like the Roman Colosseum. Bright orange and white beams of light (our school colors) shone out to space from the top of the building, and the steps leading up to the entrance were covered with a red carpet. The floor space, which probably holds close to two thousand people for concerts, was divided up into areas for tables and chairs, a food and drink area, and a big dance floor. The DJ spun your typical radio-friendly prom fare.

It actually turned out to be a really fun night. I was glad I got to experience *senior* prom, in the so-called proper way. I had my punch, I slow-danced with my man . . . I even snuck a flask in, to complete the prom experience. But I mostly just shared that with the boys—Gainesville had ruined alcohol for me . . . for at least another couple of weeks. (Come on, let's be realistic!)

At ten o'clock—kind of early in the night, but I'd asked a certain someone in student government to make it that way—the prom-queen results were announced.

And I guess Bridget and I weren't the only ones who were tired of our prom-queen antics. Apparently, most of the school was, too, because guess who won?

Environmental Club President, and future savior-of-the-world, Annabelle Turner. I couldn't think of a better choice.

Before heading to the penthouses, I had to make a quick stop at Vanessa's.

It was time to get into my anti-prom dress.

(Yeah, yeah, I know I could've just stored it at Lucas's or Laura's, but a girl needs to make an entrance!)

Okay.

Think tacky metallic turquoise bridesmaid's dress, cut super-low in the front (for maximum death-by-cleavage) and on a forty-five-degree angle on the bottom, the shortest point being midway up my outside right thigh. Throw in some calf-length silver tights, clear stiletto heels (purchased at the Gainesville porn store, of all places!), a couple pairs of extra-long fake eyelashes, glittery triangular mega-earrings, and enough silver eye shadow to give the Tin Man a new paint job, and you have what

I call the Martian Streetwalker. The *perfect* look for an anti-prom penthouse party.

Oh, and for good measure—and since a bunch of people already saw me with my hair all did-up at Hard Rock Live—a blue beehive wig. Why the hell not, right?

I don't think Randy knew what he was getting himself into with me.

We had our limo drop us in front of the condo. Immense potted palm trees flanked the automatic doors at the entrance, and Mitsy had even arranged for a red carpet to be laid down all the way to the elevator bank.

I saw Carl, my #1 Main Man Doorman, and gave him his usual shake-o'-the-booty greeting.

He tried to remain dignified but looked like he was about to bust out laughing (in a good way). "Why, Miss Diaz, you look quite . . . metallic this evening."

"Don't I *know* it, sweetie!" I replied.

Carl leaned slightly to the side, looking behind me and Randy. "Ah, Mr. Ellison," he said to Lucas, "coming home for the evening, as well?"

"Yep." He was grinning ear to ear, arm in arm with Zach, who despite his total hotness as a woman was looking infinitely better in Lucas's good suit. "And you remember Zach, right?" he asked Carl.

"Of course—how are you, sir?"

"Great!" Zach said.

"Um, Carl," Lucas continued, "he's not banned from the building anymore, just so you know." He looked at Zach, whose mouth was agape.

"You *banned* me?" Zach asked incredulously.

"Hey, what'd you expect me to do?!" Lucas laughed.

"Can we go up, please?" I begged, starting for the elevators without waiting for a response. "Later, Carl!"

As the four of us rode the elevator up to the penthouse floor, Randy asked me, "So what can I expect at an anti-prom?"

"You know, the typical . . . *un*spiked punch, people *not* in tuxes, good music, ritualistic slaughtering of a virgin . . ."

"So it's okay I left my skis at home?"

Lucas and I laughed. "Yeah, I don't think Mitsy throws those kinds of parties." Actually, I didn't really know *what* kind of parties Mitsy threw. I mean, she was a woman of utmost class and taste, but had I ever truly seen her party-planning potential played out in full effect?

Even if I had, I don't think it could've prepared me for this.

The elevator doors opened to reveal the entire penthouse level lit up only by strings upon strings of white icicle lights. The door to Lucas's condo was propped open and flanked by two topiary bushes sculpted into heart shapes. One thing that did look out of place was the six-foot-seven bouncer-type guarding the door.

"Dears!" I heard. I turned to see Mitsy coming down the hall-way from Laura's side of the building, her arms in the air in anticipation of the big hug I was set to give her. After gushing over my outfit, she asked me, "What do you think?!"

"It's *incredible*!" I said, hugging her tight. Then I whispered, "What's with the bouncer guy?"

"Madge, I love *you* . . . but do you expect me to trust all these whippersnappers?" She raised an eyebrow, then continued, "And I have Carl on the lookout downstairs. I don't want anyone walking out with anything."

"Cool with me! We're goin' in."

"Be my guest, as always."

I led my posse into the condo's main continuous room, which had been cleared of most of its furniture. On a marble table set in the middle of the foyer stood a gigantic vase, carved out of a block of ice, holding around three dozen red and white roses. On a direct axis with this vase, deeper into the condo, right in the middle of the cleared-out living room, stood a round table, which held a chocolate fountain surrounded by mounds of strawberries, pineapples, and bready cakes.

I went straight for a chocolate-covered strawberry (Mitsy had gotten dark chocolate—it was my lucky, heavenly day!), then took in the rest of the scene around me. It'd taken some time for me to get dressed at Vanessa's (plus she lives out in BFE), so by now, the room was wall-to-wall people. Well, *floor-to-ceiling-window* to *floor-to-ceiling-window* people.

The couches had been pushed to the far corner of the room, to face out over the city, and everyone was hanging out and mingling around, ambient techno music pulsing in the background. The kitchen counter was overflowing with sodas, juices, and catered snacks—oh my God, crab cakes!—and everyone looked to be having a really good time. Within seconds, Lucas and I were swarmed with grateful guests wanting to tell us how amazing the party was.

"There seems to be something missing, though," Lucas said to me, after we'd schmoozed a bit. "Where's the dancing?"

"If you want dancing, you should go to Laura's down the hall," Mitsy said, appearing out of nowhere, sipping from her signature martini glass. "I don't want you kiddies scuffing up the floors."

With that, we led our dates back out into the hallway. I could hear the music *blasting* from the other side of the building before we even got there. How had we missed that before? My question was answered upon entrance—it hadn't been loud before, because it hadn't gotten *going* yet. Because the scene I walked into was almost otherworldly.

Where Mitsy's side of the anti-prom was all class, Laura's side was all party. Some totally fierce Kylie remix was blasting through her sound system—which I'm assuming was the absolute best *lotsa* money can buy—and with all the people dancing enthusiastically to the beat, the room looked like it was practically *moving*. Laura's view over the city was just as breathtaking as Mitsy's, and the heat lightning bouncing from cloud to cloud in the distance over Disney only added to the surreal effect of the strobes on the dance floor.

I spotted Laura dancing in a far corner, pouring champagne

into Jonathan's mouth, and was just about to go over to say thank you when Randy tugged on my arm.

"Yeah?" I asked.

He gestured at the other corner of the room, where Bridget— *Bridget?!*—was standing, all alone and looking a little dejected.

"Maybe you oughta go over and say hi," he suggested.

"Yeah. Yeah, okay," I said, and excused myself from my boys for a minute.

"Hey, loser," I said jokingly, walking up to Bridget.

"Hey, loser, yourself," she replied, doing a double take at my outfit. "Oh my God. That's . . . kind of brilliant. You think your sister could do something like that for me, only toned *down* a little?"

"Vanessa can do anything," I said proudly.

"Good. You'll have to hook us up later."

"Um, all right." I smiled. "Cool." (I'd already asked Steve and Lance to document the evening for their Wednesday morning show, hoping it might eventually turn into something else for my sister, but this would work out just fine, too!)

"So . . ." I said, "are you okay? I didn't expect to see you here."

"Why? Did you think 'cause Annabelle won prom queen that I'd just go home and shoot myself or something?"

"No, I just figured you'd have an after-party of your own to go to," I replied. "I heard your boy and a bunch of your other friends rented out a villa by Universal."

"Well, yeah," she said. "But that doesn't mean I couldn't stop here first."

"Okay . . . so . . . why're you standing all by yourself over here?"

She let out a little huff of breath. "I just didn't want everyone to think the only reason I went to all their shit these last few weeks was to get their votes. . . . 'Cause it wasn't."

"No?"

"No. So I'm here."

"Okay, then," I said. "Well, lesson one: Don't look so above it all. Get out of this corner and come dance with me."

"I . . . I actually can't really dance."

"No? Well . . . let's make that lesson two." I smiled and put my arm around her, leading her into the madness. "Think of the headlines in *Teen People*: 'Martian Hooker Madge Diaz Teaches Teen Starlet Bridget Benson to Boogie.'"

"I'll get my PR people on it right away." And we started to dance. Her moves weren't that bad, actually, for a white girl with no ass to jiggle (and even less rhythm to jiggle with). She had a bit of the trainwreck-Britney-at-the-VMAs look going on, her brow furrowed as she tried to keep track of the beat. But she'd be all right.

"There're my two daredevils," I heard a sexy, rugged voice say behind me. I turned around to face Randy, who'd come up behind me. After shooting a knee-buckling smile at Bridget—okay, I was *still* a little peeved that she won that ski contest—Randy craned his neck down, and I felt a little prickle of stubble as he kissed me on the neck.

Girl, let me tell you about *goose bumps*!

"Hey, *ladies* . . . and gentleman," Lucas said, joining our little dance area and riding up on Bridget. A minute later, he whispered something in Bridget's ear that made her smile. When he was done, Bridget stopped dancing to turn around and hug him. Hard. It must've been good for her to hear nice things about her mother, for probably the first time in a long while. You gotta love that Lucas Ellison. The boy was golden.

As was his little Zachary, who appeared now with a bottle of champagne, which we passed around from person to person.

"Hey," I said, pointing the bottleneck at Bridget in a toast, "here's to you, lady. You put up a hell of a fight." I winked and took a swig, then passed it to her.

"Oh, no thanks. I don't think so." Bridget's face scrunched up in disapproval. "You know how many germs are probably on that thing?"

"What? No, forget about it—alcohol *kills* germs," I told her. "Right?"

She shrugged.

"Well . . . do it . . . do it for Octavian the Octopus." I smiled, feeling all warm and fuzzy inside. It was nice to have a break from all the hate, to have an old friend back.

Bridget smiled back and took the bottle. "Okay," she said, "I will." And she gulped it down—an impressive amount, considering her shabby funneling skills. "Thanks, Margarita," she finally said, when she came up for air. "Thanks for everything. I mean it."

"Don't mention it," I said. "And hey—you should call me Madge."

"Got it." She nodded, and smirked mischievously. "And, by the way? That was *super*-cheesy, Madge."

"Oh, shut the hell up." I laughed, smacking her shoulder. "Let's just keep dancing."

And so we did. And you know what? It felt a helluva lot better than any cheap-ass tiara would've!

Acknowledgments

· ·

This infamous "Book 2" took a lot out of me, and at times I became something of a moody and reclusive friend, brother, and son . . . so first and foremost, I'd like to thank my friends and family—um . . . *especially* my family! (Mama, Papa, Jessica, and Katherine)—for putting up with me, and for understanding.

Perhaps the one who's had to deal with me at my very worst is my beyond-words amazing boyfriend (and soon-to-be husband), Billy Merrell. Billy, I owe so much of this book to your love and patience, and to our always interesting guest-room brainstorming sessions. Thanks for always being willing to help, and for believing in me and my ridiculous ideas. Well . . . *most* of them!

The logical next group of people to thank is The Bitches, my novel-writing group. Thanks, boys (Nick Eliopulos, Jack Lienke, and Dan Poblocki), for the extremely helpful feedback, and for being both so hard and so kind to me. If it weren't for you, I wouldn't have had the confidence to cut out those two super-boring characters, so I—and my readers!—owe you big-time.

(Oh, and *extra* thanks goes out to Dan and the wonderfully skanky girls from Jersey and Long Island who were at Christina Aguilera's March 2007 show at Madison Square Garden. Without you guys, this book wouldn't have had such an . . . interesting title!)

For Susan Jeffers Casel—my CE guru, dear friend, and mentor—thank you for the constant support and wisdom, the champagne shenanigans on your deck, and of course for your kick-ass copyediting job on this book.

So many thanks to my very trusting and perceptive editor, Jennifer Klonsky, who is a *master* at making me feel confident in my writing yet mindful of how much I can improve it. I don't know what I would've done without you. And I of *course* have to thank everyone else at Pulse for treating me and my books so well: Russell Gordon, who designed the *unspeakably* fabulous front cover (which exceeded my already high expectations!), Mike Rosamilia for the fantastic interior layout, as well as Bethany Buck (eternal gratitude for everything!), Michael del Rosario, Jaime Feldman, Caroline Abbey, Brenna Sinnott, Carey O'Brien, and I'm sure many, many others.

And how could I not thank the *real* Lady Pearl, for giving me permission to use her stinging and jaw-dropping one-liners, and for making me laugh, cringe, and cower in fear (but all in good fun!) on countless Thursday nights at the University Club. College wouldn't have been the same without you!

And . . . (I hate to utter such a cliché, but it's totally how I feel!) *last but not least*, I want to thank my fans (oh my *God*, I have *fans!*) for all their kind, excited, and insightful messages about the first book. Seriously, people—it makes my day/night/ *week* when you write, and many of your words did wonders at bolstering my self-confidence, without which, who knows if I could've finished this book on time. Writing a second book is apparently very tough on your psyche, so hearing that I did a good job on the first one helped me out a *lot*! (And I hope you all enjoyed this one.)

Love what you just read?

Here's a peek at another Nico Medina book,
The Straight Road to Kylie

••

*Join seventeen-year-old out-and-proud Jonathan Parrish
and his friends as they celebrate Joanna's eighteenth
birthday. Everything's a harmless swirl of music and
dancing, until Jonathan makes a very BIG mistake. . . .*

. . . .

Appropriately enough, "Me So Horny" kicked in just as Trent
Kessler came through the front door with Alex Becker. God, Trent
looked gorgeous; Joanna was right to have been crushing on him
since God-knows-when. He had on a pair of very faded jeans that
hung halfway down his perfectly toned surfer-god bubble butt
(which is probably why the damn pants weren't slipping down to
his ankles) and a tight vintage T-shirt that read daytona beach.

"I see Alex is in her usual garb," I said to Carrie as we spotted
them and waved them over to us.

"Aww, take it easy on her," Carrie said.

"Oh, I totally am—I love her to death, but she acts like she's
still getting used to her post-pubescent body. And she'd be totally
cute if she just retired those old jeans and big baggy shirts."

"If you say 'makeover,' I am so outta here," Carrie told me jokingly. "Now shut up, they're coming over."

Trent ambled in, his right hand running through his curly blond hair. Mmm!

Alex clomped awkwardly—but cutely and charmingly, nonetheless—over alongside him.

"Dude," he said (I know—how appropriate, right?), "you're, like, the only other dude here!"

"The curse of being a gay boy in high school, I suppose," I replied. "Hi, Alex."

"Hola, Jonathan."

"Joanna wants her fucking rug back."

"I don't know what you're talking about," she said, all deadpan.

We smiled at each other and broke out into laughter.

Maybe I should mention that Alex Becker is the other girl in my Spanish group with Joanna. She was my mistress in the last skit, who'd stolen Joanna's—or, rather . . . Soledad's—husband (me) and alfombra (rug). Boy, did it get messy that day! Totally fun.

"You guys are crazy," Trent said. "So, seriously, no other dudes?" he asked. "We're not gonna break out the Ya-Ya Sisterhood or something, are we?"

"But then we get in our panties and have a tickle fight!" I giggled. "But what do you care if you're the only available boobylover in the room?" I asked. "This should be a dream come true for a red-blooded all-American boy like yourself."

"No, man, I think I need a drink first," he said. Awww, how cute. Surfer-boy was the nervous type. "What do you guys have?"

Perfect.

"Well, why don't you go see the birthday girl? She'll hook you up." I couldn't resist, and pointed him in Joanna's direction.

"Awesome." And he was off.

"So, lady, what can I get you?" I asked Alex.

"I dunno—something sweet?"

"Vodka and cran?"

"Uh . . . sure," she answered. "What service!"

"Pleasing you is my pleasure," I said (God, do I have to flirt with everyone?), and walked to the kitchen, where Joanna was nervously—but not too nervously (I was proud of her)—giving Trent a tour of the alcohol table. I poured Alex and myself two generous vodka crans, squeezed a bit of lime into them, added a glug of orange juice, and headed back to the living room. I swung my head around as I walked away, waggling my tongue at Joanna and checking out Trent's adorable ass at the same time. I believe in multi-tasking.

The dance party had gotten nuts, and I was loving every drunken minute of it. In hindsight, maybe I didn't really need to try to drink my weight in alcohol, but I was feeling euphoric as I bounced from girl to girl on the living-room-slash-foyer impromptu dance floor we had cleared, grabbing waists, riding asses, and shaking my nose in cleavage all along the way.

At one point, I couldn't help but notice that I was surrounded by a crowd of girls, all sort of tag-team nasty-dancing with me. It was a sort of gay Lord-of-the-Dance-esque orgy, but with clothes on, and with all the girls' boyfriends standing off to the side, looking perplexed, jealous, and intrigued, whispering to one another. At one point, this girl Kristen Samuels whispered sloppily into my ear, "Tom never dances with me like this—I wish he would!" I laughed, glanced up at her boyfriend, Tom Matthews—who was this muscular, brown-haired football stud I'd had the hots for since tenth grade—and politely passed her on to him, saying, "You should take her to some backseat somewhere."

If this was the extent of the action that I was ever going to get—girls riding me, having their dance-floor way with me, while their hunky boyfriends gave me smoldering looks—then I'd take it. I have to admit, I kind of liked it. Not as much as I'd enjoy a reciprocal sexual attraction, but oh, well. Not like that was gonna happen.

I surveyed the scene—the party seemed to have reached epic proportions:

I saw Kenny Daniels taking over my place in the sea of hot-and-bothered girls who had boyfriends who wouldn't dance with them. Whatever. So not touching that, ever.

I spotted Joanna and Trent sort-of-talking-sort-of-dancing at the far end of the room. Good!

A few feet to the left, I saw Shauna sandwiching Jake McKay

with Marie Acosta. Go, Shauna! I wondered how drunk she must be to act so boldly.

And then I spied Carrie leading Latest-Conquest Nick upstairs, presumably to one of the "chill" rooms. Glad somebody was getting some action tonight. Carrie was always getting action, actually—with plenty of guys, and even a few girls. But guys were easier. Apparently. Not like I knew, or would ever know. "Ugh—I am not gonna turn into a bitter drunk gay boy," I said out loud to myself, looking around and noticing a couple people looking at me strangely. I laughed. I should have known then how drunk I was.

And then I saw Alex, dancing by herself near the window. She turned her head and saw me, and waved. I smiled back, took a swallow from my beer, and danced over to her, mouthing the words to "Like a Virgin." She laughed as I held out my hand, gesturing her to dance with me. She accepted, and I semi-bowed/semi-fell to one knee and gave her delicate hand a not-so-delicate kiss.

"Very gentlemanly, Jonathan," she said through a gutteral, gurgly, groggy-drunk laugh as she wiped her hand on her jeans.

I grabbed her by the waist and locked hips with her, swaying back and forth to the synthy eighties beat. And then she was smiling at me, really big.

"And kudos on the CDs," she continued. "It's quite a mix you have. . . . Marilyn Manson followed by Madonna?"

I said something idiotic like "Variety is the spice of life" or something. Then, "Oh, whoa, was that cliché or what? God, I'm drunk—did I say that out loud?" I leaned forward and gave her a peck on the cheek.

She threw her head back and laughed some more (she must've been pretty loaded; I'd never seen her act so wild), and I tilted her body back, supporting it with my right arm, while we continued to grind our hips back and forth, back and forth, forward and backward.

"Jesus, Jonathan, you're an incredible dancer," she said, clasping her hands behind my neck. "A girl needs to be on birth control to dance with you—"

"Aaaaaahhhhh!!!!!" I interrupted her. I couldn't help it—Britney had come on. My favorite club mix. "I fucking love this remix—the beat is just brutal!"

Our dancing and grinding pumped up into hyper mode. We shook our bodies to the relentless beat. We vibrated our pelvises to the intense rises and buildups. And our bodies erupted, arms and torsos flying and flailing, to the techno explosions that followed. Our bodies contorted, our muscles screamed against the lactic-acid buildup (I guess health class taught me some stuff), and we could feel the sweat dampening our clothes.

"Don't you love it!" I beamed.

"Totally," Alex said through ragged breaths, leaning forward to kiss me on the cheek now. She was getting totally into it.

And then I started to notice things: some of the other party-goers looking at us, talking into one another's ears. Trent looking away from Joanna momentarily and staring at Alex, then me, then quickly away (kinda weird). Alex's incessant grinding against me, even when the song slowed down and blended into the next. How my hands were totally grabbing her ass, and hers mine. And the weird, never-quite-before-seen bedroom eyes I think she was making at me.

"But," she said, "I think I need a break—I might've pulled a leg muscle thanks to you. Do you wanna come take a breather with me?"

"Sure."

Apparently, noticing strange things and connecting them in your brain to possible consequences is something that gets screwed up with copious amounts of alcohol.

We stumbled off the dance floor and through the kitchen, slowly lumbered up the stairs, and wound up falling down very ungracefully ("Timberrrrrrrrr!" was all that was running through my head) onto the bed in one of the empty guest rooms. (Guest room? Again, not thinking.) I could have easily just passed out right there. I mean, why not? I'd already had a ton of fun, my girlfriends were occupied with other guys, and I sure as hell wasn't gonna hook up with Kenny Daniels or anything. . . .

"Hey, Jonathan," Alex interrupted my dizzy thoughts, "are you and Kenny together?"

I let out a burst of laughter. "No!"

"So are you seeing anybody?" She sat up in the bed and pulled her knees up to her chest, hugging them.

I laughed again. "Other than my left hand and a few teen heart-throbs in my dreams? Hardly." I sat up, too, and leaned my head against the wall for support. It wasn't doing so well on its own.

"Well, why not?" she asked. "You're totally hot, and such a sweetheart."

"Oh, go on," I chuckled. "Haven't you noticed? I'm, like, the only gay guy at Winter Park that is less than hideous!"

"Well, Kenny isn't hideous."

"In ways he is, though." I exhaled. "I don't want to date some pill-popping kid who puts on house music to make out to, you know? Plus, I don't think he'd want to date, really. He's just kinda sleazy . . . and I'm not really interested."

"Huh."

"But, you know, it's kinda starting to suck," I said. "I'm seriously, like, the only gay guy at Winter Park I'd date. And I'm not gonna go online to meet anyone, 'cause that kind of freaks me out, so what does that leave me?" Why was I just going on and on about this? All of a sudden, the words just kept coming out of my mouth, and I couldn't stop. "And, God, I can't take one more party where I see everyone else coupling off and leaving me with nothing. . . . It's getting old. Anyway, Carrie has been promising to introduce me to some of her other gay friends from Dr. Phillips—their magnet program's for drama and the arts, so that school is crawling with 'mos."

"That's nice."

"Yeah, but I'm sick of waiting!" I said. "God, I just think sometimes it'd be easier to be straight. Maybe then I could couple off with someone and head to a guest room. . . ."

I realized my slipup and the resulting awkwardness, and looked at Alex and laughed nervously.

"Well, I'm not dating anyone, either," Alex said now, wringing her hands, like she was drying them off with a hand towel but without the hand towel. "I haven't ever, really."

"That's kinda hard to believe," I told her. "I mean, you're way cute—maybe you just don't know how to work it."

"Hey, same for you, Jonathan! You're totally hot."

"You said that already."

"Did I?" She looked away from me and studied her feet, hugging her knees closer to her chest. "Anyway, it's so annoying—and this party's gotten me thinking. . . . I'll be eighteen soon, too. I mean, that makes me a woman, right?"

"Well, technically doesn't womanhood start the day you get your first period? I think I learned that on a Cosby Show rerun."

She laughed loudly at this. "God! You're so funny!" she choked out. "The thing is," she continued, "I still don't feel like a woman yet, I don't think. I feel like I need to go through some rite of passage or something."

The only light in the room was coming from a little lamp on the bedside table and a sliver of light peeking in from the hallway. I could hear Kylie singing "In Your Eyes" through the din of the happy partygoers and longed to be down there. Away from this room. And this situation . . . whatever it was. I'd never been seduced before, but this was starting to feel like it . . . and I didn't know what to do. If I couldn't handle getting myself a glass of water, how could I take care of this situation?

"So maybe I should just have sex once to get it over with, right?" she blurted out.

Whoa! Um, okay. Twisted. Weird. Illogical. Sad. Interesting. "Sure, why not? As long as you're safe." Who was I to lecture while intoxicated? Didn't they give tickets for that?

"Well, it should be with someone I care about, I think . . . so it's special." She leaned closer to me and put her hand on my knee. "Someone like . . . you? What do you think?"

"Who-ho-ho-hooooah," I managed, drunkenly trying to swat her hand away like a fly. "Are you serious?"

"Well, yeah . . ." She pulled her arms back to her side of the bed and resumed her former knee-hugging position, all of a sudden looking crushed. "You were kinda flirting with me a lot while we were dancing and I thought you wanted to . . . I dunno. But maybe you could? If you don't mind, that is. . . . I didn't think you would, actually. . . . Is that crazy?"

"Mind? Alex, I'm gay! Of course I mind. I like guys. I think boobs are nothing more than superfluous orbs of fatty tissue. I impersonate Cher after too many cosmos. I drink cosmos! I consider Madonna to be higher than God. And Kylie Minogue to transcend even Madonna's status! Are you seeing a pattern? Plus, I'm . . . I'm not in the frame of mind. It'd be . . . taking advantage of me if you made me have sex with you. I don't even know my own name right now. Am I making sense?" I was scrambling for a way out of this.

"Sure, you're making sense. . . ." Alex said, looking kind of embarrassed. "But consider it," she continued, seeming to get more confidence. "We know each other really well, and you've been a great friend to me since I met you. Remember when you stuck up for me in Señora Lopez's class that time? In the middle of class, right when she was reaming me for not knowing the past tense of some verb, and you just raised your hand and were all like, 'Señora Lopez, why do you hate Alexandra?' She didn't know what to do—it was so wonderful!"

"Actually, it was '¿Por qué detestas a Alexandra?'" I corrected her.

"Exactly! You're brilliant. And when we would eat lunch together sometimes in junior year and you'd listen to all that stuff about my parents and everything?"

"Yeah," I said, softening up a little. "I remember. I mean, it was no big deal or anything—I was just helping out."

"I know. But that's why you're so special to me."

"I dunno, Alex—"

"And you're just such a sweet, amazing guy," she continued, interrupting me, clearly aware that she was on a roll, "and I know I can trust you to be gentle with me, and to just be . . . well . . . Jonathan about it. You mean a lot to me, and it'd mean a lot to me if you were my first."

Well, actually, this was really nice to hear. I wished it was a guy saying it, but beggars can't be choosers, I suppose. Alex was a good friend, and I liked the idea of being her first, and being someone she could trust. And getting genuine physical attention for once was also pretty cool . . . even if it meant sleeping with a—

Wait. Hello, this is Logic checking in. "But won't things get weird?" I asked.

"I dunno," she said. "Probably not."

"'Cause you don't, like, have a crush on me or anything, do you?"

"Me?" she laughed. "Well . . . no! That'd be crazy . . . because you're gay, right?"

"Way gay," I clarified. "So we couldn't get weird, okay? Wow." I paused, contemplating. "Have you considered a career in selling insurance? You've almost got me sold."

"That's the sweetest thing anyone's ever said to me," she said, laughing again.

Could I? Would I? I was, of course, still pretty shaky on the idea. I mean, come on! Having sex . . . with a girl? Was I this desperate for physical affection? It would be special . . . for her. Because when I pictured myself losing my virginity, it was with a guy, not a girl. So losing my girl virginity wouldn't exactly do anything for me. So, by that rationale, maybe . . . I could do it?

"I don't know, Alex. I think . . . maybe . . ." I stammered. "But, maybe it's just because I'm so wasted. I mean, don't you think I'm too . . . wasted?" For lack of a better word. Apparently.

"Well, let's see. . . . Pop quiz: What did Madonna say to her cabdriver when she first arrived in New York?"

"'Take me to the center of everything!'" I replied proudly.

"Then I think you're good to go."

"Wait! That one was too easy—!"

And I don't know what came over her, but the next thing I knew, Alex was straddling me and holding me in a wet, tongue-y lip-lock. Hate to admit it, but it was pretty great—kissing is just fun in general, regardless of gender. After a little while of that, she started rubbing against me as if we were back on the dance floor and putting her hands up my shirt. This was bizarre. It felt all wrong. But I just couldn't stop. It wasn't like I was enjoying it, though. I mean, yes, after five minutes or so, I popped a boner, but I was a seventeen-year-old guy—I could give myself an erection by fumbling around for my cell phone for too long!

O, Madonna (Ciccone) in Heaven, if only I wasn't so knowledgeable in useless pop-culture trivia, I could be back downstairs, dancing and drinking at the party. (And now I could hear a Garbage remix playing. Dammit!) Alex would have determined that I was too drunk to screw without remorse, and she would have left me alone. But no. Now she was taking my pants off tentatively—and I was letting her!—and going into her purse for a condom. I couldn't believe it was all happening!

So maybe it was the alcohol. Maybe it was my sudden lack of assertiveness. Or maybe I was just happy to have someone other than Kenny Daniels want me for once. It was nice. But I finally decided to throw caution (and gayness) to the wind and go with it. So that is how it happened.

How I went to "the center of everything" (for some people, at least) without even asking (or wanting) to.

So, after the clothes came off and the condom went on, I sort of lost track of what was happening. I had no idea what the hell I was doing, but I just let my instincts take over. I mean, biologically speaking, maybe I was meant to do this. To spread my wonderful seed. The world needed more Jonathan Parishes, right?

I'll spare you the dirty details, but let's just say that my heterosexual instincts sucked. It was so awkward. I was bungling everything—knocking over the lamp, accidentally banging Alex's skull against the headboard, and at one point unknowingly humming that freaking Hanson song "MMMBop" to keep some sort of a rhythm going. It was utterly ridiculous. All I could hope was that everyone's first time was this weird, and that I hadn't screwed up everything for Alex. And I could not stop hoping against hope that she wouldn't get completely naked, leaving me to face actual breasts head-on, and thus undoubtedly ending the entire sexual act. That would kind of suck for Alex, too.

"Are you humming?" Alex asked me as I stared at Mrs. Marin's floral-patterned guest-bed pillows (who the hell still buys floral, anyway?). "Wait, let me rephrase that—are you humming 'MMMBop'?"

"Look, just . . . just . . . keep that bra on."

BRIAN McCABE

NICO MEDINA's first book, *The Straight Road to Kylie*, came out when he was twenty-four, whereas Medina *himself* came out when he was eighteen. A graduate of both Winter Park High School and the University of Florida, he now lives, works, and plays in New York City. A fat, fabulous, and tacky girl at heart, if Mr. Medina *were* a woman, he would want to dress just like Madge Diaz. To learn even more about the author, check out his temple to good-natured narcissism at www.nicomedina.com.